COLIN BROOKS

Paint

Copyright © 2021 by Colin Brooks

All rights reserved. No part of this publication may be reproduced, stored or transmitted in any form or by any means, electronic, mechanical, photocopying, recording, scanning, or otherwise without written permission from the publisher. It is illegal to copy this book, post it to a website, or distribute it by any other means without permission.

This novel is entirely a work of fiction. The names, characters and incidents portrayed in it are the work of the author's imagination. Any resemblance to actual persons, living or dead, events or localities is entirely coincidental.

Colin Brooks asserts the moral right to be identified as the author of this work.

Colin Brooks has no responsibility for the persistence or accuracy of URLs for external or third-party Internet Websites referred to in this publication and does not guarantee that any content on such Websites is, or will remain, accurate or appropriate.

Designations used by companies to distinguish their products are often claimed as trademarks. All brand names and product names used in this book and on its cover are trade names, service marks, trademarks and registered trademarks of their respective owners. The publishers and the book are not associated with any product or vendor mentioned in this book. None of the companies referenced within the book have endorsed the book.

First edition

ISBN: 978-1-7369676-1-4

Editing by Dominic Wakeford

This book was professionally typeset on Reedsy.
Find out more at reedsy.com

I dedicate this novel to Ryan, for always believing in me, and to "the illustrious, the beautiful, the talented, the incomparable" Nicky Monet for continuing to inspire me and helping me get my heel in the door in the drag scene.

Contents

Acknowledgement   iii

I   Part One: Fall

Chapter 1	3
Chapter 2	12
Chapter 3	22
Chapter 4	33
Chapter 5	43
Chapter 6	54
Chapter 7	61
Chapter 8	73
Chapter 9	83
Chapter 10	90

II	Part Two: Winter	
Chapter 11		101
Chapter 12		113
Chapter 13		124
Chapter 14		136
Chapter 15		147
Chapter 16		162
Chapter 17		167
Chapter 18		172
Chapter 19		178
Chapter 20		187
III	Part Three: Spring	
Chapter 21		201
Chapter 22		206
Chapter 23		213
Chapter 24		220
Chapter 25		226
Chapter 26		232
Chapter 27		240
Chapter 28		247
Chapter 29		258
About the Author		268

Acknowledgement

There are a lot of people who I need to thank for their support, and I want to preface this by acknowledging that I will more than likely forget someone and am sorry in advance.

I want to thank the talented Candace Neal for her beautiful work on the cover, and for putting up with all of my ideas and requests despite having no idea what I was doing a majority of the time. I want to thank my partner, Ryan, for encouraging me to keep writing and supporting me when I doubted myself or this project. I want to thank my friend and real-life drag mother, Nicky Monet, who helped me get my foot in the door to start performing, taught me almost everything I know about drag, and let me know when I looked horrible with a light read before helping me look better. I want to thank my parents for always giving me their support in everything I've done and letting me be my own person, even when they had no idea what I was doing or disagreed with my choices (like when I moved to Chicago for five months, which I am still sorry about).

I'd be remiss not to thank my friends who contributed in bringing this novel to life by helping me hack it to bits and put it together again—Claudeen and Lexi. I had no budget for this novel and could not afford much professional help, so their constructive criticism and opinions helped shape this into what it is now.

I cannot thank Dominic Wakeford enough for working with me on editing my novel. His skillful eye caught any tiny mistakes or errors I made, and his constant assurances helped me to move forward with *Paint's* publication. I've said it to him about a trillion times, but I'm so grateful for all of his help and his kind words.

Finally, and I know how cheesy this sounds, I'd like to thank whoever else is reading this acknowledgement. I've wanted to be a writer since I was a little kid, so your support just by reading this means the world to me. I hope I will keep you entertained and be able to show you that there is more to life as a queer person than just coming out like you see in every movie.

I

Part One: Fall

Chapter 1

In the compact, crowded parking lot behind the three freshman housing buildings at the University of Central Florida, Tucker Peterson stood against the side of his mother's off-white Ford Explorer, sweating in the humid August heat.

In every parking spot, and even some grassy areas that weren't parking spots at all, sat vehicles stuffed with moving boxes for their own freshman family member. He watched as girls his age ran across the lot to hug their friends, as their parents trudged behind them with multiple moving boxes in their arms. He could see the desperation on their faces as they tried to get their children moved in quickly before the inevitable afternoon thunderstorms began, and fluffy gray clouds rumbled gently overhead in confirmation of what was coming.

Tucker's mother slammed the trunk of her Explorer shut, startling Tucker back to reality, and shoved a box marked 'TUCKER BATHROOM' into his arms. She wore a black UCF hat that covered her short dark hair, an old gray t-shirt, jean shorts, and running shoes. Her mascara was smudged, giving away the fact that she had been crying.

"Okay," she said, "I think this is the last box."

Before Tucker could respond, she grabbed his shoulders and pulled him into an awkward hug, separated by the box in his arms. Tucker could feel his mother's shoulders gently shaking as she silently cried, kissing the side of his head.

"Mom, stop!" Tucker protested. "I've been sweating since we got here."

"You lived inside of me for nine months," his mother said, still not letting him go. "I don't care about a bit of sweat."

"Well, I do!" he laughed, pulling away from her embrace.

Tucker and his mother had always had a close relationship while he was growing up—the two differed in personalities, as his mother was a loud and stubborn woman from Pennsylvania and he was more quiet and introspective, but they'd always gotten along great and complemented each other's traits. "Like opposite ends of a really fun and cool magnet," as his mother would often remark, causing Tucker to groan and roll his eyes at her. He secretly enjoyed how out-of-touch his mother was with what verbiage was "cool" or "trendy", making her sound like a mom on a family-friendly '80s television sitcom.

The two walked towards Tucker's new building, which had the words 'LIBRA' painted on the top of it. The other buildings had 'GEMINI' and 'CANCER' painted on their own respective walls, and Tucker couldn't help but feel thankful he wasn't living in a building with 'CANCER' on it, like it was a bad omen.

His room was on the third floor, and his mother opened the door to the stairwell once they were in the lobby before he could even try for the elevator.

"Mom, it's so hot!" Tucker complained. Hot weather anywhere in the world was unpleasant, but there was something about Florida's damp, oppressive heat that seemed to suck all the energy out of you the moment you stepped outside.

"Sweating is good for you," she countered. "It lets you know that your body's working and you're exerting energy."

"I'm well aware," he replied sourly, readjusting his hold on the box as he entered the stairwell.

As soon as they got to the third floor, the nearby elevator doors opened and what seemed like forty people poured out. He wouldn't admit it, but knew his mom was wise to take the stairs.

Each floor had a common area with bright white cinderblock walls, beige and gray checkered carpeting, and some cheap-looking furniture haphazardly placed in the center of the room. Other residents were already

CHAPTER 1

making themselves comfortable, moving the furniture around so people could sit with their friends, laughing and yelling, oblivious to the sweaty, red-faced families trying to move around them to get to their destinations. Tucker's room was in the very back, a straight shot from the doors to the common area.

"I can't believe this place is so messy already," Tucker's mom muttered to him as they approached his door. The two chuckled as he placed his student ID up to the scan lock above the door's handle and swung it open after a confirming beep.

Inside were two elevated beds, tucked into the corners of either side of the room. Like the common area, its walls were bright white, and the carpet was the same beige-gray checkered combo. Boxes from their previous trips to his room were stacked under his bed, and Tucker dropped his next to the others.

"Well," Tucker sighed, turning to look at his mother, "I guess this is it."

As if on cue, tears began rolling down her face. Tucker pulled his mother into an embrace, each of them hugging each other tightly. Though Tucker was excited for this new chapter in his life, living in his own and discovering who he could be without having to hide any parts of himself, he felt a heaviness in his chest as he realized his mother would be heading home alone.

"I'm sorry," his mother sniffled, "I said I was done crying."

"It's okay," Tucker said, pulling apart and wiping tears that had pooled in his eyes. "This isn't goodbye, just see you later. Remember, I'm only two hours away from you guys."

"I know," his mom said, wiping her own eyes. "I've just never had to do this before. You're my baby!" Without warning, she pulled Tucker into another hug, holding on tight.

"And you know your father wanted to be here too, to say goodbye," she said, her voice muffled in Tucker's hair. "He wanted to get the day off so badly."

"I know," Tucker said into her shoulder. "It's not his fault his boss is an ass."

"Hey, hey," she said, standing back and holding Tucker by the shoulders. "You may be a college kid now, but you don't need to start cussing all the time."

Tucker laughed and hugged his mother once more, quickly letting go before she could hold on to him for any longer.

"Okay, now get back on the road before it starts to rain," Tucker said. "I'll see you and Dad in a couple of weeks for Parents' Weekend, right?"

"Wouldn't miss it for the world," his mother said, smiling sadly. "Alright, I'm going. You be good, you hear? It should be good, but let us know if your car gives you any trouble and we'll give you some money to get it looked at. And don't forget to look for a job."

Before Tucker could respond, his mother grabbed the nearest box and opened it, pulling out its contents and placing them on the bare blue plastic mattress.

"I should help you unpack before I go," she muttered.

"Mom, go!" Tucker laughed. He snatched the box from her hands and placed it back on the floor.

"Okay, I'm going!" she said, throwing her hands up in mock defeat.

"I love you, Mom," Tucker said, his mouth quivering as he forced himself to smile.

"I love you too, Tucker," she said, her voice breaking as tears appeared in her eyes again. She quickly wiped her face, took a deep breath, and walked toward the door, looking back at him once more before exiting. Tucker could hear her loudly excusing herself as she made her way through the common room and couldn't help but laugh at the image of her shoving oblivious kids out of the way.

He began unpacking his boxes, placing his clothes in the dresser next to his bed, and had only gotten through a few of them before there was a knock at the door. Tucker, expecting his mother making a dramatic re-entrance to say goodbye again, threw open the door and was met instead with a floating stack of large brown boxes.

"Hey," came a deep voice from behind the stack. "Thanks for getting the door."

CHAPTER 1

Tucker stepped aside, and the boxes moved into the room, carried by a guy slightly taller than him. He dropped the boxes next to the other bed in the room with a loud thud and turned to look at Tucker. He was tall and skinny, with sun-kissed tan skin and a mop of shaggy hair the color of sand on his head.

"You must be Tucker," the guy said, walking toward him and extending his hand. "I looked you up online when we got our room assignments last month. I'm Mike. Nice to meet you!"

"Yeah, you too," Tucker said, wiping his sweaty palms on his shorts and shaking Mike's hand.

"Wow," Mike said, looking around the room, "this place is depressing. It looks like we're in a jail or something."

"I was just thinking the same thing!" Tucker said. "Like, they couldn't put up some wallpaper or get some better carpeting or something?"

"Exactly," Mike laughed. "Did you just get here too?"

"Yeah," Tucker said. "My mom just left a few minutes ago."

"It's nice that she helped you move," Mike said. "My parents both had to work, so I'm doing this all by myself."

"Oh, do you want some help?" Tucker asked, putting the toiletries he had in his hand down.

"No, it's cool," Mike said. "I've only got a few more boxes in my car. Thanks, though."

Tucker nodded once in response, and focused his attention back to his moving boxes, trying hard not to turn and look when he saw Mike take his shirt off to wipe his sweaty face out of the corner of his eye. Mike looked deceptively skinny, but had abs and a fairly defined chest hidden under his clothes that made Tucker's mind wander to what the rest of his body might look like.

Mike pulled a fresh shirt out of one of his boxes and left the room without a word as he was pulling it over his head. Once the door closed behind him, Tucker let out a breath that he didn't realize he'd been holding and nervously ran a hand through his hair.

"Pull yourself together," Tucker muttered to himself. "He's just a guy —

there's going to be a lot of them here."

By the time Mike banged on the door again with another armful of boxes, Tucker had already unpacked most of his clothes and was working on putting sheets on his new twin bed. He let go of the fitted sheet he was attempting to wrap around his mattress, letting it snap back into a pile, and quickly opened the door for his new roommate.

"Thanks again," Mike said breathlessly as he entered, throwing the boxes down near the previous stack he'd brought in. "Why the hell did I think it was a good idea to change my shirt before I was done moving? It's so hot outside!" He pulled the neck of his shirt up, exposing his lower abdomen as he wiped the sweat from his face. Tucker looked up at the ceiling, trying to keep his hormones under control.

"I know, it's like walking through hot soup," Tucker joked, looking back at Mike after a moment. "Are you from out-of-state?"

"No," Mike said, "which makes me feel even more dumb! I've lived here my entire life, so you'd think I'd know how awful August in Florida is. Are you from Florida too?"

"Yeah, I grew up a couple hours away from Orlando," Tucker said.

"Where at?" Mike asked, grabbing a plastic cup from one of his boxes. He walked over to the sink near their front door and flipped on the tap, filling his cup with water and taking large gulps.

"It's a small town. You probably haven't heard of it," Tucker said. "It's called Weeki Wachee."

"Oh, yeah!" Mike said, putting his cup down next to the sink. "I've heard of that place! With the mermaids, right?"

"That's us," Tucker said. He reached into a box next to his feet and pulled out a poster, showing Mike. It was a picture of smiling women in multi-colored mermaid tails and matching seashell bikini tops underwater with the words 'VISIT THE MERMAIDS OF WEEKI WACHEE SPRINGS' across the top.

"Wait," Mike said, coming over and analyzing the poster, "this is what the mermaids looked like? I didn't know what I was expecting, but they're hot!"

"I guess," Tucker said, shrugging.

CHAPTER 1

"You don't think so?" Mike asked.

"Not really," Tucker admitted, turning slightly to tape the poster on the wall near his bed. "They're all pretty, but I don't look at women like that. I'm gay, so it doesn't do much for me."

"Wait, you are?" Mike asked, his eyebrows raised.

Tucker turned back to Mike, catching his eye and holding his stare, mentally challenging him to respond negatively. "Yeah, I am."

Tucker only then noticed how hard his heart was pounding. He had come out to his friends in high school and didn't deny it if people asked because he wasn't ashamed of it, but he still wasn't used to admitting it out loud. Though he knew it was impossible, he still felt those same nerves he had back home of being outed to his parents before he could tell them his way. They were generally kind people and Tucker knew it was irrational, but the possibility that they'd hate him or disown him entirely scared him. Having no known queer adults that his parents interacted with, he was unsure how they felt about the LGBT community. He'd meant to come out to them before he moved, but felt like the moment was never right and chickened out.

Mike was quiet for a moment, and Tucker could almost see the wheels turning in his head as he processed this information, but then he patted Tucker on the arm, walked back to his boxes, and unpacked again.

"That's cool, dude," Mike said as he started taking clothes out and putting them in his dresser, which was identical to Tucker's. Though his words were nonchalant, Tucker could detect the nerves in Mike's voice as he started to babble. "I mean, I'm cool with that. I've never met a gay guy in real life before. I watched an episode of *Glee* once with my sister and that had a gay character in it, which was cool too. But I don't really watch that show. I'm not gay."

"Dude, relax," Tucker said with a relieved chuckle. "I know you're not gay. I'm no different from you except for the fact that I'm into guys instead of girls. I'm not an alien or something."

"Cool," Mike said with a reassuring smile.

The two continued to get their room set up in silence, Mike unpacking his boxes and Tucker finally getting his fitted sheet on his mattress. Tucker felt more relaxed now that Mike knew he was gay and hadn't flipped out and gone on a homophobic rant or tried to convert him, but he could tell his revelation had made Mike feel slightly uncomfortable for a moment.

Satisfied with the progress he'd made with unpacking so far, Tucker applied a fresh layer of deodorant and grabbed his wallet.

"Hey, do you want to go grab some dinner at the dining hall?" Tucker asked. "I'm starving and the rest of this can wait until after."

"Sorry, man," Mike said. "I've already got plans with some friends from back home after I finish unpacking."

"Oh, okay. Some other time then."

"Totally."

Tucker walked towards the door, stopping to check his reflection in the mirror above the sink before stepping out. The redness in his face from moving in the heat had finally gone away, and his dark hair wasn't as messy as he was expecting from sweating all day either.

"Hey, Tucker?" Mike said, stopping Tucker before he opened the door. Tucker turned and looked back at his new roommate, who stood with his hands in his pockets and a careful look on his face. "I just wanted to put it out there that it's not because you told me you're gay or anything. That was just a coincidence. I was surprised for a second, but I'm totally cool with it."

Tucker shot him a quick, reassuring smile to ease any guilt Mike might have been feeling. "Yeah, you said that already," Tucker joked. "Seriously, it's cool. Don't stress about it. I'd be hanging out with my friends too if any of them had moved in today. I'm gonna go, so I'll see you later if you're gone by the time I get back."

"Definitely," Mike said, visibly relaxing. "See you later, man."

Tucker turned and walked out the door with a smile on his face, feeling confident about his new relationship with his roommate. The common area had emptied since Tucker had begun unpacking and the sun had set, yet the room seemed almost brighter now that the white light from the harsh fluorescent bulbs overhead lit the room instead of the sunlight through the windows on each wall. He felt his stomach growling and walked briskly to

CHAPTER 1

the entrance of the common area where the elevator was located. There was a hand-written sign on the elevator doors warning that it was under maintenance the rest of Saturday night and all day Sunday, but would be working again when classes began on Monday.

"Great," Tucker muttered to himself, throwing the doors to the stairwell open and taking the stairs down to the lobby two at a time. When he got there, he was greeted with a downpour of rain and crackling thunder that shook the windows.

"Oh, come on!" he protested to no one in particular, as he was the only one in the lobby. "It was fine two seconds ago!"

There was a newspaper stand next to the doors leading to the rest of the campus, so Tucker grabbed two copies and quickly unfolded them to make a makeshift umbrella, and raced out into the storm.

Chapter 2

The thing about Florida thunderstorms is that they come hard and fast when you're least expecting them, but never stick around for too long. Tucker, a Florida native, knew this and hoped it would be the case as he threw the lobby doors open and sprinted down the wet, slippery concrete path that led from his building to the main sidewalk, which connected around the entire campus of the University of Central Florida in a giant circle. His hopes were quickly dashed as the newspapers he held above his head immediately soaked through, and he threw them in a trashcan on his way to the dining hall, Knightro's, which was named after the school mascot.

It was a short walk from his building, and Tucker knew where he was headed thanks to a map of the campus that was included in the school's free app, but the two-minute journey proved more than enough time to soak Tucker from head to toe. He ran down the walkway from his building and across a small lawn where the mailboxes for his section of dorms were, trying to get under some cover as fast as possible. He slipped on the wet concrete just as he was approaching the entrance to Knightro's, landing on his arm and earning a stinging cut. Other students waiting for the rain to stop under an awning that covered the dining hall's entrance gave him slightly concerned looks as he got back to his feet, but nobody said anything to him or offered any help.

Tucker looked down at his feet to avoid their stares, feeling his cheeks flush with embarrassment, and walked quickly through the hall's front doors and into the adjacent bathroom, locking the door behind him. He pulled his shirt off, wringing it over the sink and holding it under the electric hand dryer on the wall, doing the same with his arms and hair afterward. Satisfied with his level of dryness, Tucker put his shirt back on and exited the bathroom, joining a nearby line for food.

The dining hall was set up buffet-style, with three different areas for classic cafeteria-style foods like pizza and sandwiches, a salad bar, and a dessert station within a half-circle in the center of the room. Tables and chairs were crammed together in designated eating areas on either sides of the room, reminding Tucker of a food court you'd find at a mall. He followed the line, grabbing a plate of pizza sitting under a heating lamp and a sad-looking salad comprising limp lettuce and a pile of shredded carrots on top, and squeezed his way through the tables occupied by excitedly chatting freshmen until he found an empty one in the corner.

Tucker took a bite of the lukewarm pizza, feeling a layer of grease immediately coat his mouth, and quickly set it back down on his plate with disgust. He pushed the salad around with a fork, hoping that there would be something better hidden under the top layer of sad vegetables, but was disappointed to find more of the same underneath.

If this is what my social life is going to be like in college, he thought, *it's going to be a long four years.*

Tucker couldn't help but feel envious as he looked around the room and noticed all the people sitting together, laughing and chatting as they ate. Even their food, which was the same as Tucker's, looked better than what he had.

Ignoring the growling protests of his stomach, Tucker sighed and got up, throwing his food in a nearby trash can as he walked back towards the entrance. The storm had subsided in the short time Tucker had been inside, but he still took careful steps as he headed back to his building.

When he got back to his room, he found it empty and assumed Mike had already left to meet up with his friends. Tucker, feeling exhausted from moving all day and in a foul mood after seeing those new students with friends already, took the silence and darkness cloaking the room as a sign to call it an early night. He stepped into the bathroom and changed into a loose shirt and gym shorts, left the light on and cracked the door so Mike wouldn't be walking into complete darkness whenever he returned, and climbed into bed.

Before he moved to Orlando for school, Tucker had always felt that he had plenty of friends. As he scrolled through his different social media accounts and saw pictures of his friend group enjoying the weekend tradition they'd always shared in high school of pizza on the beach, Tucker felt pangs of regret shoot through his stomach. *Or was that just hunger?*

Tucker had felt so excited to come to UCF and begin his new life as an adult, but in that moment, seeing his friends moving on without him, he felt nothing but loneliness and jealousy. He had nobody here with him—no support system, no friends to hang out with, no real company at all. It wasn't as if it was a surprise to him; he knew that none of his other friends had chosen to go to this school, but thinking he'd be alone and actually experiencing it were two very different things.

He set his phone down with a huff, eager to stop feeling so upset, and closed his eyes, willing himself to sleep. It did not come for what felt like hours to him, and he tossed and turned in his new twin bed, desperate to get comfortable as his mind continued to race. Finally, another thunderstorm began, and the familiar pattering of rain on the window and low grumbles of thunder lulled Tucker into a dreamless sleep.

* * *

He awoke the next day to find Mike's bed still empty, and no sign that he'd ever returned during the night. He felt slightly alarmed by this revelation, but convinced himself that everyone was an adult and entitled to their own choices, and just because Mike had been nice to him did not mean they were automatically friends.

Still, Tucker couldn't help but feel anxious by Mike's absence, so he got up and quickly dressed, determined to shake those feelings and any lingering ones he still felt from the night before. Opening up the school's app on his phone and going to the map, Tucker left his room to embark on his own

CHAPTER 2

personal treasure hunt to find where his classes would be the following day.

Even though the campus had been bustling with the new student body the day before, Sunday on campus felt almost eerie with how quiet and empty it was. The sun was high as Tucker followed the walkway from his building to the main sidewalk that circled the entire campus and was sweating heavily within a few minutes. Towards the front of campus was the Administration Building, where the President's office was located and where the Financial Aid Department could be found. In front of it sat a giant fountain, with enormous concrete steps leading down to its edge like seats in a coliseum. The jets shot water up and out in multiple streams, and reminded Tucker of pictures he'd seen of the fountains in Las Vegas.

He stopped for a minute, taking in the sight of the water glistening in the sunlight, and felt a moment of calm as he listened to the water splashing paired with the silence of the campus. He felt a drop of sweat fall into his eye, stinging slightly, and the moment was over.

Swearing under his breath as he rubbed his right eye, Tucker continued his self-ran tour along the sidewalk until he came to a covered set of stores. There were tables spread out down the walkway under the awning, and a set of patio couches sat in a semi-circle on the other side. The group of stores comprised a bookstore, a coffee shop, a women's clothing boutique, and a skateboard repair store. Only the bookstore was open, and Tucker relished the faint breath of air conditioning he felt as passed by the open front doors.

There was a line that stretched from outside the building and wound all the way through the store, and sweaty red-faced students stood with their faces glued to their phones as they waited to get inside to purchase their textbooks prior to classes starting. A guy in jean shorts and a black tank top with a rainbow on the front exited the building with a bag on his arm as Tucker passed and offered him a quick smile as he looked Tucker up and down appraisingly. Tucker's eyes widened in surprise at the stranger's attention and quickened his pace, feeling his face redden from the attention instead of the heat outside like everyone else.

In the center of campus was the Student Union, a large red brick building with a giant UCF logo painted on its front. Inside, it housed another dining area with restaurant outlets from around the city, a computer lab, and multiple floors above filled with tables and chairs that overlooked the first floor. Tucker cut through the building, eager to get out of the heat, and came out the other side to a back patio surrounded by trees with even more tables and chairs. There was a walkway that cut through the trees to reveal a sprawling, green lawn that had buildings on each side.

Using the app for guidance, Tucker found his classrooms with little issue, and returned to the dining hall across campus for a celebratory lunch. Lunch, it turned out, was anything but celebratory, as the hall was closed for cleaning before school started the next day, according to a sign taped to its front doors.

Tucker, now having not eaten a proper meal since before moving in the day before, took it as a sign to order in. He went back to his room, which still showed no signs of Mike having come back, and ordered a pizza. He spent the rest of the day picking out an outfit for his first day of school—new black and white sneakers, jean shorts, and a black UCF shirt—and relaxing before the stress of school officially kicked in.

It wasn't until well after the sun went down that day that Mike, looking disheveled and exhausted with dark purple bags under his eyes, came back to their room and went to bed without saying a word to Tucker. He tried not to take the silence personally, reminding himself again that they were roommates, not friends. But having nothing else to do and no responses yet from the texts he'd sent his friends that day, he shortly followed suit and went to sleep early, anxious for his first day of school.

* * *

If his walk around campus had been indicative of what Sundays would look like for Tucker, then he wanted nothing to do with Mondays. Tucker awoke the next morning to the sound of the door slamming behind Mike as he left for class. Groggy-eyed, Tucker reached for his phone to check how much time he had left before his alarm, and threw it to the ground in shock. The

CHAPTER 2

phone read 9:03 AM, which was three minutes after his first class began.

"Shit!" Tucker yelled, flying out of bed and tumbling to the floor. He grabbed the outfit he'd laid out the night before and changed as quickly as he could, snatched his backpack off of the floor, and ran out of the room as fast as his feet would go. He swung the door open, almost hitting one of his neighbors in the face, and yelled an apology over his shoulder as he dashed out of the common room and down the stairs.

By the time he'd remembered where he had to go and raced across campus, there was less than fifteen minutes left in his class period. Tucker pushed the doors to the Mathematical Sciences building open and ran down the hall, reading classroom numbers on the doors until he arrived at the correct room, the second-to-last door in the hall. He slowly twisted the handle and soundlessly slipped inside, followed by the loud slam of the door behind him. The class, a room of thirty individual desks facing toward the whiteboard at the front of the room, turned to stare at him. The professor, a thin, short man with tufts of dull brown hair on either side of his head and almost translucent skin indicative of his old age, stopped what he was writing and slowly turned to look at Tucker with dead eyes.

"Hi," Tucker said sheepishly.

"Can I help you, young man?" the professor asked, disdain obvious in his tone.

"Professor Whitley, I'm so sorry I'm late. I accidentally set my alarm for 8:00 PM instead of 8:00 AM and completely overslept," Tucker said in one breath. "I promise, I won't let it happen again."

"What is your name?" Professor Whitley asked.

"Tucker Peterson, sir. I'm here for your General Psychology course. That's now, right?"

"Well, Mr. Peterson," Professor Whitley said, ignoring Tucker's question, "I do not tolerate tardiness in my class, no matter what the excuse. I try to be lenient on the first week, but this class begins at 9:00 AM sharp and I will be locking the doors when I begin my lectures starting next week so that late students like yourself will not interrupt and learn your lesson. Remember that for next time."

This was him being lenient?, Tucker thought, feeling his brows furrow in frustration. The older man walked to his desk, which was nestled into the corner of the room parallel to the door, and brought Tucker a piece of paper, placing it in his hands with more force than necessary.

"This is my course syllabus," he advised, his tone sharp. "It has my tardy policy on it, as well as my grading scale and an assignment schedule for our semester together. Read it. I suggest you try hard not to be late again. Two unexcused absences after today will lead to a whole letter grade drop. Now, I'm going to go back to my lecture, and I suggest you find a way to get the notes you've missed from today."

In all the movies and TV shows focused around college, there's always that one professor who seems rough around the edges, but always comes around to the students and eventually shows their heart of gold. *This wasn't one of those cases. Professor Whitley was just an asshole*, Tucker thought bitterly.

Without waiting for Tucker to find a seat or even respond, he turned back to the board and began writing terms down again, picking back up where he left off in his lecture. The students, who had been sitting in a stunned silence as Tucker was made an example of, all watched him out of the corner of their eyes as he moved to the only empty desk available in the very back of the room.

He sat down, and the chair creaked loudly in protest, only earning him more looks from his other classmates. A girl sitting to his left, with dark brown skin and caramel-colored hair pulled back in a bun, wearing bright pink glasses and a yellow floral jumpsuit, passed Tucker her notes before he could even turn to her. There was a pink sticky note attached to it that said "I'm Kiara" with a smiley face and her phone number. Tucker pulled the note off and quickly took a picture of her notes on his phone, making a mental note to write it all down later, and added Kiara's contact information to his phone. He introduced himself on the same sticky note and reattached it to her paper, passing it back with a grateful look.

In the ten minutes remaining in class, the professor continued his lecture about the basics of general psychology and seemed to never stop to breathe. Tucker, wary of any other interaction with the man, stared at his notebook

CHAPTER 2

intently and tried to note everything that sounded important. Which, Tucker quickly realized, could be basically everything. Professor Whitley didn't seem like the type that would talk just for the sake of talking. Or the type to own a beating heart.

Eventually, Professor Whitley concluded the lesson for the day, and all the students in the room sprang up and quickly packed their things.

"Hey," Tucker said to his desk neighbor, "thank you so much for your notes."

"No problem," Kiara said with a smile.

"I'm Tucker, by the way," he said, throwing his backpack on his right shoulder and extending his left hand.

"Oh, I saw the show," she laughed, shaking his hand. "I'm Kiara."

"It's nice to meet you."

"Likewise. I hope you don't mind me giving you my number—I got the feeling like you might need a new friend after watching that fiasco."

Tucker laughed. He was absolutely mortified by the first impression he'd made on his *first* new teacher on the *first* day of classes, but Kiara's gentle teasing actually made him feel better.

"You know, you're my first friend here now, so I don't mind at all."

"I'm honored!" Kiara said. "I have to run to my next class, but text me if you want to grab lunch or something. I'd love to get to know you better, New Friend Tucker."

"I'd love to," Tucker said earnestly. "I'll text you!"

Kiara, who had just zipped up her own backpack, offered a wave goodbye and walked out the door. Tucker, who had momentarily forgotten how mortified he felt, caught the judgmental eye of Professor Whitley as he was leaving the room and felt his face get hot all over again.

It was the first day! What kind of asshole singles out a lost student on the first day in front of everyone? *This kind of asshole*, he thought to himself bitterly as he stormed back to his room. He had a break for a couple hours between classes and wanted to actually clean up now that he had time.

As he entered his room, he was surprised to see Mike sitting in his bed, watching a daytime court show on a television set on the wall that he must have hung while Tucker was out.

"Oh, hey!" Mike greeted him. "How was your first class?"

"Awful," Tucker complained, throwing his backpack on his bed. "I set my alarm for the wrong time and only had, like, ten minutes left in class by the time I got there. And my professor, who seems like a complete dick, by the way, ripped me a new asshole in front of the entire class!"

"Damn," Mike sighed. "That sucks, dude. I'm sorry."

"Whatever," Tucker said, shrugging his shoulders. "What about you? I heard you leaving this morning. How was class?"

"Well, it started out kind of annoying," Mike said. "I got to the classroom and there was a note on the door saying class was cancelled. So it ended up being cool, but I wish I didn't have to walk through this heat to find out. She sent us the PowerPoint of her lecture and gave us all perfect scores for the day since it was her fault, though. So college kind of rules!"

"Well, I'm glad you had a good first experience," Tucker grumbled.

He walked to the sink and wet his hair while he brushed his teeth, trying to get the obvious bedhead tamed before going out in public again, and eventually gave up and put on a plain black baseball hat. There was a bright blue flyer on the counter advertising all the first week activities the school was putting on. Determined to turn his day around, Tucker snatched the flyer and put it in his pocket.

"Hey," he said, grabbing his backpack, "I'm going to go check out all the stuff the school's doing for the first week at the Student Union. The flyer says there's a guy who breathes fire! You want to come?"

"Dude, that sounds awesome!" Mike said excitedly. "I wish I could, but I have to start studying in a minute for my Biochemistry quiz on Friday."

Tucker blanched, his eyebrows shooting up in surprise. "You have a quiz already? It's the first day!"

"Yeah, I guess someone forgot to mention that to my professor. He sent me three emails before I even woke up this morning about it! Let me know if there's anything cool there, though. I may have to take a study break later and stop by."

"Alright, I will," Tucker said. "Have fun studying!"

CHAPTER 2

Mike let out a groan and turned off the TV, pulling a textbook out from behind him. Tucker grabbed a piece of gum from his dresser and popped it in his mouth as he headed out the door again to visit the Student Union, fixing a smile on his face to make himself feel better.

Chapter 3

Tucker didn't think it could be possible, but it felt even hotter than before when he left the air-conditioned dorm hall and ventured toward the Student Union. Unlike the day before, there were people everywhere he looked as he followed the walkway—staff members dressed in heavy suits despite the heat, obvious new students nervously looking at their surroundings to determine where they were, people sitting by the fountain singing along to a guy playing guitar, and, to Tucker's surprise, a mob of angry adults yelling into megaphones. They screamed about repenting to anyone that was unlucky enough to pass them and held signs saying things like "God Saves" and "You Will Burn in Hell". The messages seemed counter-intuitive, Tucker considered amusedly as he passed, but refused to make eye contact with them in case they tried to pull him into a conversation he had no interest in being a part of.

   He didn't have a problem with religion, though he had realized as he got older that it just wasn't something he was interested in, but knew that these people were extremists who did not truly represent any religion's intentions. He could hear a woman getting into a screaming match with one of the men holding a megaphone, calling them pigs and hypocrites, which made Tucker smile with satisfaction. Two could play the screaming game, he reasoned.

   Tucker cut through the covered storefronts as he had the day before, noticing a plaque drilled to the wall that notified him he was in "The Breezeway", and emerged on the other side to what he could only think was an outdoor flea market. There were booths and tables set up in every available space, leaving a small walkway for people to pass through, and

CHAPTER 3

were advertising everything from protein powder to the school's student government.

Tucker noticed one booth in particular that had a rainbow canopy to provide some shade and a matching rainbow tablecloth taped to the folding table, and decided to start there, taking in all of the sights and sounds as he walked. As he got closer, he heard a shrill voice yell, "Hey kid, come here!". Confused, he stopped and looked around, trying to find who was yelling.

"Yeah, Mary, I'm talking to you," the voice yelled again. "Come over here. We don't bite unless you pay extra!"

Tucker turned his head toward where he thought the voice was coming from and made direct eye contact with the person, who was standing at the rainbow booth. The voice belonged to a drag queen, who was dressed in a skintight black leotard and shiny black boots that went up to her thigh, a tall blonde wig, and beautifully applied makeup consisting of neutral tones and a bright red lip. She towered over the other person behind the table, a very attractive shirtless man with rippling chest muscles evident under a thin layer of golden-brown hair and gorgeous tan skin that glistened in the sunlight.

"Sorry, are you talking to me?" Tucker asked, walking over to the booth. "My name's Tucker, not Mary."

"Don't mind Jamie," the shirtless guy said, offering a brilliant smile. "'Mary' is just another term of endearment, like how queens say 'girl', 'she', 'bitch'... you know."

"I'm not sure I do," Tucker said, confused. He'd never been around drag queens before, since there were none he knew of in small-town Weeki Wachee.

"I'm David," the guy said. "Are you new to UCF?"

"Yeah, today was my first day," Tucker said.

"That's awesome!" David said enthusiastically. "I remember my first day here. I'm in my third year now. How are you liking it here so far?"

The drag queen, Jamie, had taken an extreme interest in her golden, rhinestoned nails on one hand and fanned herself with a giant foldable fan that said 'BITCH' in the other. It was obvious she had no ties to the school, nor cared about the conversation if she wasn't involved.

"Well," Tucker sighed, "I set my alarm for tonight instead of this morning, so I was super late for my first class, and my professor bitched me out in front of everyone. So, so far, not so good. But the fountain's cool, I guess."

"I wish that bitch would have tried that with me!" Jamie interjected, snapping her fan closed and pointing at Tucker with it. She spoke with her hands, accenting every other word with a flourish of her clicking nails. "I would have let him have it in front of everybody, honey!"

"That sounds terrible," David said, ignoring Jamie's outburst. "But the good news is you're here with us now! I'm president of the UCF Queer Alliance and we're partnering with Haven, a local queer club downtown, to let new students know about the different student nights they have, some future collaborative events we'll have going on with them, and some job openings they have right now at the club. I'm a bartender there and it's a really fun place to hang out."

Tucker's mother's words rang in his ears, reminding him of her request that he look for jobs.

"That's really cool!" Tucker said, grabbing a glossy red pamphlet on the table that had both organizations' information on it. "What are you guys hiring for right now?"

"The only entry-level job that's open right now is for shot boys," David said, earning a confused look from Tucker.

"Can you carry a tray with little cups on it?" Jamie asked, noticing Tucker's expression.

"I've never tried, but I'm sure I could," he answered hesitantly.

"That's the spirit!" David said, reaching across the table to pat Tucker on the arm encouragingly.

"Girl," Jamie said, "if I can do it, I'm sure you can do it."

"Am I allowed to sell shots if I'm under twenty-one? I'm only eighteen."

"You're not the first to ask this, and you definitely can under the club's supervision. Can you come by tonight at 8:00 for a test run?" David asked. "The address is on the pamphlet you just grabbed. Beat me to it," he added with a wink.

CHAPTER 3

"Yeah, that'd be great!" Tucker said excitedly, ignoring the confusion and heat in his cheeks he felt from David's wink.

"Sickening!" Jamie exclaimed, throwing her fan open again with a loud crack. "David, give the boy a condom, would you?"

"Oh, uh," David stammered, looking slightly embarrassed, "the UCF Queer Alliance always promotes safe sex, so we're giving condoms away. Take one."

He held out a small plastic tub filled with condoms. Tucker delicately reached into the tub, as if the condoms would cut him, and grabbed two, shoving them in his pockets.

"Thanks," he said sheepishly, not wanting to look David in the eye. He was sure David was just being friendly since he was new, but the guy was cute and Tucker didn't want to embarrass himself.

"So, is there any special dress code or anything I should know about for tonight?"

"No, girl," Jamie replied, rolling her eyes dramatically. "The skimpier you dress, the more the older guys will tip you—they're a bunch of perverts. But you can wear whatever you want."

Tucker was shocked by Jamie's frankness. It wasn't lost on Tucker that older men sometimes went for younger guys, but nobody had phrased it like that in front of him before.

"And if you're interested," David said, obviously trying to move the conversation along and shooting Jamie a sideways glance, "the Alliance is having a meet-and-greet tomorrow afternoon in the building next to Knightro's for anyone interested in joining or just finding out what we're about. You should stop by!"

"I'd love to," Tucker said with a grin. "I live right by there, so it should be easy to find."

"Oh," David said, grabbing the flyer out of Tucker's hand, "let me give you my number in case you have any questions in the meantime. I'm a night owl thanks to the job, so feel free to text me whenever."

Pulling a pen from his jeans pocket, he quickly scribbled his number on the bottom of the pamphlet and handed it back to Tucker with another dazzling smile.

"I'll keep that in mind," Tucker said, carefully folding the pamphlet and putting it in his pocket. "I'm going to go grab some lunch, but it was great meeting you both and I guess I'll see you soon!"

"Bye, girl," Jamie said with a wave of her fan. "Wear something that makes your ass look good!"

Tucker managed a nervous laugh as he walked away and heard David chastising Jamie for being so rude, which made him smile. Though it was jarring at first, Tucker found that he liked Jamie's way of speaking. She seemed like the type to always speak honestly, for better or worse, and Tucker appreciated that.

A majority of the other vendors at the Student Union were there advertising for their businesses and selling things like gym memberships and spray tan appointments, but no fire-breather, Tucker noted with disappointment, so he quickly made his way through the maze of booths and wandering students and walked into the building to get a quick snack before his next class.

Sitting at a tall metal table near the door was Tucker's new classmate, Kiara, eating a sandwich as she pored over a thick textbook. She looked up as the doors opened, noticing Tucker, and waved him over.

"Hey!" she said with a mouth full of sandwich. "Fancy meeting you here. I know I said I wanted to be friends, but are you stalking me now?"

"Oh, absolutely," Tucker joked.

"Please, take a seat," Kiara said, throwing her backpack onto the floor.

"Are you sure?" Tucker asked. "I don't want to interrupt your studying."

"What, this?" Kiara asked, lifting the thick book on the table. "No, this is just some reading for fun. Please, I'd love the company!"

"I don't think I've ever read a book like that for fun," Tucker said, hopping to reach the seat of the tall plastic chair.

"You should try it!" Kiara said, balling up her now-empty sandwich bag and tossing it into a nearby trash can. "This one is super interesting—I'm reading about theatre history and how it's changed so much, and all of the different types of plays that have come and gone."

"Oh, are you a theatre major?" Tucker asked.

CHAPTER 3

"Sure am!" she replied. "What about you?"

"I'm not sure yet," Tucker sighed. "Nothing's really called my name so far, you know? I'm basically here right now because my parents told me I needed a degree to get a good job, but I have no idea what I want to do with my life, so who knows what that good job would even be."

"There's lots of people like that, so no need to stress over it. Besides, you don't have to pick a major until your third year at the latest, so you have plenty of time."

"So if you're majoring in theatre, do you want to be an actress?" Tucker asked, eager to steer the conversation away from him.

"I mean, I wouldn't say no if Broadway came calling, but I like the behind-the-scenes stuff better," Kiara said. "I'd much prefer to be a director or a writer."

Tucker shifted his body to turn more toward Kiara, and the folded pamphlet in his pocket fell out and onto the floor unnoticed by him—Kiara, who saw it fall, reached down and grabbed it, and gasped dramatically.

"Excuse me, sir, but is this a phone number I see?" she asked, her tone dripping with excitement. She waved it in front of Tucker's face like a fan, and he grabbed it from her hands.

"Oh my god, I didn't even feel it fall out of my pocket!" he said, ignoring her question.

"Whose number is that?" she pressed eagerly.

"Just some guy I met at a booth outside," Tucker said with a shy smile. "It wasn't a flirting thing, he was just being helpful since I'm trying to get a job."

"Bullshit it wasn't a flirting thing!" Kiara said, lightly smacking his arm. "People don't just give strangers their numbers for no reason."

"You just gave me your number this morning in class!" he countered.

"Yeah, and my reason was that I wanted you to be my friend," she replied. "I've met people that go to Haven," she said, pointing to the pamphlet, "and I can confidently say that he does not just want to help with your job."

"You weren't even there!" Tucker said with an exasperated laugh.

In high school, Tucker found himself in multiple situations throughout his four years where he was convinced a guy was into him, just to have his dreams dashed time after time. He was starting over here and vowed he wouldn't make that same mistake again.

"I didn't have to be there to know what's going on," Kiara retorted. "You're super-cute, so there's no reason why he *shouldn't* have given you his number with an ulterior motive!"

Tucker blushed at her compliment, but scoffed anyway. He had just met David and didn't want to ruin a possible friendship/potential job opportunity because he thought the guy was attractive.

Kiara checked the time on her phone and swore, quickly shoving her book back into her backpack.

"I really need to set an alarm for my classes," she huffed. Tucker felt a strong sense of déjà vu, remembering his own sense of panic earlier that morning. She slid off of her chair, slinging her backpack across her right shoulder, and walked backwards towards the doors Tucker had entered earlier.

"Text me later and give me an update!" Kiara called before turning around and pushing the doors open, speed-walking out of view. Tucker shook his head in amusement before following Kiara's lead, determined to be early to his remaining two classes of the day.

He still had plenty of time before his next class, American History, so Tucker bought an overpriced granola bar from a nearby vending machine and strolled across campus towards the building where it was held. He arrived with plenty of time to spare, so he took out the notebook he used earlier for Psychology and copied down Kiara's notes from the photo he took on his phone. More people showed up as it got closer to the beginning of class, and Tucker was surprised to see the class would hold students of all ages, not just first-years like he'd expected. Even the more experienced students, though, failed to meet his gaze as he looked around, staring at their feet or out the window with bored expressions.

Maybe it was the movies Tucker had seen over the years, but he'd expected more from his college experience so far. He had seen no fraternity or sorority recruitment yet, or any a capella groups performing around campus. Everyone seemed focused on simply minding their own business and making a point not to look at anyone else in the eye as they walked from class to class until their day was done.

His American History class, held in an auditorium housing over a hundred students, and his English Composition class after that came and went without any notable experiences. After his fiasco that morning, though, Tucker couldn't be too upset with the monotony that encompassed the remainder of his day. He'd made sure to be early and got a good seat close to the back of the rooms, but still close enough that the professors could see he was paying attention to them. His American History professor, a tall blonde woman in her late thirties, and his English Composition professor, a skinny bald man who looked to be in his late twenties and seemed to have just graduated because of his own obvious nerves, came across to Tucker as professional and inclusive, and seemed to understand the stress of the first day, letting their classes end early after introducing themselves and going over their course syllabi.

Tucker hurried back to his dorm once his last class let out, eyeing the thick dark clouds overhead that threatened to open up at any second with each menacing rumble, and immediately started combing through his wardrobe to find something suitable to wear for his job trial that evening. He heard Jamie's parting words ringing in his head, and chose a simple black t-shirt and a pair of jean shorts that fit snugly, accenting his curves like Jamie'd suggested. Mike was nowhere to be found again, and Tucker felt relieved to have some time to himself before he had to leave that evening.

Relief quickly turned to panic, though, as he sat alone in his room with his thoughts spiraling about the many ways that he could mess this opportunity up, including a particularly outrageous scenario where he somehow served the patrons poison instead of alcohol. He wanted to call his mom and let her know how his first day went and about the new job opportunity before remembering where the job was, making him feel nauseous at the thought of having the dreaded coming-out conversation. There wasn't really a way to spin it to where his mother wouldn't question his choice to work at a drag bar without inquiring about his sexuality as well, and his nerves were too high already without adding that to the mix.

Instead, he pulled up Kiara's contact information and sent her a text, hoping she wasn't too busy to talk and keep him occupied.

TUCKER: I'm nervous.

Immediately, the thought bubble appeared in their text chain, showing that Kiara was responding.

KIARA: What for?

TUCKER: What if this all goes horribly wrong?

KIARA: You're carrying a tray, Tucker. There's not much that can happen.

TUCKER: But what if I'm no good?

KIARA: Then you're no good and you find a job somewhere else.

TUCKER: You make it sound so easy.

KIARA: It is easy! You just need to relax and remember that you'll be fine, and it won't be the end of the world if you suck.

KIARA: But you will not suck.

TUCKER: How would you know? You only met me this morning!

CHAPTER 3

KIARA: And you only met me this morning, but here you are looking for my advice. My phone is about to die, so I have to go, but stop freaking out because it's going to be fine. Have fun!

Tucker didn't know what he was expecting to get out of the conversation with Kiara, but her unfaltering confidence in him did nothing to calm his nerves. He knew she was right and there would be no true repercussions if he didn't do a good job tonight, but that didn't stop the nervous butterflies in his stomach from fluttering.

When it was finally time for him to leave, Tucker triple-checked that the pamphlet David had given him was folded up in his pocket, took one final look in the mirror to make sure he looked okay, and headed out the door towards where his ancient black Honda Civic sat in the parking lot. The GPS said that Haven was only about twenty minutes from campus, and Tucker arrived about a half an hour before the agreed upon start time. He parked in the adjacent gravel lot and passed a door to what looked like a hotel lobby. Looking around, he noticed numbered rooms above him, indicating Haven included a place to stay for interested patrons if they were willing to pay.

Tucker paced outside of the entrance, offering shy smiles to men who passed him and looked him up and down appraisingly. Jamie walked out the front door without noticing Tucker, wearing a full face of makeup, a tank top, and basketball shorts, and pulled on a lit cigarette. Tucker nervously approached, offering a half-hearted wave as Jamie looked up from her phone and caught his eye.

"Hi," he said sheepishly.

"Hey, girl," Jamie replied, unfazed by his apparent nerves.

"I don't know if I should do this," Tucker blurted out. "I've never even been to a club before."

"Mary, it's easy," Jamie said, taking one final drag from her cigarette before flicking it onto the ground and snubbing it out with her flip-flop. "You just walk around with a tray and people buy the shots from you. They're all a dollar, so it should be pretty simple for you to keep track of your sales."

"But what if I mess it up?" Tucker asked.

"It's the easiest job you could have," she said, shaking her head in exasperation. "If you screw it up, there's no hope for you. Don't have children."

"You know what? You're right," he said. "It's going to be fine. Fuck it, let's do this."

"Girl, *you* do this. I have a show to do," Jamie retorted, unimpressed with Tucker's sudden bout of bravery and already looking at her phone again. "Have fun," she said without looking up, waving him inside.

Tucker, leaning into his newfound confidence, offered Jamie a smile she didn't see, walking through the front doors that led to the club. The bouncer, an older man standing behind a glass countertop centered in the small red lobby, noticed Tucker and gave him a small nod.

"You have your ID?" The bouncer asked.

"Oh, yeah, sorry," Tucker said, trying to fish his wallet out of his tight pants. There was a line forming behind him of club-goers eager to get into the club and grab a drink, and he could hear their impatient muttering as he tried to pull his ID out with his sweaty fingers.

"Let the kid take his time," the bouncer boomed to the people behind Tucker.

"Sorry about that. Here you go," Tucker said as he finally pulled his ID out and handed it to the man. The bouncer quickly glanced at the ID before handing it back to Tucker and waving him inside.

Tucker, having no idea where he was supposed to go, felt the pounding beat of a song blasting through speakers deeper within the building and followed the vibrations through a dark hallway lined with mirrors towards what he hoped was the right destination. He took a deep breath, wiped his sweaty palms on his shorts, and pushed through the double doors at the end of the hallway as he entered the heart of the club.

Chapter 4

As Tucker exited the dark mirror-lined hallway, he was met with soft red lighting and the sounds of a remixed pop song blowing through the speakers set up around the club that rattled in his ears. The room he was in housed more mirrors on the walls, two long black couches tucked into the corner of the room to his left, and a square bar with a counter on each side and a bartender in the middle of it to his right. There was an open doorway straight ahead from where Tucker stood that led to the dance floor, and Tucker could see club-goers drinking cocktails out of clear plastic cups as they chatted with one another on the sides of the dance floor or danced with each other in the center of the room, lit by the flashing lights and the disco ball above their heads. A DJ was speaking into a microphone, but Tucker couldn't make out what she was saying from the room he was in.

Having no other guesses as to where he should be, Tucker turned to his right and headed to the square black bar, catching the eye of the muscular bald bartender, clad in a tight navy blue tank-top and short black shorts, as he approached.

"Hi, honey, what can I get you?" the bartender yelled over the music, dancing back and forth to the music as he worked.

"I'm Tucker," he yelled back. "I'm supposed to give out shots tonight."

"Oh, perfect!" the bartender said. "Give me one sec' to set them up and then you can get to work!"

"Okay, great," Tucker said with an enthusiastic smile, eager to show that he was happy to be put to work. "Do you know where David is? He's the one that set this up for me."

"I think he's on break right now," the bartender yelled over the pulsing beat echoing through the club, not looking up as he quickly poured the shots and placed them on a black plastic tray.

Tucker was disappointed David wasn't here to talk to before he started working, hoping to get some words of encouragement from him. Not because he thought he was cute, Tucker rationalized, but because he was a familiar face and someone on the inside that could vouch for him. The bartender slid the tray toward Tucker, interrupting his wandering thoughts.

"Is there anything I should know before I get started?" Tucker asked loudly.

"It's pretty easy," the bartender said, echoing what the others had promised earlier. "Smile, be friendly, and sell the shots. They're all a dollar tonight and they're all vodka. Think you can handle that?"

"Definitely," he replied, sharing another confident smile with the bartender, who offered a dazzling white grin in return.

"Then go get 'em, tiger," the bartender said, tapping on the tray. A group of men approached the bar to the right, and the bartender turned to get their drinks started, ending the conversation.

Tucker carefully lifted the tray and, once he felt secure with it in his hands, walked through the open doorway towards the dance floor. Men in the room quickly flocked towards him in an almost comedic fashion, throwing dollar bills onto the tray and taking shots off. Tucker was so overwhelmed with everyone that he couldn't see who was doing what, but he felt multiple hands quickly grasp his butt, confirming Jamie's statement about older men from earlier that day.

After most of the shots were paid for and taken, the crowd disappeared as quickly as it appeared, leaving one guy who looked to be around Tucker's age. He'd apparently waited for the rest of the crowd to disperse before approaching and now stood casually in front of Tucker with his hands in his jeans pockets. The guy was slightly taller than Tucker and had short, curly brown hair, caramel-colored skin, and wore a maroon tank top with his jeans that revealed a patch of dark chest hair underneath with a gold chain nestled in it. He had sharp features, a defined jaw that was accentuated by a shortly cropped beard, and full lips turned up in a confident smirk as he

CHAPTER 4

approached.

Wordlessly, he placed a dollar on the tray, took the last remaining shot, and slightly threw his head back as he swallowed the liquid, all while keeping eye contact with Tucker. Tucker felt almost hypnotized by the handsome stranger and watched him take the shot, unable to take his eyes off of him.

"You're cute," the stranger said over the music. "You new here?"

"Yeah," Tucker replied, blinking slowly as if he was waking up. "Today's my first day. I'm just on a trial right now."

"Very cool," the stranger said, his confident smirk playing at the edge of his mouth. "What's your name?"

"Tucker," he replied. "What about you?"

"Adrian," the guy replied, momentarily placing a strong hand on Tucker's arm. "It's very nice to meet you, Tucker. What are you doing after this?"

"Oh, I'm not sure. They'll probably give me more shots to sell or something now that these are gone," he said.

"No," Adrian chuckled, "I mean, what are you doing after you get off of work?"

"Oh!" Tucker said with an embarrassed laugh. "I'm not too sure. I'll probably just go home, depending on when I get done. I've got an early class tomorrow."

"You go to UCF?" Adrian asked.

"Yeah, I just started," he replied. The other patrons had barely spoken a word to him before taking their shots to go, so Tucker had no idea what was happening with Adrian. He was handsome, Tucker noticed approvingly, so he was happy to make small talk with him.

"That's awesome," Adrian said, showing off a gorgeous smile. "Well, you should come hang out at my place instead. You can always crash there and go to class in the morning. It'll be fun."

"I don't think I'll be able to," Tucker said apologetically. He was certainly in uncharted territory now, and didn't know how to navigate the conversation professionally without coming off uninterested in the handsome stranger. "But if I get off soon, then maybe I can stop by for a little!"

Adrian replied, but a new song started blaring through the speakers and

Tucker couldn't hear anything but the sounds of extremely loud house music for a few moments.

"Sorry, what did you say?" Tucker yelled over the music. Adrian took a step closer to Tucker, putting a hand on his arm and his face next to Tucker's ear.

"I said, trust me, I can help you get off soon," Adrian murmured huskily, his beard tickling Tucker's neck as he spoke. His warm breath and sensual words against Tucker's ear sent a tingling sensation down his spine, and Tucker shuddered slightly. Tucker, shocked and aroused by Adrian's bold statement, was unable to speak for a moment, which caused Adrian to smirk once again. Outside of the porn he'd occasionally watched once he was sure his parents were asleep, Tucker had never heard someone be so forward before and had no idea how to respond.

"I'll see you around, New Guy Tucker," Adrian called over the music, patting Tucker on the shoulder as he passed him and disappeared into the crowd of dancing people.

That was the first time he was ever aware that a guy was coming on to him, Tucker realized as he wandered back to the bar to get more shots. He still couldn't believe how frank Adrian had been, and how hot he'd found it! He scanned the crowd as he maneuvered around the patrons towards the bar for another glimpse of Adrian, but couldn't find him anywhere. The bartender had his back to Tucker, but there was another tray full of shots waiting for him as he approached. Not wanting to interrupt the bartender, Tucker wordlessly exchanged his empty tray for the full one and headed back to the dance floor.

He was again met with a flock of gay men as transactions were made and shots were taken from his tray. After the rush ended, he still had a few remaining and milled around the dance floor for other patrons to approach. Another DJ's voice boomed on the microphone from inside a tinted booth in the far corner of the room, this one a deep baritone, announcing the start of the drag show. People from the other rooms in the club streamed in, dollar bills already in their hands and eagerly waiting to tip the performers.

"To start out the evening," the voice boomed, "please help me welcome to

CHAPTER 4

the stage the illustrious, the beautiful, the ever-talented Jamie Kahlo!"

The music started and a slow, sultry jazz song Tucker didn't recognize began to play as Jamie, now clad in a fully rhinestoned burlesque outfit consisting of a corset and many straps secured around her body that accentuated her curves, took the stage, a spotlight shining on her as she walked. She lipsynced the words as the song progressed, keeping eye contact with different members of the crowd as she moved. She started slowly taking off her gloves, then a portion of her outfit to reveal a rhinestoned bra and corset set, before later taking those off to show Jamie's breasts (which Tucker did not realize were real and not another drag illusion), covered only by rhinestoned pasties. She unleashed flips and cartwheels as the song swelled towards the end, and the crowd went crazy—screaming and clapping and throwing money on the stage for her as trumpets blared and she hit her final pose.

Tucker was entranced by the performance, not taking his eyes off of Jamie as he took people's money and handed them the remaining shots on his tray. He had never seen anything like Jamie's act before. Sure, he'd seen drag queens on TV before, but this was entirely different. Jamie was real, she was raw and electric. The audience could see that she put herself into everything she did onstage with such gusto that the crowd had no choice but to holler and cheer and shower her with money. She was stunning. It was in that moment that Tucker thought to himself: *I want to be just like her.*

Finally noticing his tray was empty, Tucker made his way back to the bar as the show continued and the next performer took the stage. The bartender he met earlier was nowhere to be found, but David had taken his place, pouring drinks and passing them towards two men as Tucker approached. David turned, ready to take the next order, and his face lit up when he met Tucker's eyes.

"Oh, hey!" David said excitedly.

"Hey, there you are!" Tucker said with a big grin on his face. They'd only met earlier that day, but seeing David only lifted his spirits even higher than they already were. Tucker confidently placed the empty tray on the bar.

"Wow, you sold all of those already?" he asked.

"Yeah," Tucker replied, "this is the second tray I've done tonight. They were just throwing money at me!"

"That's amazing!" David said enthusiastically. "I haven't seen shots sell that fast in a long time."

"Oh, I didn't really do—"

"Would you like to become a permanent shot boy?" David interrupted. "You're a natural."

"Wow, yeah, that'd be amazing!" Tucker said with a surprised laugh.

"Great!" David said. "Here, give me the tray and all the money you got and come back in a little while to collect your tips. Sound good?"

"Yeah, that sounds great," he said with a grin, sliding the tray towards David. "Hey, in the meantime, do you know where Jamie went? I just saw her perform, and she was amazing, so I wanted to congratulate her."

"She always is," David nodded knowingly. He pointed to his right, toward a door on the other end of the bar. "You see that door over there? The dressing room is through there and down the hall."

"Thanks," Tucker said, offering David another smile before heading towards the door. As he passed the doorway to the dance floor, Adrian walked through, brushing shoulders with Tucker.

"Oh, sorry," Tucker said, turning towards Adrian before realizing it was him. "Oh, hey!"

"Hey!" Adrian smiled. "Looks like you got off pretty early, huh?"

"Yeah, they just made me the official shot boy," Tucker said proudly. "I guess you'll be seeing a lot more of me now."

"Sounds great to me," he said with a laugh. He grabbed Tucker's hand and lightly pulled. "Come dance with me."

"I can't," Tucker said apologetically. "I have to go find Jamie. Rain check though?"

"You know where to find me, New Guy Tucker," Adrian said with a smile and a wink, patting Tucker on the arm before turning around and heading back to the dance floor. Tucker watched him leave for a moment before focusing his attention back to the dressing room, surveying the club as he walked toward the door. As David described, there was a small hallway

CHAPTER 4

behind the door dimly lit with overhead lamps, and another door with a giant high heel attached to it on the other side.

Tucker pushed the door open, almost immediately hitting something as it swung open.

"Ow, Jesus!" Jamie yelled indignantly from behind the door. "Somebody's in here!"

"I'm so sorry!" Tucker said as he quickly slipped into the room and closed the door. "I had no idea you were behind there."

Tucker quickly looked around the small dressing room, which was lit solely with light bulbs surrounding a large vanity mirror where Jamie sat, and contained a short clothes rack against the opposite wall filled to the brim with various costumes. There were wig heads mounted on the wall displaying differently colored and styled wigs, and there was a small mountain of shoes tucked in the corner of the room next to the clothes rack.

"Yeah?" Jamie asked impatiently, snapping Tucker back to attention.

"Oh...," he said slowly. "I just wanted to say you did a great job. I watched your performance and you were really, really good."

"Thank you, I know," Jamie said, giving Tucker a playful wink from the mirror.

"Oh, okay," Tucker mumbled, feeling his face grow hot from embarrassment. He had no idea what possessed him to want to come backstage and talk to Jamie, but he just had the feeling that he had to talk to her after seeing her performance.

"But thanks," Jamie said, noticing Tucker's reddening cheeks in the mirror and softening her tone. "You're sweet."

Tucker smiled at her reflection, feeling appreciative. Just like David, he had only met Jamie earlier that day, but he really enjoyed being around her and wanted to be her friend.

"Oh, hey," he said, "thanks for the heads-up about the job earlier today. I got hired as a permanent shot boy!"

"Good for you," Jamie said as she applied more blush to her cheeks. "I told you it was easy."

"Yeah, you were right," Tucker admitted. "And I think this guy was hitting on me? I'm not totally sure though."

"What do you mean?" Jamie asked, her eyes narrowing in confusion. "Was he or wasn't he?"

"I don't know," he said truthfully. "I've never had a guy hit on me before."

"How has that never happened to you before?" she asked, putting her brush down on the makeup-stained black counter attached to the mirror. "Girl, *everybody* gets hit on."

Tucker shrugged. "I'm one of the only gay guys I know of in my town, and I'm not even fully out, so there wasn't really anyone to hit on me."

"Hold up," Jamie said, turning around in her chair to look Tucker in the eye, "your *town*? Where'd you come from, Kentucky or something?"

"Might as well have," Tucker laughed. Feeling more comfortable in their conversation, he sat in the empty chair next to Jamie. "So, how did you learn to do drag and stuff?"

"'And stuff'?" Jamie asked. "You're going to have to be a bit more specific than that."

"You know," Tucker said expectantly. "All the dancing and learning to strip and cartwheels and stuff—how'd you learn all of that? You looked so cool."

"Lots of practice," she replied, turning back to the mirror to continue touching up her makeup. "I've been doing drag for years."

"Did you go to school for it or something?" Tucker pressed.

"School?" Jamie asked incredulously, turning back toward Tucker again. "Bitch, I didn't even graduate high school. No, I didn't go to school for drag. It's just something you learn."

"Do you think you could teach me?" Tucker blurted out before the words even registered. *Was that something you could ask someone?*, he wondered. Before Jamie could answer, a stern-looking woman wearing all black and a headset on her head opened the dressing room door. Her nametag said her name was Tanya, Tucker noticed.

"Jamie, you're about to go on," the stage manager said.

"I know, bitch!" Jamie said playfully, turning toward the woman. "I hear the music. It's got a long intro, so I'll be there in a second."

The stage manager sighed, but seemed satisfied with Jamie's answer and

CHAPTER 4

disappeared. Jamie turned to Tucker and threw her phone at him. "Put your number in my phone," she instructed. "We'll talk."

"Okay!" Tucker said excitedly, quickly inputting his information and handing the phone back to her. Jamie grabbed the phone, tucked it into her bra, pulled up a tight red strapless dress and exited the dressing room without another word. Tucker could hear the crowd's cheers moments later as she took to the stage, and he felt a sense of admiration all over again. She definitely had an air of confidence that, mixed with her frankness and attitude, could be perceived as rude or cocky, but Tucker thought she had been nothing but genuine and helpful since meeting her earlier that day, and he admired that.

The dressing room's door swung open again, surprising Tucker and hitting him in the shoulder. He swore, and David slipped into the room, quickly shutting the door to avoid further injury.

"Shit, I'm sorry," David apologized. It was his turn to look embarrassed, and Tucker could see redness blooming on his cheeks.

"You're fine," Tucker assured him quickly. "I just did the same thing to Jamie."

"I just wanted to give you your tips," he said, handing Tucker a wad of dollar bills. "It's not much today, but you'll get more once you start working full shifts."

"Great, thank you," Tucker said appreciatively, pocketing the money. "And thank you again for helping me get this job. I really, really appreciate it."

"Don't mention it," David said with a smile, placing a hand on Tucker's arm. His touch lingered as the two stared into each other's eyes in silence for a moment, but what felt like hours to Tucker, before David cleared his throat and took a step back, pulling the dressing room door open.

"Okay, well, I'd better get back to work," David said, clapping his hands together and pointing at Tucker. "Enjoy the rest of your night, and I'm sure I'll see you around campus soon."

"Yeah, you too," Tucker said dazedly as David turned and left the room. Tucker turned to the mirror once the door closed and exhaled deeply, staring at himself wide-eyed in disbelief. His disbelief quickly turned to joy, his face reflecting it with a big smile as he exited the dressing room towards the entrance of the club. He looked for David as he left, trying to acknowledge him once more, but David was quickly pouring drinks as the line at the bar grew.

Tucker waved farewell to the bouncer as he walked out the door toward his car and sat in silence for a moment to decompress before starting the engine and pulling onto the road towards campus. Once he was back to his dorm and in bed, Tucker triple-checked that he set his alarm for the correct time before falling asleep, his mind lingering on the baffling interactions he'd had that evening.

Chapter 5

"The guy said *what?*" Kiara asked, not bothering to finish chewing the bite of her sandwich she'd just taken before interjecting. Tucker had texted her the following morning after his Computer Sciences class ended, eager to tell somebody what had happened the night before at Haven. Between the interaction in the dressing room with David and Adrian's shameless flirting, Tucker needed to talk and Kiara had been more than happy to listen. The two sat at the same tall table they had the day before in the Student Union, chatting like they'd been friends for years instead of days.

"I know!" Tucker laughed. "He was really cute, too, so I just kind of stood there in shock for a minute. But I didn't give him my number or anything, so I guess that's that."

Kiara playfully smacked his arm with her lunchbox in response. "Have I taught you nothing?" she asked.

"We've been friends for two days now, so not really," Tucker answered with a shrug.

"Okay, so you didn't give him your number," she said, "but what about David? There's no way you can think he's just trying to be your friend now."

Tucker blushed and looked down at the table, suddenly interested in its design as a smile grew on his face. "I don't know, maybe," he said shyly.

"Hey, eyes up here," Kiara demanded, snapping her fingers in front of his face. "I want you to look me in the eye as I tell you this—he likes you, Tucker. You should text him."

"Text him *what?*" Tucker asked with exasperation. "'Hey David, I know we just met yesterday and you're two years older than me but I think you're cute'? That would go over horribly!"

"I disagree," Kiara said, taking another bite of her sandwich. She chewed, but did not swallow before she continued speaking. "Maybe not those exact words, but if you start up a conversation and just be yourself, things will fall into place!"

"Be myself?" he asked incredulously. "Who are you, my mom? That's awful! In all the movies you've seen and books you've read, when someone is told to be themselves, does it ever work? No!"

Kiara rolled her eyes and continued eating, unbothered by his rant. Without her rebuttal to further the conversation, Tucker resorted to stewing in silence as she finished her lunch. He couldn't believe that 'be yourself' was the best suggestion Kiara could come up with! Desperate for more advice, he made a mental note to reach out to one of his friends back home, Brooke, later that day to get a second opinion. She wouldn't be familiar with the situation, of course, but Tucker had seen her flirt with boys in their class since the third grade and knew that if anyone could help him, it'd be her.

As if she could see the wheels turning in Tucker's head, Kiara shook hers in disappointment. "I know that this whole flirting thing is new for you," she said, "but I think you should trust me on this one. I wouldn't steer you wrong on purpose!"

"I know," Tucker sighed. "I just don't want to mess anything up, especially now that he got me this job. What if you're wrong and he fires me?"

"Then he's a dick," she said. "But I doubt that will happen. I don't want to stress you out any more, though, so let's change the subject."

"Okay, how were your classes so far today?" he asked.

"Boring," she sighed, waving her hand dismissively. "New topic. Do you have any plans this weekend?"

"Not really," Tucker said, shrugging his shoulders. "It's my birthday on Saturday, but I don't think I'll do anything."

He had never been much of a birthday party-type of guy, preferring to just celebrate it with his parents over dinner and then hang out with some friends. It wasn't that he was antisocial, but he just never saw the big deal when it came to birthdays.

CHAPTER 5

Kiara smacked his arm with her lunchbox once more. "You didn't tell me that! Let's do something!"

"I don't know, I'm not much of a partier," he said. "Besides, I'm only turning nineteen. It's not that big of a deal."

"Then we can sit in your room all night and agonize over David some more," she retorted. "But I'm not letting you sit there all alone on your birthday, whether you want to or not!"

"Fine," he said with a laugh, putting his hands up in mock surrender. "I will let you take over my birthday."

Kiara squealed and clapped her hands with delight. Tucker couldn't help but laugh at her enthusiasm and felt thankful all over again that she'd passed him her notes the day before. With the enormous class sizes in his other courses, he had been worried he wouldn't be able to make any friends.

"Okay," she said, hopping off of her chair and grabbing her belongings, "I've got to run, but I'll text you and we'll figure something out for this weekend. It's going to be fun, I promise!"

Tucker waved goodbye as she rushed out the door and pulled out his phone, dialing Brooke's number. It rang only twice before she picked up, screaming his name in greeting.

"You're alive!" she said. "We were beginning to worry about you!"

"Hey, phones work both ways," Tucker pointed out, a smile on his face. He hadn't realized how much he'd missed his friends back home until talking with Brooke, and a feeling of relief flooded through him that they hadn't forgotten about him in the few days he'd been gone. The two caught up, exchanging stories of what Tucker's classes had been like so far, and what Brooke's baby brother had drawn on the wall this week. When they ran out of small talk, Tucker took a deep breath to steady himself before the inevitable onslaught of questions from Brooke began once he brought up his boy troubles.

"So, I need to talk to you about a boy," he said.

At the same time, Brooke said, "Hey, so Micah's been asking about you."

Tucker blanched at the mention of his friend's name, rendering him momentarily speechless. Micah had been the closest thing Tucker had ever had to a romantic relationship, and the two ended whatever they had in a big fight a week before Tucker left for college. They weren't dating, and they'd never kissed, but there was a spark and a connection between the two that was palpable, and Micah wanted to cut things off before Tucker left, much to Tucker's dismay. Their friend group had their suspicions about the two, but neither had ever divulged what feelings they had for the other, much less to the group.

"I don't really want to talk about Micah right now," Tucker mumbled. He'd been hurt by Micah's abrupt ending of their friendship, or whatever they'd had, and he had pushed those feelings as far down as they could go until now.

"Did you guys get into a fight or something?" she asked. "We were talking about you at the beach over the weekend and he barely said a word. He just looked upset."

"Like sad-upset or mad-upset?" Tucker asked before he could stop himself. He knew that it didn't matter either way, but he couldn't make himself stop caring just because he was hurt.

"I don't know," Brooke said. "He was the last to show up and the first to leave, and we haven't really talked much since then."

"He'll be fine," Tucker said, eager to move the conversation along.

"I guess," she sighed into the phone. "So what were you saying about boys?"

Tucker quickly reiterated the events of the previous day, pausing at different points as Brooke let out cries of excitement or frustration at his tale.

"So what do I do?" he asked.

"Text him!" she yelled. "This guy David obviously thinks you're cute. He was flirting when you met him, he got you a job, you had that moment in the dressing room, so what are you waiting for?"

"I guess I'm just scared," Tucker said, laying his torso on the table.

"Tucker, you've seen me use my powers for good and for evil over the years," Brooke said, "so you know I know what I'm doing when it comes to boys. I'm telling you, as a flirting genius and your friend, to text him. You don't have to be overly sexual or anything, but just establish the connection

CHAPTER 5

and let your personality do the rest."

"Oh, so be myself?" Tucker asked sarcastically. "I know you can't see me right now, but I'm rolling my eyes."

"Look, *you* called *me* for advice, remember?" she asked with a laugh. Tucker joined in on the laughter, and the conversation shifted topics again as the two joked and reminisced about memories they'd created just weeks before, but felt like much longer since Tucker left. The conversation eventually ended, and Tucker left the Student Union in high spirits, even though he'd received basically no substantial advice from either friend.

He walked across campus toward his next class, and sat on a rusted green metal bench outside of the building overlooking the expansive green lawn that sprawled across the property, playing mental ping pong with himself the whole way there about what he should do. He nervously bit his lip and pulled out his phone. He'd input David's contact information the day before, fearing he'd lose the pamphlet he'd given him. Taking a deep breath, Tucker started a new message and wrote:

TUCKER: Hi David, this is Tucker. I just wanted to say thanks again for getting me the job and wanted to know if I could take you out to coffee as a small thank you.

He pressed send before he could change his mind and exhaled sharply as he picked up his backpack and went inside.

Tucker's last class of the day was Astronomy, and he could focus on nothing else besides his phone, which he glanced at every thirty seconds, much to the professor's noticeable chagrin when he looked up and caught her eye. She was an older black woman who wore thick-rimmed glasses and had short, black hair with gray showing at the roots, and spoke about the cosmos so passionately and eloquently from the minute class began that Tucker eventually gave up on a response from David and paid attention to her lecture. When the class ended and a majority of the students had poured out of the classroom, Tucker approached the professor on his way out.

"Professor Thomas," he said, stopping at her desk, "my name is Tucker and I just wanted to apologize for having my phone out at the beginning of class. I was waiting to hear back about something important, but I know you saw me and I didn't mean to be rude."

"Young man," Professor Thomas said, taking off her glasses to look at him, "I have been teaching for many years, and we are living in the age of technology, so you are not the first to look at their phone in my class. I'd appreciate if you didn't from now on, or to at least do it more discreetly than you were today, but I accept your apology. This class can be fun if you pay attention, so I suggest you try it!"

Tucker smiled. "I will, I promise," he said, nodding his head.

"Good," she said, returning his smile. "I'll see you next class then, Tucker. It was nice meeting you."

Tucker's smile grew into a grin as he left the room, relieved to have had a much better interaction with one of his professors than he'd had the day before with Professor Whitley. He reached into his pocket and checked his phone, and his grin faded as he stared at his blank notifications screen.

CHAPTER 5

He's probably just busy, Tucker thought to himself. But even he knew what being blown off looked like, and was beginning to suspect that's what was occurring. He headed back to his dorm, eager to relax for the rest of the day after the constant rush he felt like he was in the day before. Mike was nowhere to be found, surprising Tucker less each time he made the discovery.

On his dresser was the half-folded pamphlet from David and Jamie's booth, and Tucker was reminded of the event David said the UCF Queer Alliance was holding that afternoon. Having nothing better to do, Tucker walked to the mirror to make sure he looked fine, and headed out the door again towards the event. There were some guys from his floor throwing a ball around in the common area, and Tucker swore he heard one of them call him a queer under their breath based on the snickers from the others, but he kept his head high as he walked out the door and into the elevator.

As a fairly feminine man, Tucker had been getting called gay since before he knew what it meant. He could be sensitive at times, but attending public school in a small Florida town had made him grow a thick skin when it came to name-calling and schoolyard bullying. He realized, however, that he'd clenched his fists in frustration as the elevator doors closed, and relaxed them again. Moving to Orlando, he'd assumed that people his age would be more open-minded than the people he grew up with back home. Evidently, he was incorrect.

The sun was lowering in the early evening sky, painting everything gold as Tucker followed the now-familiar path toward Knightro's. He passed its front doors as he made his way further down the covered walkway toward a tinted glass door with a rainbow painted on it, assuming that was his destination. He took a deep breath, trying to calm his heart that he could hear thumping in his ears, and pushed the door open. It clicked and barely moved, much to Tucker's frustration. *Was he at the wrong place?,* he wondered. He could see lights on inside, so he thought he was right. He tried again, pushing the door a few times to no avail. Finally, he saw a shadow approach the door and pushed it open with ease from the inside.

David, wearing a black shirt with the UCF logo and a rainbow on the front, stood with the door extended in one hand, giving Tucker a quizzical look. "It's a pull, not a push," he said.

"Yeah, that makes sense now," Tucker muttered, his face immediately burning with embarrassment.

David laughed, shouldering the door as he placed a hand on Tucker's back and steered him inside. The room itself looked plain, with the same white cinderblock walls Tucker had in his dorm room and a faded gray carpet. The group assembled on the mustard yellow L-shaped couch in the center of the room, however, had obviously tried to make the space their own. There were posters covering each wall with positive mottos, helpful hotlines, and upcoming events, multiple tables and chairs set up around the room for more personal work, and what looked like a small coat closet in the corner.

"Everyone," David said, "this is who I was talking about yesterday. This is Tucker!" He turned to Tucker and pointed his hand to the small group seated on the couch. "Tucker, these are the other members of the Queer Alliance."

Tucker felt his stomach flip—David had been talking about him? Was it just a recap of their conversation at the booth, or did he get more personal with the story? He gave his head a small shake, trying to clear it and stay in the moment so he didn't look odd.

Everyone offered Tucker a small wave as David brought him to the couch and introduced the members individually—there was Gray, who was thin, blond, and pale and said they identified as non-binary; Darcy and Addie, a lesbian couple that looked like polar opposites: Darcy was short, stocky, pale, and had big, bright red hair, whereas Addie was tall, tan, and had sleek black hair that extended to the small of her back; Jai, a gay Indian man who looked to be the oldest of the group by the small amount of gray in his sideburns, with a short-cropped black beard and small circular glasses; and Kenny, a self-identified bisexual man who was barrel-chested and shorter than the rest of the group, wearing a tank top that showed off the nest of chest hair he was sporting underneath. Tucker repeated their names as he said hello, and sat next to Gray on the end of the couch once introductions were finished, David taking the other end next to Jai.

CHAPTER 5

Tucker sensed a lot of nervous tension in the room, and nobody made any noise aside from a sniffle or a cough until David explained, "This is the first meet-and-greet we've done, so everyone's still feeling kind of uncomfortable."

"Trust me, I know the feeling," Tucker said cheerfully, trying to break the tension. Nobody responded, all of them staring at their phones or out the window. Tucker met David's eyes, who gave a small encouraging nod. "Back home, I tried to get a Gay-Straight Alliance started at my high school with some of my friends—I was the only gay one, but they were sweet for trying. We had a meet-and-greet in the school courtyard to try to get the word out, and I don't think I've ever felt so judged and uncomfortable in my entire life."

"I had one in my high school, too," Darcy finally said, looking up at Tucker with a small smile. She gave Addie's hand a small squeeze, encouraging her to follow suit.

"I did too," Addie said sheepishly. "I was the Vice-President."

"I didn't know you were Vice-President, Addie. That's really cool!" David said brightly. "Guys," he continued, "you really don't need to be nervous around Tucker. He's new, just like some of you were last year when you joined—like Jai!"

Jai nodded his head in agreement but said nothing. Kenny stood up, and the group looked at him expectantly, waiting for him to speak, but he pulled out his phone and walked towards the door as he quietly answered a phone call.

Tucker chuckled, and Gray started to laugh as well—a loud, almost maniacal laugh that was extremely infectious, and soon everyone was laughing for no real reason at all. Tucker took advantage of the moment and began recounting the story of his awful first college experience in Professor Whitley's class the day before, and soon everyone was chatting and mingling like how Tucker assumed they normally would.

When the sun was just barely visible through the building's windows, Tucker took it as a sign to head back to his room. He thanked everyone for making him feel welcome and headed to the door, David right behind him. Tucker found it a little strange that David had never responded to his text, nor did he mention it during the time they were just hanging out, but decided to leave it alone and tried to push it from his mind. Before exiting, he turned to David to thank him for being so welcoming, but before he could say anything his phone rang. He pulled it out and was surprised to see that it was his mother calling. David seemed slightly shaken by the call, as if his focus was interrupted, but smiled and waved to Tucker, mouthing a silent goodbye. Tucker returned his smile before walking out the door and answering the call.

"Hey Mom," he said as he walked.

"Hi honey!" her voice crackled through the phone's speaker. "Can you hear me okay? I'm driving right now."

"Yeah, I can hear you fine," Tucker laughed. She asked that same question every time she called him from the bluetooth speaker in her car, which she'd had for years now, and he gave the same response each time.

"I was just calling to see how school was going now that you've been to all of your classes!"

"They all went fine," Tucker lied, grimacing at the memory of his encounter with Professor Whitley. "How are things at home?"

"It's so quiet now! Your father and I miss you! I think I'm getting empty nest syndrome already."

"I miss you guys too," Tucker said as he approached his building. He entered the empty lobby and pressed the elevator button, waiting for the chime it made when its doors opened. It pinged a few moments later, and he stepped in. "Mom, I need to tell you something."

"Honey, speak up, it's getting hard to hear you," her voice crackled. He could hear her fine, but noticed the sound of static in the background.

"I should've done this before I moved like I promised myself I would," Tucker sighed, "but I guess better late than never. I'm gay, Mom."

He waited with bated breath for her response as he continued to rise in the elevator, but heard nothing but silence on her end. He thought the signal might have dropped, so he checked his screen and saw that the call was still going.

CHAPTER 5

"Hello?" he asked.

"I'm still here," she said softly. It wasn't the softness he was used to from his mother, a kind filled with emotion and love. This was colder, more sterile. He swore he felt his heart stop beating for a moment as the elevator doors opened on his floor, unsure if he could muster the strength to move from where he stood. He anticipated her next words, her upcoming rejection, and felt cold dread seep into his stomach as he came to the realization that he was about to face one of his worst fears.

Chapter 6

"Did you hear what I said?" Tucker asked softly, fighting back the tears already pooling in his eyes. He rushed through the empty common area and into his room, silently thanking Mike for not being there.

"Yes, I heard you," his mother said, her tone even and emotionless.

"Okay, well, do you have a response?" he asked, letting his tears fall down his cheeks. He feared the answer, but wanted to hear it from her.

"I don't know," his mother sighed. "If this is what you choose, then it is what it is. I just don't think you should tell your father right now. He's pretty stressed with work."

"I see," Tucker said, his mouth forming a tight frown as he tried to stop the tears, his sadness quickly morphing into anger. "I won't tell him, then. And for the record, I didn't *choose* this, Mom. It's who I am. So get on board or lose your son."

"Tucker, don't be so dramatic!" his mother said, her tone rising.

Tucker ended the call and sat on his bed with his phone face-down, letting his tears fall. His phone vibrated softly on his comforter, alerting him to what he assumed was his mother calling him again. He was hurt and disappointed, but felt tears coming from a place of anger as well. He had imagined the worst—her screaming at him and disowning him, or calling him despicable names, but somehow her indifference hurt worse than that. A parent was supposed to love unconditionally, and for her to react that way—for her to tell him not to tell his own father who he really was—hurt him more than any name she could have called him.

The door unlocked with a beep from the automatic lock and Mike began

CHAPTER 6

to walk into the room with a few friends in tow. Noticing Tucker on his bed, Mike turned and quietly said something to his friends, who nodded and walked back into the hall, the door closing behind them.

"Hey," Mike said, approaching Tucker's bed, "you okay?"

"Yeah," Tucker sniffled, wiping his face with the back of his hand. "You know, just the usual."

"What happened?" he asked, his eyebrows furrowing with concern.

"I just came out to my mom, and instead of telling me she loved me and that it didn't change anything, like what every kid hopes for when they think of coming out, she told me not to tell my dad that I *chose* to be like this because he was stressed out at work," Tucker explained, acid dripping from every word.

Mike's eyes widened. "Dude," he breathed, "that's fucked up."

"Yeah," Tucker laughed ruefully.

"I'm really sorry, Tucker," Mike sighed, patting Tucker on the shoulder. "I know I didn't handle things super gracefully when you told me, but for what it's worth, I know you didn't choose to be gay."

"Thanks," Tucker said, offering Mike a sad smile.

"I've been doing some research," Mike added, "about, like, gay culture and stuff like that so we could talk about it. Did you know that Neil Patrick Harris is gay? I've seen him on TV and I had no idea!"

Tucker laughed, a true, honest laugh, and it was his turn to pat Mike on the shoulder. "Yeah, Mike, I did," he said, sniffling once more.

"Damn," he said, "I really thought I was going to surprise you with that one!"

"The fact that you looked that up because of me is surprise enough," Tucker replied with a smile. "I appreciate it."

"Hey, do you want to go grab some food with me and my friends?" he asked, motioning behind him to where they stood outside their door.

"I'm good. Thank you, though. You guys go have fun," Tucker said. With the rollercoaster of emotions he'd been on the last few hours, the last thing he was interested in was eating.

"Alright, but text me if you change your mind," Mike said, turning and heading back out the door.

Tucker's phone buzzed again, and he ignored it. If his life were a movie, he considered bitterly, this would be the point where he'd run to his lover for a long embrace to show that love comes from all places, not just family. But his life wasn't a movie, he reminded himself as he reached into one of the dresser drawers he'd designated for snacks and grabbed a bag of chocolate candy, stuffing a handful in his mouth. He was living real life, and real life sucked sometimes. He was less than a week into his college experience and had no idea how he was going to survive four years if it continued like this.

There was a knock at the door, cutting through the silence in the dorm room and startling Tucker. Curious, he went to the door and tried to spy on whoever was there through the peephole, but found that it had been painted over. "I'm going to have to tell someone about this," he muttered under his breath as he swung the door open, not bothering to hide the annoyance on his face.

Standing in his doorway was Kiara, arms crossed over her chest, reflecting the same look of annoyance on her face.

"Where have you been? I've been trying to call you!" she said, pushing her way into his room.

"How do you know where I live?" Tucker asked, truly bewildered by his unannounced guest.

"It wasn't that hard to figure out," Kiara said, jumping up to sit on his bed. Noticing the bag of candy, she reached in and grabbed a handful.

"Kiara," Tucker sighed, trudging back to the bed, "now is really not a good time."

"I just came over because I got bored and I wanted to find out if you talked to that guy. Did something happen?" she asked.

Tucker nodded, afraid that his voice would give his hurt feelings away if he spoke, and felt tears appearing again. He looked up at the ceiling, trying to keep them at bay. "I just told my mom I was gay, and she told me not to tell my dad. She said I chose this."

Kiara's mouth dropped open, showing off the chewed pieces of candy she had yet to swallow. "Oh, Tucker," she said, sliding off the bed and pulling

CHAPTER 6

him into a hug, "I'm so sorry." Tucker hugged her back, and the two stood in their embrace.

"It's okay," he mumbled into her shoulder, "I guess it could always be worse. She didn't disown me or anything."

Kiara pulled back, looking into Tucker's eyes. "Just because she didn't try to exorcise the gay demons out of you or whatever bullshit crazy homophobes try to pull doesn't mean it's okay. Maybe she needs time, but I want you to promise me that you'll make sure you're your own priority in case they try to change you to make themselves feel better, okay? My dad tried to do that with my sister when she came out, and it was heartbreaking to see her hiding who she was to make him comfortable."

"I promise," Tucker said, nodding his head. Kiara pulled him back into a hug, and the two eventually separated. "How have we only been friends for two days?" he asked with a laugh, wiping his eyes.

"Time is irrelevant," Kiara shrugged. "If you've got the connection, then you've got the connection. Doesn't matter if it's been hours, days, or years, you know?"

"I guess I do now," Tucker chuckled. He hopped on his bed, legs dangling over the side, and patted the spot next to him as an invitation for Kiara to join him. She hopped up and threw her arm around his shoulders.

"Okay, so what happened with the guy?" she asked.

"Honestly," Tucker sighed, "nothing. I texted him after lunch, but he never responded. Then I went to the Queer Alliance headquarters for their meet-and-greet, and he was there and was super friendly like he usually is. He didn't mention my text or anything, so I guess I was right and he was just being nice."

Kiara gave him a skeptical look, which made Tucker laugh again. "I sincerely doubt it."

"I'm telling you!" he insisted. "Was he a little touchy when I was there? Yes. Did we have that weird moment in the dressing room last night? Yes, I will give you that. But I think today made it obvious that he's just trying to be my friend, and I'm okay with that."

"You liar!" she said, shoving him lightly. "I don't believe for a second that you're fine just being friends. I found him online, by the way, and he's cute!"

"How did you find him online? Where?" Tucker asked. "You don't even know his full name! *I* don't even know his full name!"

"Never underestimate my skills," she said, pointing a finger in his face. "His last name is Gibson, by the way."

"That doesn't answer my question," Tucker said, rolling his eyes.

"And I don't plan to," she retorted. "Look, all I'm saying is that you shouldn't give up so easily if you like him. But I'll drop it for now."

Tucker laid back on the bed, sighing loudly as he stared at the ceiling. His day had ended so well yesterday and he had been in such a good mood, but that was all overshadowed now by his feelings of sadness and betrayal after the call with his mother. Out of the two, he'd imagined that she would be the easier one to come out to, and now he was even more scared of how his dad might react. He was technically an adult, but he loved his parents and wanted to still be their child, and knew that if things got worse, one of the two parties would cut the other from their lives.

Kiara gave Tucker's arm a reassuring squeeze and hopped down from his bed. "I'm going to give you some alone time," she said, handing the bag of candy she'd been holding to him. "You've got my number, so call me if you want any more company, okay?"

Tucker sat up and gave her a half-smile in response. He was still upset, but felt comfort in how Kiara and Mike had been there for him. Mike, who had become so flustered at the mention of Tucker's sexuality only a few days ago, but had taken the time to try to learn something so he had common ground with Tucker. Kiara had quickly become his best friend at school, and Tucker was so thankful that the empty desk in General Psychology that first day was next to her. It reminded him of the phrase "chosen family" and how family doesn't always refer to blood. He found solace in the fact that, if things went awry with both of his parents, it didn't mean he wouldn't have a family anymore.

Kiara returned his smile and patted his knee before turning and leaving the room. Tucker, wanting nothing more to do with that day, swung his feet up on to the bed, rolled under the covers, and went to sleep without

CHAPTER 6

bothering to turn any lights out or undress.

* * *

The rest of the week seemed to fly by in a blur for Tucker. He still felt quiet and numb from his conversation with his mother and simply went through the motions to make it through each day. He rarely checked his phone, giving up on a response from David, ate in silence and let Kiara do most of the talking during their now-daily lunches in the Student Union, and took notes for his classes each day, heading home after they finished to do homework or sit on his bed and watch videos on his phone until it was time to go to sleep. Even Professor Thomas, who'd quickly become his favorite teacher that semester because of her wit and her warm demeanor, couldn't get Tucker out of his funk while he was in her class.

On Friday, he'd made sure he was one of the first people to arrive for his General Psychology class with Professor Whitley, who seemed to look through him when he walked into the room. He wasn't expecting the man to throw a party when he saw Tucker arrive on time, but it frustrated him that he wasn't even acknowledged or offered a general "good morning" like how any normal person would greet another. Still, he went to the seat he'd sat in on his first day and waited for Kiara to show up, drumming his nails on the desk in impatience. She finally arrived just before class started, and they barely exchanged greetings before Professor Whitley began to lecture in a monotonous tone about the differences in the id, the ego, and the superego.

At lunch, Tucker's phone calendar reminded him of his birthday the next day, which he hoped that Kiara would forget, as he was trying to. He was in no mood to celebrate anything. Based on her plans, he would not be so lucky.

"I know you said you weren't much of a partier," Kiara said after they'd finished eating their lunches, "but I wanted to do *something* to celebrate! It's nothing crazy, but would you meet me outside of your building tomorrow afternoon?"

"For what?" Tucker asked cautiously.

"Don't worry about it!" she retorted. "It's nothing to stress over, but it's my gift to you. So will you?"

"I guess," Tucker said with a shrug of his shoulders. He had no other plans and was not in the mood to sit alone in his room anymore, since Mike was hardly ever there anymore, so Kiara's mystery plans were better than anything he could think of. Kiara had continued to chat about the latest fun fact she'd learned from her theatre history textbook (something about a playwriting nun), and Tucker was only half-listening as he considered what scheme she could've cooked up for him. She eventually seemed to realize her knowledge was falling on deaf ears, and bid Tucker a cheerful farewell before she left for her next class. He did the same, returning to the robotic state as he ventured to his next class, until he was done with school for the week.

He'd gone to bed that night feeling a mix of emotions—sad, upset, angry, disappointed, anxious, and frustrated more so than anything else. He'd felt frustrated that his mother reacted the way she did. He'd felt frustrated that Professor Whitley seemed so disconnected from the students he taught. He'd felt frustrated that he had listened to his friends and hoped that David would like him. More than anything else, he'd felt frustrated that he couldn't let the events from the week go, clinging onto every negative experience he had as if he was collecting reasons why he should drop out. He fell asleep that night feeling defeated, wishing that he'd stayed home with his friends and never come to the University of Central Florida.

Chapter 7

Tucker woke up the next morning to his phone vibrating loudly on his dresser. He rolled on his side and picked it up, quickly scanning the notifications from his various social media accounts. Distant relatives and friends from school that he hadn't spoken to in years wished him a happy birthday, and he had two missed calls from his mom. He deleted all of them and rolled onto his back. Once again, Mike had never returned from wherever he went with his friends the night before, so Tucker stared at the ceiling in silence.

I'm nineteen now. Happy birthday, me, he thought to himself drily. His phone buzzed again, this time his dad calling. Trying to talk to his dad as if nothing happened after his call with his mother seemed impossible with how he was still feeling, so Tucker let the call end. Unlike his mother, his dad left a voicemail for him, so he input his password and played it on speaker.

"Hey, bud," his dad's deep southern voice boomed through the speakers, "it's your dad. You're probably still sleeping since it's your day off, but I just wanted to call and say happy birthday. Alright, well, I'll talk to you later."

Tucker smiled, hearing his father's familiar gruff tone. His world had changed entirely within the week and his father had no idea, and the innocence in his message made Tucker's heart swell. For the first time in days, he had hope for his family again. His mother didn't react well, but his father was his own person. Tucker couldn't think of anything else to do but hope that things would be different when the day came that he came out to his father, but he knew that wouldn't be anytime soon.

Noticing how late in the morning it was, Tucker slid off of his bed and stepped into the bathroom, turning on the shower and letting the water run hot. He took a long, luxurious shower, relishing the surprisingly strong water pressure. After he dried off, he dressed in shorts and a floral short-sleeve button-down shirt, unsure of what Kiara's plans for the day entailed. He grabbed a granola bar from his snack drawer and sent her a text, letting her know he was awake and dressed. When she didn't immediately respond like she normally did, Tucker set his phone down and finished his breakfast.

Within five minutes, there was a knock at his door. Tucker opened it and came face-to-face with a half a dozen balloons, each sporting a different message such as "It's a girl!" and "Congrats, grad!".

"Can you believe the store didn't have a single birthday balloon?" Kiara huffed from behind the bunch. Tucker stepped aside and she entered, shoving the strings into his hand as she passed. "Happy birthday," she added with a grin.

"Thanks," Tucker laughed, closing the door. "So, it's now my birthday. Can you finally tell me what we're doing today?"

"Oh my god, Tucker, relax," Kiara said, rolling her eyes. "I'll tell you in a little while. Can you manage?"

"I don't think I have much of a choice," he responded, his eyebrow raising inquisitively.

"Do you even have a roommate?" Kiara asked, pointing at Mike's unmade bed. "I'm starting to get the feeling you're just staging this to make it look like you have one."

"Basically the same thing," Tucker laughed. "Since we moved in last week, I think I've seen him maybe twice. He's always out with his friends doing who knows what."

Kiara shrugged and hopped onto Mike's bed, pulling out her phone and firing off a quick text.

"You always ask me, but it's my birthday so I'm turning it around on you," Tucker said with a smirk. "Are you texting a boy?"

Kiara threw her head back and let out a loud, fake laugh. She shook her head slowly as her phone buzzed, her fingers flying as she typed out another message. "If only you knew," she finally said.

CHAPTER 7

"I mean, that's why I asked," Tucker muttered.

The two sat in companionable silence, Kiara's phone occasionally buzzing with another text alert. Tucker scrolled through the happy birthday messages he'd received online, thanking each person for their message.

Eventually, Kiara hopped off the bed and grabbed the balloons Tucker let float in the middle of the room.

"Okay," Kiara said, clapping excitedly, "it's time!"

"Finally!" Tucker huffed. Kiara's teasing and pointless hints had made him excited for her plans, and he was eager to see what she'd cooked up for them.

Kiara led the way, walking quickly through the common area and down the stairs for the lobby. Once they reached the ground floor, Kiara made Tucker hold the balloons in front of his face to act as a blindfold and she pulled him by his arm out the door and into the courtyard. Tucker could hear whispering, but he had no idea what was happening.

"Okay," Kiara finally said, "you can look!"

Tucker moved the balloons and was met with a chorus of "surprise!". His friends from home—Brooke, Taylor, Mara, and Micah, Tucker noted with surprise, crowded around him in a half-circle. They laughed and enveloped Tucker in a group hug before he could say anything, making him laugh as well. He could hear Kiara giggling and clapping close by, obviously pleased with herself.

"Oh my god," was all Tucker could manage, a bewildered smile on his face.

"I got you," Kiara teased in a sing-song tone.

"How...?" Tucker asked, unable to finish his sentence as his mind attempted to wrap around the situation.

"It wasn't that hard," Kiara shrugged. "I just found your profile online, went through your old pictures to find your friends, sent them messages to set this up, and have been texting them all morning to find out when they got here."

"You're an evil genius," Tucker laughed, pulling Kiara into a quick hug. He released her and turned to his friends, repeating himself by yelling "Oh my god!"

They laughed and all started talking over one another, excited to catch up with their estranged friend. Even Micah, who Tucker still couldn't believe had agreed to come after their last interaction, seemed happy to see him. They sat at a picnic table in the courtyard and caught up, Tucker filling his friends in on his first week in college (excluding his coming out and David), and each of them giving him an update on anything exciting in their lives. Brooke was single again, which shocked no one, Taylor and Mara, tan twins with sun-bleached blonde hair, were attending the local community college to get their Associate's Degrees, and Micah, taller than the rest of the group with brown hair and light green eyes that seemed to glow in the sun, shrugged and said, "nothing much" with a smirk. Though Tucker had only been away from home for a little over a week, it felt like a lifetime apart now that they were all together again.

Kiara listened with intent, laughing as she heard stories from their years together in grade school they'd repeated to each other a hundred times. Tucker was relieved that she was mixing in with the rest of the group so well, and she was even jumping in on some of the teasing jokes the group made at one another's expense. After they were all caught up, Kiara offered to show everyone around campus, so they began their trek around UCF's vast grounds. She led the group with Brooke next to her, Taylor and Mara right behind them, and Micah and Tucker took up the rear.

"Hey," Tucker said, offering Micah a small smile as Kiara spouted off random facts from the front of the group.

"Hi," Micah smiled back. "Happy birthday."

"Thanks," Tucker chuckled. "To be honest, I'm surprised you're here."

"I...," Micah began, trailing off. "I am too, but I'm happy I came."

The group continued the tour, and after a few minutes Micah put a hand on Tucker's shoulder and slowed their pace down, putting a bit of distance between them and the twins.

"I want to apologize," Micah sighed. "I know I acted like a dick. I... I didn't know what was going on with us, and you were leaving, and I just kind of reacted. But it wasn't fair of me, and I'm really sorry."

Tucker was taken aback. This was the most candid Micah had ever been

CHAPTER 7

about their friendship, and he was speechless. He'd thought a lot about what he wanted to say the next time he saw Micah after their last conversation, but anything he'd planned was now gone from his mind.

"Can we be friends again?" Micah asked.

"I don't know," Tucker sighed. "Were we just friends, Micah? I don't know that I wanted to just be your friend by the time you ended things. I thought you might have felt the same, but you quickly changed my mind when you said you didn't want to talk to me anymore."

"Can we talk about this later?" Micah asked, lowering his voice. "Just you and me? I don't feel like now is the best time."

Tucker stared at Micah for a moment, then sighed and looked towards the disappearing tour group ahead of them.

"Yeah, Micah, we can talk about this later," Tucker finally said. "Let's catch up with the others."

The two speed-walked and caught up with the group, hearing Kiara call over her shoulder, "...and this used to be a chemistry lab, but now it's a theatre!"

Tucker laughed, imagining Kiara sitting in her room trying to memorize her lines before giving the tour. She seemed entirely too prepared to just be casually talking about everything she passed. For the next hour, the six of them walked the entirety of UCF's campus, stopping in the Student Union to sit in the air conditioning and point out what table Kiara and Tucker had lunch at. Taylor took a picture of the table, oooing and ahhhing like a tourist on Hollywood Boulevard, making Tucker chuckle. By the time they made it back to Tucker's dorm, it was already almost 4:00 in the afternoon, much to Tucker's surprise.

"You guys go up to Tucker's room," Kiara instructed, "and I'll be there in a minute. I'm going to grab some food for us." She hurried off in the other direction, and Tucker took the rest of his friends up to his room. As he suspected, Mike had still shown no signs of return. Brooke, Taylor, and Mara jumped onto Tucker's bed, and Micah and Tucker sat on the floor facing them. He was painfully aware of how close his hand was to Micah's, their fingers centimeters from touching, and feelings from high school began flooding back. Tucker took a deep breath, trying to clear his mind, and focused on Brooke's phone case in her hand, which was filled with a pale pink liquid and little floating multicolored stars.

The group sat in comfortable silence, checking their phones and relaxing in the air conditioning until Kiara banged on the door, startling everyone. Tucker jumped to his feet and opened the door to let her in. She rushed in with a few plastic bags on her arm and dropped them on the floor at Tucker's feet. She began unpacking wordlessly, handing individually wrapped sandwiches to Tucker. After the bag of food was empty, she threw it to the side and unpacked the next bag, which was filled with bottles of alcohol. She placed a jug of vodka, a bottle of tequila, and a twelve-pack of beer on the counter.

"Ta da!" Kiara sang, gesturing towards the bottles with her arms, fingers waggling.

"Oh my god!" Brooke gasped, sliding off of Tucker's bed and walking to the beer, ripping a hole in the cardboard box and cracking one of the cans open. "You have a really good friend, Tucker," she said after taking a long gulp. Mara and Taylor joined Brooke, cracking open a beer and unwrapping a sandwich.

"Where did you get all of this?" Tucker asked, astonished.

"When will you learn to stop asking questions?" Kiara asked, placing her hands on her hips in mock exasperation.

Micah wordlessly leaned over, tapping Tucker on the back of the knee. Tucker handed him a sandwich and passed another to Kiara. He unwrapped the last one for himself, taking a bite of the pre-packed turkey sandwich Kiara prepared and moaning appreciatively.

"I wanted to make sure we all had something in our stomachs," Kiara said around a mouthful of sandwich, "because we're going out later!"

Brooke, Taylor, and Mara cheered, raising their cans in salute before chugging the rest of its contents. Tucker said nothing, but met Kiara's eyes with a raised, questioning eyebrow. He turned to Micah, who was looking at him with the same look. Tucker simply shrugged in response and took another bite of his sandwich. After they'd finished eating, Kiara passed out

CHAPTER 7

shots, and Micah stood up, wiping his hands on his pants.

"I still have to work in the morning, so I think I'm going to head out," he said to the group but looking directly at Tucker. The rest of them groaned and booed him, but Tucker gave him a small nod in response. He knew that Micah was even less social than he was, and had an aversion to alcohol because of his late alcoholic mother.

"I'll walk you down," Tucker said.

Micah nodded, and the two headed out the door, walking down the stairs to the lobby in silence. When they reached the lobby, Micah turned and faced Tucker, the two only inches apart.

"I'm sorry I have to go," he said apologetically.

"Don't worry about it," Tucker responded, giving him a reassuring smile. "I know you're not a partier."

"And I thought you weren't either," Micah responded, his tone questioning.

"I guess I'm making an exception today," Tucker said with a shrug, maintaining eye contact with Micah as if to dare him to say something about his choice. The two stared at each other in silence, and Tucker's breath hitched. It had been a while since they'd been in the same room, let alone as close as they currently were, and Tucker realized he had forgotten how handsome he thought Micah was. Micah cleared his throat and took out his phone, checking the time. He looked back up at Tucker, his face moving even closer to Tucker's. Tucker didn't dare breathe, scared he would ruin whatever was happening at the moment. Micah seemed to think better of whatever he was considering and turned away.

"I'll call you later," Micah said, not looking at Tucker. Tucker's face fell, and he was brutally reminded of how Micah used to make him feel in situations like these, always too scared to do what he wanted to do, leaving Tucker feeling undesirable and alone.

"Yeah, sounds good," Tucker said flatly, turning toward the stairwell and throwing the door open. He didn't wait for Micah to leave or respond and headed back up the stairs toward his dorm without another word.

When he opened the door to his room, Kiara greeted him with two shots in her hands. The room chanted, "shots! shots! shots!" until Tucker drank them, shuddering at the sensation as it hit his throat and stomach. She took the empty glasses out of his hands and placed another in his palm, moving his hand toward his mouth. Tucker, still readjusting from the first shots, shook his head in protest, but took the shot anyway and spluttered as the liquid went down his throat.

"You've got to catch up to us!" Taylor laughed.

"I was gone for five minutes!" Tucker said in-between coughs.

"You can do a lot of damage in five minutes," Kiara pointed out.

Tucker handed Kiara the empty shot glass and sat down on the floor with Brooke, Taylor, and Mara, who had migrated from his bed in his absence. Kiara rinsed the glasses out and joined them, and the five of them laughed at the redness blooming in each others' cheeks as the alcohol set in. As the sun continued to set, the girls went to go grab the extra clothes they'd packed in their cars and Tucker quickly freshened up. Once they'd returned and changed, they each took one more shot and Kiara called to get them a car. It being a Saturday night in a college town, it didn't take long for someone to pick them up and they were soon on their way to wherever Kiara planned next.

Tucker, feeling warm and loose from the shots, took no notice of where they were going and instead focused on the lights from the city as they passed buildings downtown, before they shortly arrived at their destination. He climbed out of the car and was surprised to see that he was standing in front of Haven.

"Yay, surprise!" Kiara cheered, and the girls whooped in response. Tucker grinned, thankful that he'd at least be somewhere familiar if they were going out. They headed into the lobby, Tucker nodding at the bouncer as he handed him his ID, and rushed to go further into the club.

Tucker looked around as he walked, still trying to familiarize himself with his surroundings, and made unintentional eye contact with David and Adrian, who were both standing on opposite sides of the bar. Tucker excused himself from his friends, who didn't take the hint and followed closely as he approached the bar.

"Hey!" David said, a grin on his face.

CHAPTER 7

"Fancy meeting you here," Tucker said, trying his best to appear sober.

"I could say the same to you," David laughed. "You here with your friends?"

"Yeah," he said, turning to gesture to the group of girls behind him. "This is my friend Kiara and my friends Brooke, Taylor, and Mara from back home. They surprised me and took me out for my birthday."

"It's your birthday?" David asked. "That's so exciting! Happy birthday!"

"Thanks," Tucker laughed.

Adrian, who was standing close by but had said nothing yet, got David's attention and ordered two shots of something Tucker couldn't hear over the music. While David was pouring, Adrian winked at Tucker, whose already warm face became hot.

He turned to his friends, who had been observing the interaction like a nature documentary, and quickly filled them in on who the two men were, excluding any romantic details to avoid embarrassment. Kiara gave him a knowing look and wiggled her eyebrows suggestively, pointing to Adrian and David with her eyes. Tucker laughed and turned away from them toward David before she could say anything.

David handed the shots to Adrian, who thanked him and walked towards the dance floor, motioning behind David's back for Tucker to join him. More people approached the bar, so Tucker said goodbye to David and headed to the dance floor, scanning the crowd for Adrian. He was leaning against a wall across from the entrance and offered Tucker a smile when he caught his eye. Tucker told his friends he'd join them soon and left the group, walking towards Adrian.

"A little birdy told me it was your birthday," Adrian said, handing Tucker the shots.

"Wow, thank you," Tucker laughed. "I had some before we came, so do you want one of these?"

"No, those are for you!" Adrian protested. "I just finished my drink when you guys got here, so I'm good. Drink up before anyone sees, birthday boy!"

Tucker shrugged and took the shots, coughing as he handed the empty plastic cups back to Adrian. He laughed at Tucker's response and threw the cups in a nearby trash can. The song playing through the speakers ended and a new one began, and Adrian took Tucker's hand and led him to the dance floor.

He put Tucker's arms around his neck, placing his on Tucker's waist and pulling him close, and the two gyrated shamelessly to the music. Adrian's gaze was hypnotic, as were his movements, and Tucker took his lead as their bodies rubbed against each other. He was painfully aware of every instance that their bulges touched through their pants, feeling physical responses from both parties as they moved to the music. He was unsure if it was newfound confidence or just the liquid courage, but Tucker pulled Adrian closer and the two kissed. Adrian's lips were soft, and he parted Tucker's with his tongue, who opened his mouth wider in response to let Adrian explore. They stayed like that, grinding against each other's bodies, their tongues grappling, until the song ended. Tucker pulled away, his face tingling from where Adrian's beard had rubbed on it, and Adrian pulled Tucker's head close again so his mouth was touching Tucker's ear.

"Come home with me tonight," Adrian murmured, his voice a hungry growl. "Let me take care of you and give you a birthday you won't forget."

"I can't tonight," Tucker said, pulling back to look in Adrian's eyes. "My friends are in town and they're going to crash on my floor. But can I get your number? I'll text you."

Adrian smiled, looking content with Tucker's response, and pulled out his phone. The two traded phones and input their information, and Adrian put Tucker's phone back in his front pocket, grazing his crotch with his fingers while he did so. Tucker's breath caught in surprise at his touch, but tried not to show it as he handed Adrian's phone back to him. Adrian looked from Tucker's pants to his face with a satisfied smirk as he took his phone back, pocketing it.

"I guess I'll talk to you later then, birthday boy," he said with a wink.

"Definitely," Tucker breathed.

Adrian looked Tucker up and down once more with satisfaction, then turned and walked towards the exit. Following Adrian with his eyes, he accidentally made eye contact with David, who was looking at him from the bar with a look on his face that Tucker couldn't decipher. It definitely

CHAPTER 7

wasn't David's usual, cheerful face, he noticed, but couldn't quite place what emotion he was seeing. Tucker glanced at the floor, his face growing hot with the realization of what he'd just done with Adrian in front of everyone at the club. He wasn't ashamed, and as far as first experiences went, Tucker was pretty pleased with himself. Adrian was now officially his first kiss, and the first guy to get to second base if that counted for anything. Tucker quickly looked up, careful not to glance in David's direction in case he was still looking, and scanned the crowd for his friends. He found the four of them sitting on barstools, and they clapped and cheered and he walked towards them, his face growing even redder from embarrassment.

"Tucker, you slut!" Brooke teased.

"I didn't know you had that in you!" Mara laughed, and Taylor's phone emitted a bright light as she took a picture of him, his hair tousled and his mouth slightly red from Adrian's beard.

"I'm drunk and it's my birthday, and I kissed a boy!" Tucker yelled, laughing and throwing his hands in the air in triumph. Some older men standing near them laughed at Tucker's outburst, cheering his accomplishment. One of them handed Tucker a shot they were holding, wishing him a happy birthday. Tucker quickly swallowed the liquid, making a disgusted sound, and he crushed the small plastic cup, which made the men laugh again.

"I need some water," Tucker told his friends, slightly stumbling towards the bar. David was watching him as he approached, a small smile playing at the corners of his mouth.

"Feeling okay?" he asked, his smile widening.

"I feel so great," Tucker said with a drunken grin. "Can I get some water?"

"Sure," David chuckled, pulling out another plastic cup and filling it with water from a spray nozzle with multiple buttons on the top. The lights seemed to intensify around Tucker and the music faded, but he shook his head in an attempt to sober up. David handed him the cup with a quizzical look but said nothing.

"Cheers," Tucker slurred, raising his cup toward David before quickly drinking all of its contents, making David laugh.

"So how old are you now, fourteen?" David asked.

"I'm nineteen, so I'm very legal!" Tucker protested. "Just because you're cute doesn't mean you can tease me on my birthday, David."

"You think I'm cute?" he asked, raising an eyebrow.

"Of course I do!" Tucker said. "Look at you—you're so hot and nice and smart and cute!"

Tucker remembered seeing David's eyebrows raise in surprise, the lights becoming harsh again, and began to hear a humming noise, entering a state of drunkenness he'd only heard of before—blacking out. When he came-to again, he was sitting in the backseat of a car, his head resting on the cool window, and heard his friends chatting and laughing next to him before he slipped out of consciousness once more.

Chapter 8

Tucker woke the next morning to the sounds of loud whispers in his room and immediately felt his head throb as if his brain was pounding against his skull to break free. He groaned, pulling the covers over his head and rolling on his side so he faced the wall, quickly falling back asleep. He awoke again a few hours later, his headache dull but now accompanied by a dry mouth and nausea. He carefully rose, squinting against the sunlight peeking into his room as he surveyed his surroundings. There were blankets and pillows folded up on his floor, but his friends were nowhere to be found.

Tucker slipped onto the floor and trudged to the sink, filling up his cup to the brim with water twice and chugging the contents. He quickly realized how bad of an idea that was, but after dashing to the toilet to vomit, he was surprised to feel so much better. He walked back to his bed and checked his phone, opening up the pending message he had from Brooke. There were multiple pictures of the five of them from the night before on the dance floor, a look of serenity on Tucker's face, that he had no recollection taking. Taylor had also sent him pictures, hers of Tucker and Adrian dancing and making out. He flushed, partially remembering the events from the night before. He texted them both, thanking them for coming and celebrating with him, and called Kiara.

"Good morning, sunshine," she said cheerily.

"Wow," he croaked, "you sound a lot better than I feel."

"I also didn't drink as much as you did last night," she pointed out.

"I had fun," Tucker said, rubbing his eyes. "Thank you for taking over my birthday."

"Anytime!" Kiara laughed. "You seemed like you had a good time—flirting with boys, making out with that guy, dancing with us..."

"I don't remember half of it," he groaned, making Kiara laugh. "Wait," he said, "did you say flirting with *boys*? As in plural?"

"Looked like it to me! We all saw you with that guy on the dance floor, but I found you drooling all over yourself talking to David after."

"Oh my god," Tucker groaned again. "I think I told David he was hot!"

Kiara cackled, and Tucker had to pull the phone away from his ear until she finished. "Well, what did he say?" she asked when her laughter finally subsided.

"I don't remember," he sighed. "God, I hope that conversation was only in my head!"

"Why don't you just ask him about it?"

"Are you insane?" Tucker said, his eyes widening. "Absolutely not!"

"You are so frustrating!" Kiara growled. "Just be open and honest!"

"I'd rather get a hangover all over again," he retorted.

"I can't help you if you don't want to help yourself. But I'm *so* going to say I told you so when you finally come to your senses and just talk to the guy."

"I have no doubt," Tucker said, smirking. "I'm gonna go, but thanks again for my birthday. I had a lot of fun, from what I can remember."

"If you thought this was fun, just wait until next year!" Kiara said excitedly.

"Goodbye!" Tucker said pointedly, quickly ending the call before she could respond again. He set his phone down, taking a long, hot shower to try and wash away the remaining alcohol in his system. He quickly dressed and jumped back on his bed, pulling out his laptop and working on different homework assignments for the rest of the day. That evening, he got a text from an unknown number telling him to call them. Against his better judgement, he did, and was surprised when Jamie answered the phone.

"Hey, girl," she said.

"Hey!" Tucker said. "Thanks for texting me. I was starting to think you might've forgotten about me. Are you still okay with teaching me drag?"

"No, I'm calling to see if you want to come with me on a cruise to Europe," she retorted, and Tucker could imagine her rolling her eyes on the other

CHAPTER 8

end. "Can you come to my house sometime this week? We're going to have a lot of work to do."

"Sure!" Tucker said, unable to keep the excitement from his voice.

"Cool. I'll text you when I'm free and we'll pick a day. Sound good?"

"Absolutely," he said.

"Okay, I'll talk to you later then. Bye!"

Jamie ended the call before he could respond, and Tucker chuckled at the similarity of the abrupt end of his call with Kiara earlier that day. He put Jamie's number into his phone and set it aside, shifting his focus back to his homework. Shortly after, his phone buzzed again, and it surprised Tucker to see that it was now David calling him.

"Hey, David," he said, answering the call.

"Hey!" David said. "Glad to hear you're alive after last night."

"Me too," he chuckled, feelings his cheeks heat again as he remembered bits and pieces of the night before.

"I just wanted to call and let you know I got your schedule, and we're going to have you working weekends from now on. Sound good?"

"Yeah, that sounds great! Thanks again for your help."

"No worries!" David said. "Okay, well, I'll let you go."

"David," Tucker blurted out, fearing he might hang up before he could speak. "I just wanted to apologize if I said anything weird last night. I wasn't thinking straight."

"You're fine," David laughed. "Nothing weird, we just chatted a little and I got you some water. You looked like you were having plenty of fun."

"Right," Tucker said, laughing uneasily.

"Alright, I'll talk to you later, Tucker."

"Bye, David," Tucker said, ending the call. He exhaled, running a hand through his hair. Tucker didn't know if he'd ever feel entirely relaxed talking to David, especially hearing his voice so close to his ear over the phone. Tucker considered texting Adrian, but thought against it and set his phone down again. He attempted to shift his focus back to his work, but between his phone calls and the lingering nausea, Tucker decided to get a good night's sleep to make up for the night before. He looked at Mike's bed, debating if he wanted to leave lights on for him, but thought against it and plunged the room into blackness, quickly drifting off to sleep.

* * *

Having a better idea of what to expect now that he was in his second week of classes, Tucker's week seemed to fly by in a series of lectures and papers as his course load continued to increase. Lunches with Kiara were now spent chatting while working on individual projects in the Student Union, and his nights were devoted to quick dinners at Knightro's and studying for his classes, anticipating their upcoming exams.

On Wednesday, he received a text from Jamie telling him to stop by whenever he finished classes for the day. He drove to the address she'd sent, which turned out to be in a large apartment complex a half hour away from his dorm, and knocked on the door. To his surprise, a tall, bald black man answered, smiling when he saw Tucker.

"You must be Tucker!" he said, showing off a beautiful white smile. "Jamie's in the drag room. Come in, come in!"

The man stepped aside and Tucker entered, surveying the apartment. The area by the door was completely open, with a kitchen nestled in on one side of the room, and Jamie had separated the rest of the space into a living room. Tucker could hear a machine whirring from another room down a hallway connected to the kitchen, and he followed the stranger towards the noise.

In the drag room, just as the man said, sat Jamie at a sewing machine, her brown hair tied up in a messy bun on top of her head and pins in her mouth as she shoved shiny pink fabric under the needle.

"Hey girl," she called over the noise of the machine, not looking up from the garment she was working on. Another guy, looking to be around Tucker's age with pale skin and curly red hair, sat by her feet and cut fabric with a pair of metal shears. He looked up and offered Tucker a quick smile before returning to his work.

Tucker stood in silence, awkwardly leaning against the wall, waiting for

CHAPTER 8

Jamie to finish. She pulled a few more pins out of the fabric as it got closer to the sewing needle, sticking them in her mouth with the others, and finally pulled the newly made garment free of the machine. She set it to the side and put the sewing machine under the table, before finally shifting her attention to Tucker.

"Welcome to my estate," she joked, her arms moving around the room. "Looks like you already met my roommate, Crystal Waters," she said, referencing the man who answered the door, "and this one at my feet is Kitty Dupree. Girls, this is the new shot boy at Haven, Tucker."

Tucker smiled at both of them in acknowledgement. He was excited to learn about drag, but also felt strangely nervous. He had never attempted anything like this before, so everything was brand new to him and he already felt clueless. Before he could ask any questions, Jamie had Tucker seated in a chair facing a small vanity in the corner of the room.

Jamie, Crystal, and Kitty took turns putting makeup on Tucker's face, first covering his eyebrows with a glue stick and some powder, to his bewilderment. Crystal, who was applying the powder, explained that this step was to cover up the texture from his natural eyebrows so he could draw on new ones. Jamie then slathered his face with foundation, setting it with even more powder, and Kitty worked on his eyes while they let the powder sit on his face to "bake", as they referred to it. After applying a layer of highlight and contour to his cheeks, they drew lips on with a liquid lipstick, completely ignoring where his lips ended and overdrawing them.

"To make them look fuller, like you just had some filler injected," Kitty explained, noticing his confused expression.

Tucker nodded in understanding, and Jamie chastised him for moving, so he tried his best to keep statue-still until instructed otherwise. After they finished his lips, they brushed off the powder on his face and applied some blush with a large brush, and finally stuck some false eyelashes on his eyelids with glue. Satisfied with their work, the queens moved and let Tucker get a good look at himself in the mirror. He watched the entire process occur, but he was still amazed at how different he now looked.

"Look at her—she's living for herself," Crystal chuckled behind him.

Jamie sat Tucker down again and continued the lesson, pulling a tight wig cap over his head to cover his hair, and carefully sat a large black wig on his head, securing it with bobby pins.

"How do you know where to put that?" Tucker asked.

"Oh my god, you really are clueless," Jamie muttered with exasperation. She pointed at the thin layer of lace attached to the front of the wig, forcefully tapping it (and his forehead underneath) repeatedly with a large red nail. "The wig is a lace front, so the lace goes in the front."

"Are all wigs lace fronts?" Tucker asked.

"No, girl," Jamie said simply.

After giving Tucker a moment to marvel at his transformation in the mirror, Kitty steered him toward the clothes rack behind him. Jamie rummaged through the hanging garments, muttering to herself under her breath, and finally selected a long-sleeved black dress made of a glittering velvet fabric. While Jamie was searching, Crystal and Kitty instructed Tucker on the undergarments he'd need—bras, tights, a waist shaper, and foam pads to make his hips look fuller.

"It's all about the illusion," Crystal advised. "You may think you look bigger, but when you have big man-shoulders, the pads even you out and make you look all curvy and sexy."

Tucker nodded in understanding, and Jamie loaned him a pair of tights and a bra, giving him a moment alone in the room to get undressed and into the garments. Tucker undressed down to his underwear and was about to pull the tights up before the realization of his ongoing cluelessness dawned on him.

"But what about my... front?" Tucker called through the door, feeling embarrassed.

"Your front?" Jamie asked, barging back into the room.

"You know," Tucker said sheepishly, motioning toward his crotch.

"Oh, you mean tucking!" Jamie said with a laugh. "Girl, you've gotta stop acting so prim and proper if you want to do drag."

"Yeah, tucking. How do I do it?"

"Well, you just kind of take the end of it and pull it down and behind me

CHAPTER 8

with one hand, and then yank your underwear up with the other like a thong to keep it in place," Jamie instructed. "It's not pretty, but it gets the job done and the tights help smooth things out. Try it, I'll look away."

Tucker hesitated for a moment, but after he was sure Jamie wasn't playing a joke on him, he did as Jamie instructed and yanked everything into place. To his surprise, it barely hurt at all and was more uncomfortable than anything, which he assumed would lessen with time and practice.

"Can I ask you a question?" Tucker asked as he was moving everything around to be sure he'd done it right.

"No, I will not tell you if I still have my dick," Jamie replied automatically.

"No, I wasn't going to ask about that at all!" Tucker said quickly. "I don't know how to phrase this delicately, but I know you have breasts and just wanted to ask—"

"Yes, I'm a transgender woman," Jamie answered, not bothering to let Tucker stumble through his awkward question.

"Thank you for cutting me off," Tucker sighed, chuckling uncomfortably.

"Is that a problem?" Jamie asked, looking him in the eye and raising an eyebrow daringly.

"No, not at all," he replied earnestly. "I've never met a trans person before, so I just wanted to be sure I don't say the wrong things by accident, is all."

"You really came from the middle of nowhere, huh?" Jamie asked, a smile playing on her lips. "To keep it brief, yeah, I'm trans, I'm a woman, and I've felt this way my whole life. It's just within the last ten or so years that I could put words to what I was feeling and get surgery to start to make myself look like it on the outside too. But you don't need to look any certain way or have any special surgery to be your authentic self if you feel that way. What my body looks like, whether I choose to show it or not, is nobody's business but my own."

"Thank you for telling me," Tucker smiled, forgetting momentarily that he was standing in the middle of Jamie's drag room with his penis tucked between his legs and his underwear yanked up behind him. Jamie looked him up and down and laughed, having apparently forgotten as well, and left the room again to let Tucker finish putting the undergarments on.

When he was dressed, the three of them entered and Jamie handed him a pair of black heels. "I had to guess on your shoe size," she said, "but this is what I got, so make them fit."

Luckily, the heel slid easily onto his foot, and Tucker was soon standing uneasily, trying to keep his balance as he took tiny steps to look around the room. The queens laughed, and Tucker joined in, imagining how ridiculous he must look. When he turned toward the mirror again, he gasped and his jaw dropped in surprise. The person standing in front of the mirror—the *woman* standing in front of the mirror—was someone he didn't recognize. He could see his mentors looking at each other in the mirror, pleased with themselves. They took his phone and took some pictures of him before helping him undress and take off his makeup. To his surprise, Jamie gave him a majority of the makeup they used on him, the dress and undergarments he wore, a different black wig that wasn't styled, and the heels, throwing it all in a large plastic bag and shoving it into his hands.

"Thank you so much!" he said in awe.

"I get so much makeup from different people—I'm happy to give it to someone who'll put it to use," she said flippantly. "But if you tell anyone I was nice and helpful," she warned, "I will cut up all your drag and put glass in your makeup."

Tucker's eyebrows shot up in surprise, but Kitty and Crystal laughed to signify that Jamie was joking.

"My lips are sealed," Tucker promised. "And thank you both for your help too."

"You come see Auntie Crystal if you need more help," Crystal said, patting Tucker on the shoulder. Referring to drag queens as 'she', even when they were out of drag and looked like a boy, was something Tucker was still getting used to, but Crystal and Kitty exuded such feminity at all times that it made things easier for him.

"I'm going to be working weekends at Haven now," Tucker advised, "so if you're there come and see me! I'll save a shot for you."

"Just one?" Kitty asked. "You really haven't been around many drag queens, have you?"

CHAPTER 8

Jamie and Crystal laughed, but Tucker just smiled, unsure of the joke. They said their goodbyes and Tucker left, throwing the overstuffed bag into the passenger seat of his car. He pulled onto the highway back towards campus, and answered the phone blindly when it began to ring.

"Hello?" he greeted.

"Tucker, finally!" his mother said through the car's speakers. Tucker cursed under his breath, mentally kicking himself for answering the call.

"Hi, Mom," he said flatly. There was an awkward silence, neither of them sure what to say.

"Did you have a nice birthday?" she finally asked.

"Yeah," he replied tersely, trying to say as little to her as possible.

"Look, Tucker, I need to talk to you," she said. He said nothing, so she continued. "You're still my son, and your father and I still want to come see you for Parents' Weekend in a few days."

"Can't," he said simply. "I work weekends now."

Granted, he worked at night, but he was not planning to divulge that information to his mother. The wounds from their previous conversation were still fresh for him, and she was the last person he wanted to see.

"Oh, you got a job? That's nice," she said cheerfully. "Where at?"

"Based on our last conversation, I don't think it's a good idea to go into details," he said coldly. He could hear her sigh angrily on the other end, but she said nothing. He had nothing else to say to her, so the two again sat in silence as he drove.

"Well," she finally said, "I'm happy that you found a job. How's school?"

"Fine," he said. "Look, Mom, I have to go. I'm driving and I have to focus on the road. I'll talk to you later."

He ended the call without giving her a chance to respond and sighed with disappointment. He still loved his mother, and it pained him to be so rude to her, but he still hadn't let go of the cruel things she'd said to him, and he would not pretend like it didn't happen to make his family happy. He drove the rest of the way home in silence, crawling into bed and continuing the cycle of classes for the rest of the week with no notable issues.

That weekend, he was in a terrible mood from seeing all the happy families around campus during the day, but pushed the feelings down and glued a smile on his face when he got to work. The club was much busier on the weekends than it was during his trial, he noted, and he left with a much bigger stack of dollar bills at the end of his shifts than he had on that first Monday. David worked weekends as well, but the two hadn't talked at all since David's phone call the previous week, to Tucker's disappointment.

After his shift on Sunday night, Tucker trudged up the stairwell to his room, taking off his clothes as soon as he got in the door and went to bed, desperate to busy himself with schoolwork again and clear his mind of his familial issues. He distracted himself as he laid in bed by thinking of drag, considering the seemingly endless possibilities of looks and performances he could do once he felt more comfortable with the craft, and drifted off to sleep that night with thoughts of wigs and heels at the forefront of his mind.

Chapter 9

The following Monday, Tucker felt much better than he had the morning prior, and leaned into his good mood as he woke and dressed. He left early, careful to close the door quietly so he didn't wake Mike, who was still snoring heavily in his bed.

Tucker pulled out his phone and sent Kiara a quick text, asking her to meet him at their usual table in the Student Union, and made sure to get there quickly so he could purchase two cups of coffee from the school's coffee shop inside and have it waiting for her. She eventually threw the doors open, dressed in a bright yellow sundress covered in daisies with matching flats, a pair of oversized sunglasses, her hair put up in a bun, and a grumpy scowl on her face.

"Good morning, sunshine," Tucker greeted with a smirk, handing her one of the coffees he'd purchased. She took a long sip and sighed contentedly, taking off her sunglasses and looking at Tucker up and down.

"You're much more manageable in the mornings when you're hungover," she replied, a hint of a smile on her lips.

The two chatted about Tucker's weekend at work while they walked to class, getting to Professor Whitley's classroom with ten minutes to spare. They sat at their desks, Tucker scrolling mindlessly through social media and Kiara doodling horrific caricatures of Tucker in her notebook, until Professor Whitely, true to his word, locked the door and began his lecture.

"This week," he began, not bothering to greet his class, "I am allowing you to work in pairs on a project associated with your assigned reading. You will demonstrate basic research techniques to analyze one of the mental illnesses listed in Chapters Four and Five and write a two-page paper, single-spaced, on the symptoms, treatments, and examples of cases regarding the disease you chose. This will be due by next Monday. Let me know if you have any questions, and get to work."

Tucker and Kiara whipped their heads toward each other and grinned, their pairing obvious. Kiara dragged her desk closer to Tuckers, the metal legs scraping horribly on the linoleum floor as she moved.

"Have you started the reading yet?" Tucker whispered.

"Not a word," Kiara replied. The two erupted into a fit of quiet giggles, conscious but uncaring of their classmates nearby shooting them questioning looks.

Kiara yanked her Psychology textbook out of her overstuffed backpack and opened it between them, and they spent the remaining time in class pretending to read and laughing at each other.

"Miss Jackson, Mister Peterson," Professor Whitley called from his desk before ending class for the day, "have you decided on your topic?"

"Not yet, professor," Kiara replied. "But we've narrowed it down!"

"Fine, email it to me by the end of the day," he said, writing something in the large binder on his desk before asking another pair the same question.

"So, what *are* we going to write our paper on?" Tucker asked as they left the classroom, Kiara lacing her arm in his as they walked.

"No clue. Want to come by my dorm later and we can actually work, since we just wasted a full class period dicking around?"

"Sure. I have no idea where you live—and unlike *some* people, no clue how to find that information so I can break into their building and harass them—so do you want to meet at our table when we're done with our classes?"

"Works for me," Kiara said, pulling away and turning toward her next destination. "I'm headed to class. I'll text you later!"

Tucker waved as she walked away, and headed back to his dorm to decompress before his classes in the afternoon. As he passed the fountain, following the walkway back to his building, a large mass of students passed him and he felt a strong shoulder bump into his.

CHAPTER 9

Tucker turned, ready to yell at the person, but came face-to-face with a grinning David, who looked very pleased with himself.

"I was about to call you so many bad words!" Tucker laughed.

"I saw you coming and I couldn't resist messing with you," David replied. "How've you been? I was bummed we were too busy to chat at work this weekend."

"Me too. I've been fine, just adjusting to college life and all of my classes. What about you?"

"Can't complain too much—I've got some tough classes this semester, but the sooner I knock them out of the way, the sooner I graduate, you know?"

"Totally."

They stood there, both sweating in the oppressive Florida heat, feeling the conversation come to a natural lull. David looked around like he was about to leave, and Tucker heard Kiara's advice echo in his head—*Just be yourself, things will fall into place!*

"I was just about to go get some food at Knightro's," Tucker lied, surprised at himself as the words left his mouth, "would you like to join me?"

"Sure, I've got some time to kill," David said with a shrug. "Lead the way."

The two made the quick trip to the dining hall, grabbing some hash browns and eggs from the serving area, and sat at a small table in the middle of the room.

"So, what classes do you have today?" David asked through a mouthful of food.

"I just came from General Psychology, and then I have American History and English Composition later today. Nothing super exciting. I'm not sure if you remember me telling you about my asshole professor, but that was my Psych professor."

"He getting any better?"

"Not really, but I've accepted it and am just trying not to piss him off again. I just need to pass the class and then I'll never have to see him again."

"I take it you're not a Psychology major, then?" David asked.

"Nope, no major at the moment. Still have no idea what I want to major in, unfortunately," Tucker replied, taking another bite of his food. David looked thoughtful as he chewed, but didn't say whatever he was thinking, to Tucker's annoyance. He was surprised that David had been so quick to agree to hang out, the two of them having only spoken a handful of times, and was ready to get to know him better.

"What about you?" Tucker eventually asked, eager to keep the conversation flowing.

"Computer Engineering," David replied, laughing when Tucker's eyes widened in surprise. "I know, you wouldn't think the bartender at Haven would be studying something so technical, but I've always liked learning about software development and stuff like that. No dream job in mind, but something in that field would be cool."

"I would have never guessed," Tucker said.

"David, hey!" a voice from behind Tucker said. David's head shot up, a look of surprise on his face. Tucker turned to see who the voice belonged to, and felt his mouth go dry as he made eye contact with one of the most attractive men he'd seen on campus yet walking toward them.

Though Tucker was seated, he could tell that the guy was tall, with dark brown skin, striking hazel eyes, and a flat-top haircut. He grinned, showing off perfect white teeth and dimples on each cheek, and waved with a muscular arm.

"Wow, Andrew! What a surprise!" David greeted.

"Good to see you," Andrew replied, towering over the two of them as he stood at their table.

"Yeah, you too," David said. "This is my friend, Tucker."

"Nice to meet you," Tucker said, offering a shy smile.

"I was just heading out, but wanted to say hi real quick. You should text me sometime! Let's catch up," Andrew said, offering David a quick wink before turning to walk away. "Nice to meet you, Tucker!"

David smiled until Andrew was out of view, then let his face drop. "Oh my god, that was so awkward."

"Oh?"

"We used to date for a little while last year. He went to New York for an internship for the summer and made it sound like he was going to stay there after, so we ended things. He's a really cool guy, but we didn't have that much in common anyway, so I was kind of glad we ended things with a clean break."

"But not so clean anymore," Tucker said, piecing the interaction together.

"Exactly," David nodded affirmingly. "My grades are always affected when I'm with someone and I really need to keep my GPA up, so I've kind of sworn off of dating at the moment anyway."

"Wow, that's very mature of you," Tucker replied, ignoring the sinking feeling in his chest. He was totally fine being friends with David, but hearing him adamantly say he would not be interested in dating anyone still stung.

"Comes with age," David replied with a chuckle. "I used to fool around a lot when I was your age, but I got that all out of my system pretty early on."

Tucker said nothing, unsure of how to respond to David's remark. David didn't seem to notice, though, as he scooped up the last of his food and threw his napkin on his now-empty plate.

"Wow, that hit the spot."

"I know," Tucker agreed. "We should definitely do this more often! It's nice to hang out outside of work."

"Totally," David replied with a grin. "I've got to get going, but I'll see you around soon, okay?"

"Oh, okay. Bye!" Tucker called as David exited the dining hall. He followed David's lead, dumping his plate in the designated area for dirty dishes, and headed back out to campus toward his next class.

That afternoon, he received a text from Kiara with directions to get to her dorm, and headed in that direction to meet her. She lived in a separate housing complex from Tucker's, but within a quick five-minute walking distance, which explained how she could make it to his building so fast. He sat on the hot, rusty bench outside of her building until she arrived, and the two took the elevator up to Kiara's room on the third floor.

Whereas Tucker and Mike shared one big room and a bathroom, Kiara and her roommate got their own rooms and only shared a bathroom and a living room containing a stained brown coffee table, a gray couch, and a large flat-screen TV, Tucker noted with jealousy. Kiara inserted her student

ID into the electronic lock on her door and thrust it open, allowing them entry.

Her room was painted white, though she had actual walls instead of cinderblocks like Tucker's, and she'd attached strings of fairly lights all around the room. The room itself was small and rectangular, containing only Kiara's tall twin bed, a dresser, and a desk. There was a humming coming from under her bed, and when Kiara lifted her large pink comforter, Tucker realized she had a mini fridge plugged in underneath.

"Thirsty?" Kiara asked, offering him a can of soda. Tucker took it, cracking it open and slurping its contents.

"I like your room," he said, admiring the posters from her high school theatre productions she'd pinned on the walls. There was a photo of her and some other girls in blunt black bobs attached to a poster of their production of *Chicago*. "This looks like it was a fun show."

"Thanks! I did what I could with the small amount of space I had," she said, hopping up on her bed and unzipping her backpack. Tucker sat on the carpeted floor, pulling a notebook out of his bag.

"So, I was doing some reading about mental illnesses in-between classes," Kiara said as she flipped through pages in her textbook, "and I think that you're a psychopath. Were you aware? That you're a psychopath, I mean?"

"*I'm* the psychopath?" Tucker laughed. "If anyone's going to go all Norman Bates between the two of us, it's *definitely* going to be you."

"That's exactly what a psychopath would say," she retorted, pointing a menacing finger at him.

"Turning the facts around to pin it on someone else is *exactly* what a psychopath would do and you know it!"

The two kept this up for another five minutes, going back and forth, accusing the other of being the crazy one and laughing maniacally until they grew bored of the joke and got to work. They eventually settled on generalized anxiety disorder for their project and sent an email to Professor Whitley confirming their topic, since they both already had a general understanding of it, and finished their paper within a few hours.

"Is it me, or was that almost *too* easy?" Tucker asked after he finished

CHAPTER 9

writing down the last sentence in their paper. "Professor Whitley doesn't seem like the type to give painless assignments."

"Who cares?" Kiara said through a yawn. "We got it done, so don't worry about it."

"Aren't you supposed to be the driven, studious one out of the two of us?" Tucker laughed.

"Too tired to care," she replied, grabbing a pillow and laying her head on it.

Tucker checked the time on his phone, surprised to see that it was already almost 10:30, and threw his school materials into his backpack. Kiara remained unmoving, a serene look on her face and her eyes closed.

"I didn't realize it was so late already, so I'm going to get going. Bye, Ki', I'll see you tomorrow," Tucker whispered, earning a grunt in response from Kiara. He let himself out of her room, taking the stairs back to her building's lobby and following the concrete path outside that led back to his own dorm.

Chapter 10

Weeks seemed to fly by faster and faster as the semester continued, and Tucker kept himself busy as September disappeared into October with a mix of classes, homework, drag, and his weekend shifts at Haven. His relationship with David had regressed from what he thought was friendship to a cordial work acquaintanceship, and the two rarely spoke unless it was while David was filling up more shots for Tucker to sell. He didn't understand why this was, since David was always friendly when they *did* talk, and ultimately blamed it on school, if only to make himself feel better.

He had seen Adrian at the club a few times but was always too busy to talk with him. Tucker felt bad, and wanted to spend more time with him after what happened on his birthday, but his continued feelings for David and the fact that Adrian only texted him in the early hours of the morning asking him to come over kept Tucker at bay.

He also had unresolved feelings for Micah, who he'd barely heard from since their last in-person conversation. Though Micah was the first guy he'd felt a connection with, each day without communication put more emotional distance between him and Tucker. However, Tucker recalled, this meant nothing if he felt the same way he did the last time he'd seen Micah, like all the days without talking and the arguments they'd had just never happened.

Kiara, who'd heard Tucker complain about his boy troubles for the last two months, had stopped giving advice. "I'll be here when you want advice," she'd said at lunch one afternoon, "but I will not give it anymore unless you ask. You obviously seem to want to wallow in your boy problems instead of

CHAPTER 10

working to fix them."

"It's not as simple as you think it is!" Tucker had protested. As usual, though, Kiara had been correct. He'd been waiting for them to come to him, Tucker realized, and waited so long that now it was too late for him to address any feelings or bring up any situations he wanted clarity on, primarily with David. So, he'd resigned to focusing on being an excellent student, both in school and for Jamie's continued drag lessons, and an exemplary employee.

* * *

Halloween landed on a Saturday that year, and Tucker had already received clearance from the club's general manager to dress in drag, so he sat in Jamie's drag room that afternoon as he got ready. He'd been practicing in his room for months whenever he was sure Mike wouldn't be there, but still could not attain the same level of polish he'd seen when the queens did his makeup that first day, or any time he'd watched Jamie paint.

The two were sharing Jamie's vanity as they got ready, and Tucker was trying to make sure his drawn-on eyebrows were even when Jamie entered the room, already in full makeup and a wig. She was playing an upbeat pop song on repeat that Tucker didn't recognize, mouthing along to the words to prepare for her performance that evening. After playing the song six more times, she seemed satisfied and changed the song to another one by the same artist, a singer named Vanity X, that Tucker had just heard on his way over to Jamie's apartment.

"Ooo, can you turn that up?" Tucker asked. Jamie did as he requested, and Kitty entered the room, dancing along to the song. She had a bottle of neon green paint in her hand and sat next to Tucker, applying it with her hands.

"Kitty," Tucker asked, turning to look at her, "is that paint supposed to go on your face? What if you go into toxic shock or something?"

"I mean," Kitty drawled as she smeared the green on her forehead, "I got it at the craft store, so I feel like I'll be fine."

Tucker caught Jamie's eye in the mirror and shot her an alarmed look, but Jamie seemed uninterested in chiming in to help and adjusted the front of her wig.

"That means nothing, Kitty," he warned. "You can buy a hot glue gun at the craft store too, but that doesn't mean you should put it on your face."

"Yeah, obviously!" Kitty scoffed.

"Give it up, Mary," Jamie said from behind them. "She'll learn once she's in the hospital."

"When in doubt, freak 'em out," Kitty muttered, moving on to her cheeks with the paint.

"Damn, I miss this bitch," Jamie said, ignoring Kitty and referring to the song.

"You know Vanity X?" Tucker asked incredulously.

"Miss Thing, I call bullshit on that. You do not know her!" Kitty said pointedly, turning to look at Jamie.

"I don't lie, bitch!" Jamie retorted. "I worked with her when I used to live in Tampa. She was just starting out, and she'd come and sing at the clubs and party with the queens."

"Are you still in touch?" he asked.

"Of course not!" Jamie laughed. "She's all rich and famous now. She told me all the time she would be, too. One time I said, 'Oh yeah? If you're going to be so famous, give me a CD and sign it so I can sell it one day and make some money off of your ass', and she did. I still have it somewhere around here too."

"Girl, how have you not told me this before?" Kitty asked indignantly.

"Because I don't need to be name-dropping to make myself seem interesting, bitch!" Jamie retorted.

"I'm so jealous," Tucker said. Jamie caught his eye in the mirror and sighed, leaning forward and taking the makeup brush out of Tucker's hand.

"Girl, come here," she said. "Your makeup looks terrible right now and I will not have you going out there looking a mess and tarnishing my good name."

"So, is she your kid?" Kitty asked Jamie, motioning to Tucker with a green-stained hand.

"Her kid?" Tucker asked. "She's only, like, six years older than me."

CHAPTER 10

"No, Mary," Jamie said impatiently. "She's asking if you're my drag kid. If I'm going to have to keep fixing you like this, I might as well name you too."

Tucker smiled, but said nothing, fearing he'd say the wrong thing and make Jamie take her offer back. Jamie took a step back, looking puzzled. Finally, a confident smile spread across her face.

"You're Karma Kahlo," she announced proudly.

"Can I ask how you come up with names?" Tucker asked. He hadn't thought of what his name was going to be and was happy with what Jamie chose, but his continued curiosity about the world of drag made him want to know how and why everything was the way it was.

"Well," Jamie said, "I originally chose the last name Kahlo for myself because of the painter Frida Kahlo. She was Mexican, just like my mom was, and I loved her paintings, so I took her name. Jamie was my nickname before I transitioned and changed my legal name, so I kept it for drag. It's androgynous and reminds me of my mom, so I thought it was a good fit."

"I chose Karma for you because it sounded fun and bitchy," she added with a shrug.

Tucker grinned. *Karma Kahlo,* he thought admiringly. He was one step closer toward being the performer he now dreamed of being, and he could almost hear the announcer introducing him to the stage. Now that Jamie had fixed Tucker's mistakes, he quickly threw on the rest of his outfit that Jamie had gifted him. He gave Jamie and Kitty a quick goodbye and went to his car, eager to get to the club and show off his look.

His phone rang and, not wanting to put the phone up to his ear in case he smeared his makeup, he answered the call using the buttons on his steering wheel that connected to the car's bluetooth system.

"Hello?" he said.

"Hi Tucker," his mother replied. Tucker's eye's widened in surprise, then narrowed in frustration. He had not spoken to his mother since the last time she'd called him, which, incidentally, was when Tucker was driving home from Jamie's almost a month and a half prior, and his feelings hadn't changed since then. He'd still texted with his dad occasionally, but hadn't mentioned anything about Tucker's mother if he'd picked up on the tension at all.

"Oh. Hi," he said flatly.

"I need to tell you something, and I need you to hear this," his mother instructed firmly. "When your father and I were growing up, there weren't any gay people that we knew. Times were different, and it wasn't something you told someone if you were. I wasn't ready for that when you told me, so I'm sorry if you were upset at how I reacted."

"Let me stop you right there," Tucker interjected, his voice cold. "First of all, 'I'm sorry you were upset' is not an apology. I was very upset, and I still am, because I trusted you enough to show you the real me, and you told me to hide my *choice*. I am who I am, and if you can't understand that because of how you grew up forty-something years ago, then tell me now so I can move on with my life. I'm gay, Mom. That isn't changing, and it isn't a choice."

His mother was silent, but he could hear her sniffling on the other end, indicating that she was quietly crying.

"I'm sorry I hurt you, Tucker," she finally said, her voice wavering. "This is all new to me and I'd be lying if I told you I completely understood, but I swear to you that I love you and I'm going to try to learn."

It was Tucker's turn to remain silent now, processing his mother's words. Though it wasn't exactly what he'd hoped to hear, Tucker could hear his sincerity in her words. He silently thanked the stoplight he was at for remaining red so he could look up to keep his tears from falling and ruining his makeup. The light turned green, and he took a deep, steadying breath before pressing his stockinged foot on the gas pedal again.

"I love you too, Mom," he said. "I accept your apology. I'm telling you, though, that I'm not changing who I am, and I will not tolerate any negativity about that from you or Dad whenever I tell him. I love you both, but I love myself too and I won't subject myself to that from my own family."

"I understand," his mom said quickly.

"Okay," Tucker said, feeling slightly relieved. "I'm on my way to work right now so I have to go, but I'll talk to you later."

"Okay," his mom said, sniffling. "I love you, Tucker."

"I love you too, Mom," he said, ending the call.

CHAPTER 10

The club was already packed when Tucker arrived for his shift, everyone milling around in costumes—a majority of which were concepts people made 'sexy', like a sexy firefighter or a sexy doctor. Tucker even noted a sexy Santa as he strutted to the bar, which was just a guy with a fake white beard wearing nothing but tight, sheer red underwear and black leather boots. David, wearing nothing but a black bowtie and a pair of black jeans, was waiting for Tucker at the bar with a tray ready, and he smiled in surprise when he caught sight of Tucker in drag.

"Wow, look at you!" David said.

"Is that a good wow, or a bad wow?" Tucker asked, laughing.

"Good, I swear!" David said.

"Thanks," Tucker said with a smile, taking the tray and merging into the crowd. He mentally praised himself for spending the last few weeks walking around his dorm in heels whenever Mike wasn't around (which was often) to get a better feel for them, now that he had to walk confidently through a packed club in them with a tray full of liquids in his hand. It being Halloween, he didn't receive as many strange looks or comments as he'd expected, and actually got a few compliments from some very drunk lesbians dressed as dinosaurs. One member of the group, dressed as a tyrannosaurus rex, even pretended to take a bite out of his fake breasts, which Tucker took as a high praise.

The night seemed to fly by as Tucker sold tray after tray full of shots, watching Crystal Waters host one of the weekly shows the club held while dressed as a slutty cave woman in a tight animal-print mini-dress and a bone stuck in her wig to hold up the ponytail. Before he knew it, the club closed for the night. He brought his last tray back to the bar, handing it and all the money he'd received to David, who had just about finished closing the bar down. He quickly counted the money, wiped down the tray, and handed Tucker a wad of cash as the two walked towards the parking lot in silence.

"David, can I ask you something?" Tucker finally said as they walked across the gravel lot. "Did I do or say something to you to upset or offend you? If I did, I'm really sorry."

"What?" David asked, looking puzzled. "No, why?"

"I don't know," Tucker sighed. "Maybe I'm just in my head, but it felt like we were becoming real friends at the start of the semester, and for the last month or so now we only talk when we're working together. I just wanted to make sure it wasn't anything I did."

"I'm sorry if I made you feel like I didn't want to be your friend," David said, stopping to look at Tucker. "I was just trying to make sure I was as focused as I could be on school, and you seemed to be plenty busy too with your friends and drag and guys and stuff, so I just figured we were doing our own things."

"Guys?" Tucker asked. It was his turn to look puzzled now, and he hoped it showed through the makeup.

"Yeah, like when you were here for your birthday and I saw you and that guy make out. That's around the time that the semester really kicked in, so I just figured that was one of the many things keeping you busy," David explained. "But I do want to be your friend, Tucker. You're a really cool guy."

"Cool," Tucker said, smiling. "And for the record, I haven't talked to Adrian much since that night. He keeps trying to make me his late-night booty call, but I'm not interested in that. I was just drunk and following his lead, is all."

"I'll make sure they edit the graffiti on the bathroom wall to reflect those changes," David joked. Tucker laughed, and the two continued walking until they got to Tucker's car.

"Oh, and David," Tucker said as he opened the car door, "I think you're a really cool guy too, and I'm happy to be your friend."

His nerve already fading, Tucker got into the car and closed the door before David could say anything else. He looked through the windshield and saw David smiling to himself as he turned toward his own car, which made Tucker grin in return. Sighing, he pulled out his phone and sent a text to Kiara.

CHAPTER 10

TUCKER: I owe you ten bucks. You were right. I like David.

II

Part Two: Winter

Chapter 11

As the Fall semester came to an end, Tucker was proud to say that he passed all of his classes with a letter grade of B or higher. Even his General Psychology class, taught by the insufferable Professor Whitley, proved to be manageable once Tucker designated enough time to studying prior to the final exam. Though he still didn't know what he wanted to major in, or why he was even there aside from a hypothetical good job in the future, he was proud nonetheless of the hard work he'd put into his first semester. His classes all held their final exams on the earlier days in the last two weeks in November the school designated for finals, which left him with an empty schedule for the first time in months.

With his newfound free time, Tucker could visit the Queer Alliance headquarters again, catching up with those he'd met at the beginning of the semester, and even helped plan a surprise party to wish Jai and Kenny a bon voyage as they prepared to graduate when the semester ended. David was often there, socializing with the others or in a quiet corner of the room studying for his own exams.

Since their conversation in the parking lot on Halloween, Tucker had been making more of an effort to talk to David, and he noticed that David was doing the same. They'd text occasionally about nothing in particular during the week, hang out together at the Queer Alliance, and still chat whenever they worked together at Haven.

Tucker had offered to help David study, so the two had spent the last three evenings making flash cards for David's microeconomics class, writing down terms Tucker'd never heard of before and quizzing David over dinner at

Knightro's or in the courtyard outside Tucker's dorm.

"So," Tucker said one evening while the two of them were studying at the dining hall over a shared plate of mediocre nachos, "I have a very important question for you, David."

"As long as it isn't another fill-in-the-blank question from this study packet, I'm all ears," David replied through a mouth full of chips and half-melted shredded cheese.

"You're going to a desert island, and you can only bring three movies and three books to enjoy for the rest of your life. What do you bring?" Tucker asked, raising an eyebrow.

"What, no food or water? It's going to be a short rest of my life!" David remarked, shoveling more chips into his mouth.

"Just pretend!" Tucker retorted, lightly shoving the plate towards David.

"Fine, let's see," David replied, looking thoughtful as he chewed. He answered once he swallowed, which felt like hours to Tucker. "For movies, I'd have to take some that bring me comfort—probably *Love Actually, Mamma Mia!*, and *Legally Blonde*."

"My god, you really *are* gay!" Tucker interrupted, laughing.

"For books," David continued with a laugh, talking louder, "I'd have to go with *The Lord of the Rings* trilogy. I've read it, like, seven times."

"And a total nerd!" Tucker said, laughing harder.

"Says the college-attending drag queen," David rebutted with a laugh. "What about you, Tucker? What're your desert island picks?"

"I'd have to go with *Silver Linings Playbook, Clue,* and *The Perks of Being a Wallflower* for movies. I'd choose the *Silver Linings* and *Wallflower* novels too, and I'd throw in *The Handmaid's Tale* just for fun."

"You'd pick the same movie and book?" David asked, looking incredulous.

"They're good both ways, and I like to see the differences!" Tucker replied indignantly, shoving a handful of chips in his mouth as David laughed.

Tucker had also promised Kiara he'd help her study, so their lunches were devoted to Tucker reading sample questions from her various study guides as she pulled at her hair in frustration while trying to think or barking out answers at him before he finished reading. Once David's exams were

CHAPTER 11

finished, he continued to join Tucker for dinners at Knightro's and was roped into helping Kiara study as well, to his apparent amusement and Tucker's horror. Even when trying to pass a crucial exam, Kiara somehow still found the time to play matchmaker for Tucker.

Kiara's last exam was on the Monday before Thanksgiving, and David invited them out to dinner at a small, family-owned Italian restaurant close to campus called Giovanna's to celebrate them surviving their first semester. An older Italian man with a thick accent that introduced himself as one of the owners was their server and told them he'd make them something special when he learned they were celebrating. They were soon brought plates piled high with pasta and a "small" side salad that looked to have had a whole head of lettuce in each bowl.

"So," Tucker asked as they devoured their meals, "what are you guys doing for Thanksgiving?"

David shoved another heaping pile of pasta into his mouth and looked down at his plate, and Kiara took a long drink of water before answering.

"Well," she said, "I actually just spoke with my parents last week and discussed it, and we decided I'd stay here for Thanksgiving so I could fly back home for Christmas."

"I didn't realize you weren't from Florida," Tucker said, shocked at himself for missing that important detail in his friend's life.

"Yeah," Kiara said, "I'm from Washington, so they're on the complete opposite end of the country."

"What made you want to come here?" David asked.

Kiara shrugged, taking another huge bite of salad before answering. "I wanted sunshine and the beach," she finally said after she swallowed, "and UCF offered me a scholarship when I applied for the theatre program, so I figured it was meant to be."

"What about you, David?" Tucker asked. "Any plans?"

"Um," David said, inhaling deeply, "I'm not on good terms with my parents, so I don't really have any plans."

"I'm really sorry," Tucker murmured sadly.

"No need to be sorry," David said, shrugging his shoulders and looking down at his plate again. "We used to be close, but they didn't take things very well when I came out, so that was that."

Tucker's heart sank, imagining what David went through. He'd thought things would be the same with his family, but was thankful his mom apologized so it hadn't come to that. Tucker wanted to give David a hug or squeeze his hand reassuringly, but he only offered David a sad smile when he looked up again.

"My sister went through something similar," Kiara said, nodding knowingly. "I'm still in touch with her, but my parents have basically stopped communicating with her. It's awful."

"Come home with me," Tucker blurted. "Both of you," he added, noticing Kiara's small suggestive smirk.

"No, I couldn't impose on your family like that," David protested.

"Please," Tucker said dismissively, "if anything, you'd be helping me! Things have been pretty tense with my mom since I came out, so I could use all the help I can get."

"I know you said you're from a small town, so I have a serious question," Kiara said. "Are there any black people there?"

"Yes," Tucker chuckled. Kiara's delivery was comedic, but it was an unfortunate yet fair question to ask.

"Then I'm in," Kiara grinned.

"What about you, David?" Tucker asked. "I'd love for you to come and I'm sure my parents would be happy to have the company, but I don't want to make you uncomfortable."

"You wouldn't!" David assured him. "I'd love to join you and your family for Thanksgiving. Thanks for inviting me."

David gave Tucker's forearm a quick squeeze, which Tucker took as reassurance that he was indeed pleased about the invite, and Kiara's eyes quickly darted back and forth from his hand to Tucker's eyes with a knowing look.

"I'm going to go call my mom," Tucker said quickly, nervously running a hand through his hair as he stood and walked out the front door. They could see him on the phone through the front windows, talking animatedly with

CHAPTER 11

his hands, and he returned to the table a few minutes later with a satisfied look on his face.

"They're looking forward to it," Tucker said, smiling at his friends. "We're going to leave tomorrow afternoon, so pack for a few days."

"Yay! Road trip!" Kiara said, clapping her hands excitedly. David laughed, and the three were soon too full from the delicious meal to talk anymore. David grabbed the check as it was placed on the table and paid for their dinner, Tucker and Kiara thanking him effusively. They waddled to their cars and headed back to their respective homes, eager to pack for their trip.

They met by Tucker's car the next day, a suitcase in everyone's hands, and after shoving the bags in the trunk they were soon on the road. Though Thanksgiving is typically known as the beginning of the winter holiday season, Orlando burned at a steady 89 degrees that day and the three were dressed in comfortable shorts and breathable short-sleeved shirts. During the two-hour drive, Tucker filled David and Kiara in on what to expect from his parents, a loud northerner and a stubborn southerner in their late forties who always sounded like they were yelling, and advised them to keep the conversation away from their jobs at Haven or Tucker's sexuality. Kiara, who had basically shoved David into the front passenger seat as she volunteered to sit in the back, had fallen asleep shortly after Tucker finished, leaving him and David to drive in silence.

"I'm kind of nervous," Tucker confessed, keeping his voice low so he didn't wake Kiara.

"Why?" David asked, matching Tucker's low volume.

"I haven't seen my parents since I moved to UCF in August. My mom didn't take things very well when I came out to her, so things have been kind of tense with us this semester. My dad doesn't even know. She apologized and we're okay now, but it's still weird," Tucker explained. David nodded in understanding.

"Well, lucky for you that you have two awesome friends keeping you company and have your back," David said, lightly punching Tucker in the arm. Tucker quietly chuckled, elbowing David back on his arm.

"Listen, if you want to pull this car over, we can fight," David challenged playfully, putting up his fists like a boxer.

"I wouldn't want to do that to you," Tucker said, smirking and staring ahead at the road. "I'd eviscerate you."

David laughed at full volume, catching himself and stopping quickly before he woke Kiara. "I'd like to see you try," David said, his voice returning to the low volume. Spoken quietly, David sounded like he was growling when he said it, and Tucker got goosebumps at the sound of his voice.

"Just wait," Tucker said, maintaining his air of false confidence. "You'll never see it coming."

David snorted quietly, shaking his head in amusement. Tucker quietly chuckled as well and felt gleeful at how naturally their conversation flowed now. To him, it sounded like David was flirting, but he reminded himself of David's reassurance that he wanted to be friends to rid his mind of any romantic hope.

The roads were clear as they got closer to Weeki Wachee, Tucker noted with surprise, as he'd expected holiday traffic to slow them down. When they turned on to Highway 50 and entered Hernando County, Tucker pulled into a nearby gas station to fill up before they continued their trip. Kiara was still asleep in the back seat, so David quietly advised Tucker he was using the bathroom and walked inside the gas station. As soon as the doors closed behind David, Kiara shot up in her seat and rolled down her window, poking Tucker's side as he filled the car with gas.

"Jesus!" he yelped at her touch. "You scared me!"

"Sorry," Kiara giggled. "I just wanted to tell you something."

Tucker said nothing, but looked at her expectantly, waiting for her to continue.

"David has a crush on you," she sang loudly, poking Tucker with each word.

"Oh my god!" Tucker whispered harshly, trying to cover her mouth with his hand as he looked around to make sure David didn't overhear her. "No, he doesn't!"

"Oh my god," Kiara said, mocking Tucker, "you are so damn blind if you really believe that. I've been awake for the last twenty minutes, so I caught

CHAPTER 11

every bit of that play-fight flirt-fest you two were having up in the front."

Tucker scoffed, but couldn't deny that conversations with David often felt like borderline-flirtations, and knowing that Kiara had heard it made him feel flustered. He finished filling up the gas tank and sat back in his seat as they waited for David to return. He walked out the gas station door seconds later, hurrying back to the car.

"Why the hell would you not have air conditioning in your bathroom when we live in Florida?" he huffed when he closed his door. His face was red and there were beads of sweat rolling down his forehead. He took the bottom of his shirt and lifted it up to his face to mop up the perspiration, exposing his glistening abdomen. Tucker fought every instinct he had not to stare, but quickly glanced and then looked straight ahead as he started the car. He made the mistake of looking in his rear-view mirror and saw Kiara, whose jaw had dropped and had a gigantic smile on her face as she jerked her head toward David. Tucker shot her the dirtiest look he could muster in the mirror before returning his eyes to the road as he put the car in gear, joining oncoming traffic and getting back on the road.

The three chatted about their finals and other small-talk topics for the remaining half hour of their trip, and were soon passing the Weeki Wachee Springs, which doubled as a water park in the summer called Buccaneer Bay. Tucker took a deep breath as the other two passengers marveled at the park, his heart rate picking up as he got closer to his home. After two more stoplights, Tucker pulled on to his street, his heart now pounding. Kiara placed a hand on Tucker's right shoulder, as if she could sense his tension.

His parents lived in a quiet neighborhood in a cul-de-sac at the end of their street. A majority of the neighborhood's residents were retirees who spent their days caring for their lawns or sitting in fold-out chairs in their driveways, keeping an eye on what everyone else was doing so they had something to gossip about with their neighbors later. His parents' house was a one-story home painted light blue, with a wrap-around porch that went around the right side of the house. Tucker pulled into the driveway, putting the car in park, and sat there unmoving.

"Tucker, you okay?" David asked.

"Yeah," Tucker said, taking another deep breath to calm himself. "It's just weird is all. So much has changed since the last time I was here."

Kiara leaned forward and rubbed Tucker's back reassuringly, the three of them sitting in silence as Tucker took steadying breaths. Finally, he exhaled forcefully and turned off the engine, throwing his door open and stepping out of the car. David turned and looked at Kiara with a look of concern, and Kiara nodded knowingly before opening her door and joining Tucker. David was the last one to get out of the car, and they walked up the porch stairs to the front door. Tucker raised his finger to the doorbell and held it there, taking one final moment to prepare himself, and pressed it, hearing the chime echo through the house.

Seconds later, the front door swung open and Tucker's father stood in the doorway, smiling. His father was shorter than Tucker's mother and stocky, almost barrel-shaped with his broad chest and wide arms. He had close-cropped brown hair and hazel eyes that revealed crow's feet when he smiled.

"There he is!" his father boomed, his Alabama accent thick as ever, as he placed a heavy hand on Tucker's shoulder.

"Hey, Dad," Tucker said, managing a smile. "These are my friends, David and Kiara."

"Pleased to meet you," his father said, shaking both of their hands. "Call me Ken."

"Thanks for having us, Ken," David said with a nod.

"Please, come on in!" Ken said, stepping out of the way as the three entered. The house was painted tan on the inside and contained three bedrooms—Tucker's parents' room was on the right, and his room and the guest room were on the left. In the middle of the home was the kitchen, and there was a dining room and living room closest to Tucker's room.

"You have a lovely home," Kiara said, surveying the pictures on the wall of family vacations, Tucker as a baby, and his parents' wedding.

Tucker's mom was in the kitchen, chopping up vegetables for a salad, and set the knife down on the cutting board as she came to say hello.

"Hi, guys!" she said excitedly, wiping her hands on her pants before shaking

CHAPTER 11

David and Kiara's hands. "I'm Pam, so nice to meet you."

"Hi Mom," Tucker said, thankful that she was focusing most of her attention on her new houseguests.

"Hi honey," Pam said, turning to Tucker and giving him a quick hug. She looked Tucker in the eyes as she pulled back and he nodded slightly, the two of them silently agreeing to not bring up their issues from the last few months. "Where are your bags?"

"Oh, we left them in the car," Kiara said. "I'll go grab them."

"You'll do no such thing!" Ken interjected. "You all stay here and I'll go get them."

"There's three, so I'll help you get the last bag," David volunteered, following Ken out the front door. Tucker could hear the two men chatting, but couldn't make out what they were saying. His father was a typical man's-man, one who enjoyed beer and sports, so he and Tucker had never had too much in common when he was growing up. He was glad that David seemed up to the task of keeping up with his father over the next few days.

"I could have done it," Kiara grumbled. Tucker snorted, and the two leaned against the refrigerator, making small talk with his mother as she returned to preparing the salad. David and Ken returned, suitcases in hand, and headed towards the two rooms.

"Now, I know y'all are adults," Ken drawled, "but I'm an old man stuck in his ways, so I hope you'll humor me when I say Kiara will get the guest room and you two can bunk in Tucker's room. Sound fair?"

"Absolutely," Kiara agreed with a grin before Tucker could object. He nervously glanced at his mother, whose attention was now hyper-focused on washing a tomato. Tucker looked to David, who gave him a small, reassuring smile.

"Alright then," Ken said, sounding pleased. He brought Kiara's suitcase to the guest room, and David brought the other two into Tucker's room. Kiara followed quickly after David, eager to get a look at Tucker's childhood bedroom. Tucker blanched, seeing the two going into his room, and hurried after them, unsure of what they'd find.

His room was painted navy blue, with a large window overlooking the backyard and dark brown hardwood flooring. There was a full-sized bed tucked into a corner, a white dresser, and an empty closet. Kiara groaned upon entering, disappointed at the lack of material to tease Tucker about, as David set the suitcases down in front of the closet doors. Tucker entered and stopped, perplexed by what he was seeing. When he moved out in August, he'd left old movie posters and pictures of his friends taped to the walls and a few old stuffed animals he'd had since childhood sitting on his dresser. He turned and walked back to the kitchen while Kiara and David were still in his room.

"Where's all my stuff?" he asked his dad, who was grabbing a beer can from the fridge.

"You moved out, so I packed it up," he grunted, looking at Tucker as if to challenge him. "Don't worry, it's all in the attic."

"You could have told me," Tucker said, holding his father's gaze. His father shrugged and cracked open the can, taking a long swig.

"Dinner's ready," Pam called, bringing David and Kiara out of Tucker's room. The three of them sat down at the polished wooden dinner table as Tucker's mother brought over the salad she'd been preparing and his father handed each of them a plate of steak and potatoes. Tucker remained quiet throughout dinner, his parents peppering David and Kiara with small talk, asking where they grew up and what their majors were before moving on to reminiscing about old family vacations to Yellowstone National Park and other stories Tucker'd heard a thousand times. Kiara, who sat across from Tucker, occasionally shot him questioning looks, and he responded with tight-lipped smiles to show that he was fine.

He still harbored feelings of resentment toward his mother, though he was trying to move on from them since she'd apologized, and he'd forgotten how frustrated he felt whenever he was around his father for long periods of time. The two of them never had too much in common, and were both very stubborn, so they clashed often. It was too late, but he was regretting bringing his friends into what he considered to be a ticking time bomb.

A dessert of fresh strawberries over vanilla ice cream followed dinner, and Tucker's parents bid the three of them goodnight shortly after, though it was

CHAPTER 11

barely after 9:00. Tucker, Kiara, and David sat on the couch, Kiara sitting in the middle, and flipped through channels on the television in the living room for another hour before they gave up and turned it off. Kiara let out what Tucker assumed to be an exaggerated yawn, knowing how dramatic she could be, and bid the two guys goodnight as well as she closed the door to the guest room. Tucker swore he could hear her giggling to herself, but said nothing.

They migrated to Tucker's bedroom and Tucker stood with his back to the door once he'd closed it, feeling awkward about the sleeping arrangements.

"So," he said, "I have a plan."

"Let's hear it," David said, standing in the middle of the room.

"You're the guest and I don't want to make things weird," Tucker began, "so you should take the bed and I'll crash on the floor. There are extra blankets around here somewhere."

"What?" David laughed. "Don't be ridiculous. There's not even carpet on the floor, and I'd still object if there was! We can share the bed."

"Are you sure?" Tucker asked hesitantly. "I really don't mind."

"We're both adults," David said, shrugging his shoulders. "It's no big deal."

"If you say so," Tucker said, drawing out the last word to give David ample time to change his mind. David laughed, shaking his head as he unzipped his suitcase and grabbed some clothes. He left the room and went to the bathroom between Tucker's room and the guest room, returning shortly after in a tight white tank top and black basketball shorts. Tucker did the same, returning from the bathroom in an old sleeveless shirt and a pair of basketball shorts.

"Last chance," Tucker warned, standing next to the light switch.

"Oh my god," David laughed. "You're being ridiculous! I said it was fine."

"Okay," Tucker said, turning off the light. The two got into Tucker's bed, laying on their backs shoulder to shoulder.

"Hey," Tucker said, his voice quieting as they laid in the dark, "thanks again for coming with me."

"Hey," came David's voice in the dark, "thanks for inviting me so I wasn't alone on Thanksgiving."

He knew David couldn't see him, but he smiled anyway, hoping that he would somehow just know.

"Hey David?" Tucker asked.

"That's me," David replied, his amused tone still evident without Tucker seeing his smile in the dark.

"Can I ask what happened with you and your family? I know it's a touchy subject, so you can say no."

"It's fine, I don't mind telling you. But it's not some big story, if that's what you're expecting. I came out to my parents when I was seventeen, right after my senior year of high school started. I thought they were mature adults with open minds, but they quickly showed me how wrong I was when they kicked me out. They said that they didn't want some fag living in sin in their house, that I was choosing this life and what I was doing was unnatural, an abomination, so they put me out on the street. I had to stay at a shelter for a couple of days, but luckily my friend Lindsay's parents let me move into their guest room until I moved to UCF at the end of that summer. I haven't talked to my parents since."

"Wow, David, I'm so sorry," Tucker breathed.

"It is what it is. I know people that had it way worse than I did, so I count myself lucky that I had a friend to help me out when I needed it."

"You still do," Tucker replied sincerely.

"Yeah, you too, Tucker," David murmured.

The two sat in silence, and David eventually drifted off to sleep, emitting quiet snores. Tucker, extremely conscious of their shared space, turned on his side so his back was facing David, giving them as much space apart as he could before he fell asleep to the sounds of David's breathing.

Chapter 12

The first thing Tucker noticed when he woke up the next morning is that he'd moved around in his sleep. As he slowly opened his eyes, he was met with the sight of David's smirk instead of the wall like he'd expected.

"You snore in your sleep. Like, *really* snore. Did you know that?" David asked, his amused smirk morphing into a grin.

"Good morning to you, too," Tucker grumbled, rubbing his eyes. "You snore too, by the way."

"Maybe, but I bet I didn't sound like a chainsaw like you," David chuckled.

"Sorry," Tucker said, his eyes still adjusting to the daylight streaming in from the window. "Did I wake you up?"

"No, I'm a heavy sleeper," he assured him. "I just woke up a few minutes ago, but that was plenty of time to hear you."

"Oh my god, shut up," Tucker laughed, making David laugh too.

The two got out of bed and left the room, David starting a pot of coffee in the kitchen while Tucker banged on the guest room to get Kiara up. His parents, as Tucker already knew, had to work all day and would be gone until the evening. Kiara opened the door, her hair flattened on one side where her head had laid on her pillow, and offered Tucker her middle finger before pushing him out of the way and entering the bathroom, slamming the door behind her. Tucker laughed, amused to be on the other side of the pounding door for once, and headed back to the kitchen. David sat on the couch, sipping his cup of coffee and watching Tucker work as he made the three of them eggs and toast for breakfast, and Kiara soon joined David. When the food was ready, the three of them sat at the table and ate.

"So," Tucker said in-between bites, "I was thinking I could show you some of the town's highlights and then we could meet up with Brooke and everyone afterward for a while. Sound good to you guys?"

"Sounds fun," Kiara said. "I haven't talked to Brooke or the twins in so long! They were such a good time."

David said nothing, his mouth full of food, but nodded in agreement. After they were finished, they each took turns showering and getting dressed, and were ready to go by late morning. They piled into Tucker's car and he drove them around town, pointing out places like the two tall brown buildings that made up his high school campus on the edge of town and the dollar movie theater where he and his friends spent every Friday night in middle school until they upped their prices. When Tucker ran out of fun stories and places to show off, which happened within the hour, he drove them back to his parents' house, texting Brooke as they went inside.

"Okay," Tucker said, flopping onto the couch, "Brooke just texted back, so we'll head out in a little while to go meet up with her. She said 'we'll be there', so I'm assuming 'we' means the twins too. Our senior year, we used to go to the beach and hang out, so we're meeting there for old time's sake. Is that cool with you guys?"

"The beach?" Kiara asked, looking alarmed. "I didn't bring a bathing suit!"

"Me neither," David chimed in.

"We just sit by the water," Tucker assured them. "There's a cute little spot we go to in the shade under some trees. Even in the middle of summer when going outside makes you want to die, it's pretty nice there."

David shrugged noncommittally, but Kiara still looked skeptical.

"You did say that you came to Florida for the beach," Tucker pointed out. "We're a lot closer here than we would be in Orlando."

Kiara rolled her eyes but agreed, and the three left shortly after for the beach, which Tucker informed them was called Pine Island. It only took them twenty minutes to get there, as Tucker's parents' house seemed centralized to almost everything around town. Tucker turned left at the Springs and followed a road lined with palm trees and the occasional boat dock that quickly changed from pavement to dirt, and Kiara marveled at the tall houses

CHAPTER 12

that sat on stilts next to the water as they got closer to the beach.

"In case the water rises during a hurricane and floods," Tucker explained.

The approaching winter holidays meant nothing in Florida, where the air didn't turn cold until at least January on a good year, and Tucker rolled down his windows to let the hot, salty sea air blow through the car. They joined the line of cars waiting to get into the crowded parking lot and found the closest spot they could once they were inside the beach's gates.

Just as Tucker described, there was a picnic table in the sand that sat under a cluster of palm trees, casting shade over the area from multiple directions. The beach was surprisingly busy for the middle of the day on a Wednesday, but Brooke had already claimed the table by the time they'd arrived. She was lounging across the tabletop with a pair of dark sunglasses on and jumped off to run and greet the three when she noticed their arrival.

"Hi everyone!" Brooke said excitedly, giving them each a quick hug.

"Brooke, this is my friend David," Tucker explained as she hugged David, who laughed in surprise at her friendliness.

"Aren't you a cutie," Brooke said flirtatiously, lowering her sunglasses to look David up and down.

"And gay," Tucker interjected, laughing as Brooke visibly deflated. She looked over Tucker's shoulder and smiled, causing him to turn as well. Taylor and Mara were trudging through the sand toward them, with Micah in tow carrying a giant multicolored beach umbrella and a canvas bag filled with beach towels slung over his shoulder.

"Hi, everyone!" Taylor said cheerfully when they were close enough.

"Kiara, so good to see you again!" Mara said, giving Kiara a hug.

"Hey," Micah said, offering an awkward half-wave to the group as he approached.

"Everyone, this is my friend David," Tucker said, introducing David to each of them. Taylor and Mara recognized David from Tucker's birthday at Haven and gushed over how much fun they had, but Micah only nodded curtly at David, his lips pressed together in a straight line. Once everyone had said their greetings, the group settled into their spot; Mara and Taylor laid their towels down in the sand, laying out in the sun while Micah set up the giant umbrella next to them, and the rest of the group sat on either sides of the picnic table.

"So I see you survived your first semester," Brooke said once they were comfortable on the wooden benches. She and David sat with their backs to the ocean, and Kiara and Tucker sat across from them. "Was it everything you thought it'd be?"

"Not at all," Tucker said truthfully. "I'm happy I'm there, I guess, but things are a lot harder than I expected them to be."

"I can tell you from experience that it only gets harder from here," David advised.

"That's what he said," Brooke murmured, causing Kiara to snicker.

"What about you guys?" Tucker called to Taylor and Mara. "How was your first semester?"

"No more school talk," Taylor groaned, "it's tanning time!"

"It was fine, Tucker," Mara answered, elbowing her twin sister in the arm.

"Micah, anything new with you?" Tucker prompted. Micah had never been a social butterfly, and Tucker found that getting him to volunteer information was like pulling teeth.

"Nope," he replied tersely, giving Tucker a disdainful look from where he was laying against the umbrella. Micah's rude response took Tucker aback, but he tried not to let it show on his face to give him satisfaction.

"I'm thirsty," Kiara piped up, eager to change the subject. "Is there a vending machine or something anywhere?"

"There's a snack bar," Taylor said, unmoving on her towel.

"I'll show you," Brooke volunteered, getting up from the table. "Anyone else want to come?"

Mara sprung up from her towel to join them, and after they started walking away David seemed to change his mind and got up from the table too.

"You want anything?" he asked Tucker.

"I'm good, thanks," Tucker said, giving him a quick smile.

David jogged to catch up with the girls, who were chatting and pointing to a shack near the parking lot where a line was formed. Still perturbed by Micah's response, Tucker stood up from the table and walked to stand over

CHAPTER 12

Micah, who was leaning against the umbrella with his eyes closed.

"Hey," Tucker said, nudging Micah's leg with his shoe, "let's go for a walk."

Micah opened his eyes, squinting at the sun, and scoffed at Tucker, but stood up anyway. They walked away from Taylor in silence toward the shore, following along the water's edge.

"Is something wrong?" Tucker finally asked when they were out of earshot.

"No," Micah said, not looking at him.

"Micah, come on," Tucker huffed. "You seem pissed. What's wrong?"

"Nothing's wrong," Micah insisted, though Tucker noticed his tone was pointed.

"Fine, don't tell me," he shrugged. The two strolled in uncomfortable silence, stepping over seashell shards and cigarette butts buried in the sand.

"Who's that guy with you, anyway?" Micah suddenly asked. "We talked on your birthday and I thought... hell, I don't know what I thought. But now you finally come home after being gone for months and show up to hang out with us with some guy we've never met? It's just weird."

"Like I said," Tucker said slowly, trying to remain calm and keep the conversation rational, "David is my friend. He didn't have any Thanksgiving plans, so I invited him to come to my parents' house. I did the same for Kiara, in case you didn't notice her."

"It's not the same," Micah said, shaking his head. "Don't you see how uncomfortable everyone is?"

"I don't think anyone is at all," Tucker retorted, his anger flaring. Any patience he had for Micah's strange possessiveness evaporated immediately, as he refused to believe that he ruined anything by bringing his new friends with him to meet his old ones. "If anything, your attitude is what's making everyone uncomfortable!"

The two had walked far enough away that there were no longer any beachgoers near them, and their volume had started to rise.

"*My* attitude?" Micah asked incredulously, turning to look at Tucker. "I haven't said anything!"

"That's my point!" Tucker argued, turning to face Micah, determined to have their quarrel face-to-face. "You've been acting so weird and cold since you showed up! What's going on with you?"

"What's going on with me is you left," he said shortly. "You were my best friend, and you left me here."

"Oh my god, not this again!" Tucker yelled, exasperated. "We talked about this, Micah!"

"You're right, sorry to bring up my feelings," Micah bit back sarcastically. He tried to turn away from Tucker again, but he grabbed Micah's elbow, holding him firm.

"Micah," Tucker said, "I thought we were over this. *You* said you didn't want to be friends, remember? I've talked to the girls since I moved to Orlando and I could've been talking to you this whole time too, but *you* were the one who started all of this and said you didn't want to talk to me anymore. Then you came to my birthday, and you said we'd talk about things later, and then that never happened. I'm just trying to be your friend, Micah, and you're making this really difficult by not talking to me."

Micah scoffed, looking down at the sand. The two stood there, Tucker holding Micah's arm and Micah staring anywhere but at Tucker, until he finally looked up into Tucker's eyes.

"Fine," he muttered. "You want to pick up where we left off and be friends again? Fine. Let's be friends again, Tucker."

"You make it sound like a punishment or something," Tucker said, letting go of Micah's arm. "I don't know what to do here."

"I don't know either, Tuck," Micah said, holding Tucker's gaze. Tucker breathed through his nose, trying to keep his feelings under control.

When they were in high school, Tucker would sleep over Micah's house and they would share his bed like he'd done with David the night before. They sat there in the dark one night, both of them staring up at the ceiling and laying shoulder-to-shoulder, and Micah had confessed to Tucker that a doctor had diagnosed him with depression earlier that week. To Tucker, it had seemed like no big deal, but he knew that Micah was not the type of person who shared things willingly with just anyone, so he'd confessed to Micah that he was gay in return. He remembered Micah turning on his side to face Tucker, putting his hand on Tucker's shoulder, and said, "I'm happy

CHAPTER 12

for you, Tuck".

After that night, it became a secret tradition between the two of them to share their feelings and secrets in the dark, and it was only in those situations did Micah feel comfortable enough to let his guard down and be caring toward Tucker, often calling him by his nickname. That tradition created a bond between the two, and though they never spoke of their feelings for each other or acted on them, the space they shared in Micah's bed became electric and almost unbearable for Tucker whenever Micah would use his nickname, always in that quiet, tender tone in the dark that pulled at Tucker's heartstrings and made his stomach drop.

"Please don't call me that unless you actually want to be my friend," Tucker said, looking away from Micah and focusing his attention on the ocean. "I'll understand if you don't want to, but don't be hurtful. You know how I feel."

"I do," Micah said firmly, nodding his head.

"Do you just want to be my friend?" Tucker challenged, looking at Micah again. His eyes widened, and he opened his mouth, but said nothing and closed it again. Tucker sighed, disappointed in Micah's hesitancy, but remained silent and waited, demanding Micah answer the question with an intense stare.

"I don't know," Micah eventually confessed. "I know you're gay, Tucker, but I don't think I am. I don't know."

"You don't have to know," Tucker assured him. "You have all the time in the world to figure it out. If you are, great. If you aren't, at least you know now."

"But when you said you didn't want to be friends anymore," Tucker continued, words pouring out of his mouth before he knew what he was saying, "you hurt me. You said that I was weird, and that you knew I liked you and it was creepy and made you uncomfortable, and a bunch of other hurtful shit. So we can talk, and we can be friends again because I've forgiven you, but figure out what you want before you seriously answer my question. I liked you a *lot*, Micah. Hell, I probably still do like you. But I won't do this again because you left me thinking I was the problem, and I'm not. I deserve to be with someone who wants to be with me, Micah."

"You're right," Micah mumbled. "I'll think about it some more."

Tucker nodded, satisfied with Micah's answer, and the two walked back to the rest of their friends, occasionally bumping shoulders playfully as they stepped. In their absence, Brooke, Mara, Kiara, and David had gone down to the shore and left their shoes and shirts on the table. Taylor had remained unmoving on her beach towel, her skin glistening under the scorching sun as she tanned. Upon seeing David's naked torso, Tucker could see Micah's body become more rigid with irritation out of the corner of his eye. Tucker ignored him, determined not to let Micah's behavior ruin their day, and ran down the beach to join his friends, taking off his socks and shoes and throwing them in the general direction of the picnic table. They landed in front of it, showering Taylor in sand, and Tucker heard her yelling a string of curse words as he reached the water.

Kiara scooped up some wet sand and hurled it at Tucker, sticking to his shirt with a wet slap. Tucker gasped, pulling it over his head and throwing it on the dry sand further up the shore. He kicked the sea at her in retaliation, but accidentally wet Brooke instead of his target. Brooke scooped up some more wet sand and lobbed it at Tucker's head, groaning when it missed.

"I got him!" David's voice came from behind Tucker. He felt David's muscular arms wrap around his abdomen and yelled in surprise as he lifted him up and dunked him in the cool ocean water. Tucker emerged soaking wet, gasping both in shock and for air, and grabbed David by the waist, pulling him under the water as well. David resurfaced, laughing in surprise at Tucker's retaliation, and the two began wrestling in the shallow water. Kiara and Mara screamed in delight as they ran back to shore to avoid getting any more wet, and Brooke stood close by, yelling, "Kick his ass, David!" and splashing water at the two whenever they got close to her.

David eventually pinned Tucker under his arms, straddling him on the shore to make sure he couldn't escape, and Tucker finally gave in. He laid there, his back against the wet sand, staring into David's hazel eyes as they both grinned and breathed heavily after their playful altercation before David got off of him and helped him to his feet. Brooke cheered for David, giving him a high-five, and the three walked back to the others dripping wet.

CHAPTER 12

Taylor was now sitting at the table and threw her beach towel to Tucker, coating his wet skin in a layer of hot sand.

"Here," she said. "You need it more than I do."

Tucker caught it and raised it in thanks, wiping off the sand and water before handing the towel to David.

"What was that you said about not going in the water?" David joked, turning to Tucker. Tucker laughed, shoving David lightly, and noticed Micah sitting behind Taylor on the bench, scowling at the two of them.

"Nobody forced you to," Micah said, clenching his jaw.

"Yeah, but it was fun," Tucker responded quickly, attempting to end the conversation before Micah spoke further.

"You should've joined us," David said, now stone-faced. "Looks like you could really use a cool-down."

"And what is that supposed to mean?" Micah asked, his tone rising.

"I can practically see the steam coming from your ears. You think I haven't noticed the dirty looks you've been giving me since you got here?" David challenged. "What's your problem? We're just trying to have fun."

"My *problem*," Micah retorted, standing up, "is that you're here. I haven't seen my friend in months, and he shows up with you. I don't know who the hell you are and I don't like you."

"Guys, enough!" Kiara interjected, but her words were ignored.

"I'm not your biggest fan either, dude," David said, stepping closer to Micah and shoving a finger in his face. His jaw was clenched and his other hand was balled into a fist at his side, prepared for a fight. "Tucker invited me here, so take whatever problem you have up with him."

"David," Tucker growled, placing a hand on his chest, "enough."

"Yeah, David, enough," Micah said, mocking Tucker in a shrill voice.

"Okay," Tucker said loudly, looking at his friends. "This has been great. Ladies, lovely to see you again. Micah, you're acting like a dick. We're gonna go."

"Me? What about him?" Micah objected, gesturing toward David, and Tucker ignored him.

Taylor and Mara sat in stunned silence, and Brooke handed Tucker his shoes and shirt without a word, an understanding grimace on her face. Tucker nodded at her in thanks, and walked toward the car without another word, not bothering to look behind him to see if Kiara and David followed. When he got to his car, they were there, and the three headed back to his parents' house in awkward silence. Tucker was mortified. He'd never seen David upset before and was shocked by his reaction, and was furious at Micah for instigating an argument right after they had what Tucker thought was a healthy conversation. Any hope Tucker was holding out for Micah to be anything more than a distant friend was fading fast.

"You should've hit him, David," Kiara said once they were almost to Tucker's house.

"Kiara!" Tucker said fiercely, silencing her.

When they pulled into Tucker's neighborhood, he sighed in defeat. "Guys, I'm really sorry about today," he said ruefully. "That was not at all what I thought it'd be like."

"It's not your fault," Kiara assured him, leaning forward and placing a hand on his shoulder. David said nothing, but Tucker noticed he'd physically relaxed in the car.

Once they got to the house and headed inside, they were quickly corralled into another awkward dinner with Tucker's parents. He was thankful for once that his parents had so many work anecdotes and stories from when Tucker was a baby to fill the silence, because his good mood had faded quickly and he was not interested in faking it for his parents' sake. Kiara had perked back up and was making light small-talk with Pam and Ken about growing up in Washington, and David's sullen silence seemed to solidify the idea in Ken's head that David was a real man's-man. For the last ten minutes they sat at the table he talked at David about his favorite sports teams and what his next truck was going to be, David only needing to nod or make a noise of acknowledgment to satisfy Ken's conversational needs.

They spent the few hours after dinner helping Tucker's mom begin the preparation of the sides for Thanksgiving dinner the following day, and his parents bid them another early goodnight. Tucker's good mood was starting to return, so the three of them played different card games at the dining

CHAPTER 12

room table until they were all yawning, signalling the end of their game.

"Can I ask you a question?" David asked Tucker as they laid in bed that evening.

"Of course," Tucker said, turning his head to look at David's silhouette in the dark.

"Is there something going on with you and Micah? Is that why he was such a dick to me today?" he asked. "Because if that's what it was, I could've told him we were just friends."

"Believe me, I did," Tucker sighed. "Things with Micah are... complicated. Well, they *were* complicated before I moved. I used to really like him and I thought he liked me, but then he said he didn't and that he was straight, but then he still acts like that around me, so I have no idea. He was my best friend, and I thought we could've been more, but he doesn't know who he is or what he wants."

"Yeah, I kind of got that vibe from him today," David said, his tone emotionless.

"But I think today solidified for me that I've moved on," Tucker said. "I should've moved on when he ended things and said I was trying to make him gay, but I forgave him. I'll probably forgive him for today, too. But just as a friend."

"That's very big of you," David murmured. "I'm sorry he said that stuff to you. You deserve better than that—in a friend and anything more."

"Thanks, David," Tucker said. He rolled over on his side so he faced the wall again and felt David's heavy hand on his shoulder for a moment.

"G'night, Tuck," he said as he yawned. Tucker's stomach filled with butterflies, and he couldn't help but smile at the familiar nickname. Tucker felt him move to get comfortable, and David was soon snoring. Remembering their conversation from earlier that morning, Tucker grabbed his phone and quickly recorded David's snore, texting the video to him with a quiet snicker and turning his phone off before he, too, fell into a deep sleep.

123

Chapter 13

The next morning was Thanksgiving, and the hours leading up to the big meal seemed to fly by in a blur. Tucker had woken up to David laughing at the video Tucker took of him snoring, but the two had little chance to talk as they slowly woke up before Kiara barged into the room without bothering to knock.

"Alright, boys!" Kiara said loudly, clapping her hands to make as much noise as possible. "Pam said she needs all hands on deck, so let's move!"

David, who seemed to be in a much better mood than the night before, sprung out of bed and exited the bedroom, while Tucker trudged behind him, rubbing his eyes as they adjusted. Kiara followed behind Tucker, grabbing him by the shoulders and pushing him forward as she walked to make him move faster.

Tucker's mom was moving in all directions in the kitchen; seasoning the turkey on one part of the counter, dicing a stalk of celery into small cubes for the stuffing on another, and stirring a cauldron of boiling water on the stove as she carefully dropped a dozen peeled potatoes into the pot. She barely acknowledged them before putting Tucker and Kiara to work, monitoring the boiling potatoes and chopping up vegetables to throw in a salad bowl the size of Tucker's head. His father, who was working outside, poked his head in the front door and requested help with setting up the deep fryer for the turkey. His mother turned to Tucker, but David volunteered before she could say anything and went outside, to Tucker's relief. Though he'd had his issues with his mother over the last few months, Tucker preferred to be in the kitchen with her than sitting in awkward silence with his father outside.

CHAPTER 13

One of the three timers his mother had set on the counter went off, and she jumped back into action.

"Tucker, drain those potatoes," Pam barked. She turned to Kiara and smiled sweetly. "Kiara, honey, I'm gonna need you to put that salad in the fridge and start working on the sweet potatoes, okay?"

"Yes ma'am," Kiara said dutifully, doing as she was instructed. Tucker shot her a questioning look, and she simply shrugged in response. He was used to her calling the shots, so seeing her obey his mother's commands was new for him.

"So," Kiara said as she sliced sweet potatoes and laid them in a dish, "I'm not the type to stray from confrontation like your son and I wanted to ask—how are you guys doing?"

Tucker and his mother both froze. Tucker was just like his mother in that they could argue all day if provoked, but typically kept feelings to themselves unless someone else brought something up.

"My family went through something similar a few years ago when my sister came out," she quickly explained to Tucker's mom, "and I've grown really close to Tucker, so I want to make sure you guys handle things better than my parents did."

"That's sweet of you, Kiara," Tucker said, eager to speak before his mother did in case she was not as welcoming of Kiara's frankness, "but I don't know if now is the right time to talk about it."

"It's taking some work," Pam said abruptly, startling Tucker. He had expected her to clam up and work in silence instead of respond, as his family was not typically the type to discuss their feelings with complete honesty. "Like I told Tucker, I never knew gay people growing up—or if I did, they didn't tell me. And keeping this from Tucker's dad is hard. I love him, but it's something I have to work through and try to understand."

"That's good," Kiara said calmly, nodding in affirmation. "My dad was the same way, and you've already made more progress than he did. I'll tell you the same thing I told him—it might not be something you're used to, but it doesn't mean it's bad or unnatural to be gay. As long as you're open and willing to learn, that's all anyone can ask for. Right, Tucker?"

She turned to look at him, and he nodded.

"Right."

"Okay," Kiara said, smiling. "This is what I like to hear. Pam, thank you for humoring me, and for just having me here for Thanksgiving in general. I'm so grateful that Tucker would not let me be alone today, and I know David is too."

His mother began to tear up, and she gave Kiara a quick squeeze. "I'm very thankful that Tucker has a friend like you," she said.

"Me too," Tucker chimed in, smiling when Kiara turned to look at him.

"Okay, that's enough emotions—let's get back to cooking!" Kiara barked, shifting back into the forceful mode Tucker knew and loved. Pam's eyebrows raised and she looked at Tucker, making him laugh. Though the conversation was uncomfortable, Tucker was glad Kiara had forced them to talk about it. Whatever tension was in the room prior had disappeared, and the three chatted lightheartedly as they prepared the meal.

David eventually came back inside red-faced, his tank top clinging to his broad chest with sweat from the ever-present Florida heat, and relayed a message from Ken requesting beer and the turkey.

"That man is going to drink himself to sleep before we even sit down to eat," Pam complained, but handed David two beer bottles from the fridge, which he put in his pockets, and the turkey on a large metal tray.

"You surviving out there?" Tucker asked David with a smirk. "You're looking redder than a lobster."

When Pam wasn't looking, David mouthed a curse word at Tucker, making him and Kiara giggle. He left the kitchen, awkwardly opening the front door with one hand while balancing the turkey with the other as he headed outside.

Once the remaining dishes were prepped and in the oven, Tucker and Kiara took turns showering and getting ready while Pam monitored the kitchen, and she left to do the same when they returned—Kiara in a cranberry-colored pencil skirt and a cream-colored blouse, and Tucker in a pair of tan pants and a navy blue button-down shirt. Tucker's father pushed the front door open and hurried into the kitchen with the now-fried turkey,

CHAPTER 13

slamming it down on the counter.

"Thanks for the help," he said sarcastically, turning to Tucker.

"Me?" Tucker asked, taken aback. "You just barged into the house with no warning! What was I supposed to do?"

"You could've done *something* aside from just standing there," his dad snapped, approaching Tucker aggressively.

"I was watching the oven timer like Mom asked," he said defensively. "I would've helped if you asked!"

"Whatever, Tucker, do whatever you want," his dad scoffed, stomping to his bedroom and slamming the door closed behind him.

"What the hell was that about?" Tucker asked aloud to no one in particular, though he looked at Kiara. She shrugged her shoulders in response. He heard the front door close, and David appeared in the kitchen, looking perplexed.

"Did I just miss something?" he asked.

"I was about to ask you the same thing!" Tucker replied. "He just came in here with the turkey and started yelling at me. Did something happen outside?"

"No, we were fine," David answered.

"He's probably drunk," Tucker sighed, shaking his head.

"You think? He seemed like he was moving fine," Kiara asked.

"Dad knows how to hide it well," Tucker said bitterly. Though his father never admitted to having a drinking problem, conversations like that were much more frequent while Tucker still lived at home and could almost always be attributed to the copious amounts of beer he'd been drinking each time.

"I'm gonna go shower before dinner," David advised, walking backwards toward the bathroom before turning and closing the door behind him.

Tucker and Kiara stood in the kitchen in silence, occasionally checking on the food in the oven, as Tucker mulled over the conversation with his father. He hadn't seen him all morning, so there weren't many other explanations for his outburst other than his drinking. The remaining two kitchen timers went off one after another, interrupting Tucker's thoughts, and he set the dishes on the counter to cool next to the turkey.

"I've never had a fried turkey before," Kiara said, standing next to Tucker so she could smell everything.

"Dad made it a few years ago and we've never gone back," Tucker explained, his mouth watering. "It's crispy on the outside, but the inside stays nice and moist if you do it right. It's delicious."

Tucker left Kiara to continue sniffing the food while he quickly set the table for dinner, eager to devour the meal he'd been working on all day. His parents emerged from their bedroom, now showered and dressed for dinner. Though it was just the five of them and there were no dress code expectations, Pam wore a red floral sundress with gold bands on both wrists and matching earrings, and Ken wore a pair of jeans and a pinstriped button-down shirt under a blue blazer. His mother fussed over the last-minute touches the dishes needed, and his father came to wait at the table.

"You did it wrong," he grumbled to Tucker as he sat down. Tucker ignored his remark, inhaling and exhaling deeply to remain calm. David emerged from the bathroom, now showered and dressed for dinner as well in a pair of jeans and a white linen button-down shirt tucked in with the sleeves rolled up to his elbows, and joined Ken at the table. Pam, satisfied with the dishes, brought the food to the table with Kiara's help, and the five of them sat for Thanksgiving dinner—Pam and Ken at the heads of the table, David on one side, and Kiara and Tucker on the other. They all complimented Pam on how delicious everything looked, and everyone helped pass a dish around the table until their plates were piled with food.

"This is the first fried turkey I've ever had," Kiara remarked once they were all eating. "I can't believe it's taken me eighteen years—this is delicious!"

"Thank you, Kiara," Ken said, nodding at her in appreciation.

"This might be the best one yet, Dad," Tucker agreed, trying to keep things positive between him and his father, who only grunted in acknowledgement as he ate.

"So, David," Pam said, trying to keep the conversation light, "what have you thought about Weeki Wachee so far? Tucker mentioned you'd never visited before."

CHAPTER 13

"I like it!" he replied after swallowing the giant scoop of mashed potatoes he'd just shoved in his mouth. "The way Tucker described it, he made it sound like it was a ghost town in the middle of nowhere or something."

Pam chuckled, but Ken cleared his throat loudly and took another long swig of beer.

"I can tell you why, David," he finally said. "He's ashamed of us. Must be why, since he hasn't come to visit!"

"That's not true at all," Tucker argued. "I've never said I was ashamed of you, and I told you I haven't been able to come home because I've been really busy with work and school."

"I'm not talking to you right now, Tucker," Ken said, his tone calm but his eyes cold as he looked at his son. "I'm talking with David, so don't be rude."

"About *me!*" Tucker defended.

"Tucker, just drop it," Pam advised quietly, giving him a sympathetic look. Tucker looked across the table at David, who sat there wide-eyed.

"Fine," he muttered, stabbing a piece of turkey with more force than necessary and shoving it into his mouth.

"The sweet potatoes came out lovely, Kiara," Pam complimented, eager to change the subject.

"Thank you," Kiara said with a grin. "Sweet potatoes were always my favorite part of Thanksgiving growing up, so my mom made it my job to make them every year so they were perfect."

"They sure are," David agreed, scooping some up with his fork.

"You're too sweet," she said.

"So are y'all dating?" Ken said, pointing to David and Kiara across the table with his fork. Kiara laughed loudly at his question, but quickly quieted when she remembered Tucker's instructions not to bring up sexuality.

"What's so funny?" Ken asked, smiling. "I think y'all would make a cute couple. Don't you, Tucker?"

"He's not really my type," Kiara lied quickly. "I'm more into skinnier guys, and David's just too muscular for me."

"Well, what about you, David?" Ken asked. "If it isn't pretty little Kiara here, do you have a girlfriend back at school?"

David snorted at the question, but shoved another helping of sweet potatoes in his mouth to avoid answering. Ken waited, to David's chagrin, as he swallowed.

"No," he answered truthfully, "I'm more focused on school right now."

"Well, you certainly won't get one shacked up in Tucker's room like a couple of queers," Ken said, chuckling at his own joke as he took another swig from his beer bottle.

"Dad, that was your idea," Tucker pointed out, unable to keep quiet any longer.

"Well, I assumed one of you'd sleep on the floor, not share the bed together like a couple of fairies," he replied, still chuckling.

"Honey, enough," Pam warned Ken.

"What?" Ken asked innocently. "I'm just joking! You boys know I'm joking, right?"

David chuckled humorlessly in an attempt to move the conversation along, but Tucker slammed his fork on his plate.

"Are you, Dad?" he asked, staring coldly at his father. "Which part of that was the joke?"

"The whole thing! I know you boys aren't gay," Ken answered, laughing to himself again.

"Well, I've got some news for you, dad," Tucker said, his voice icy. "I *am* gay."

His stomach dropped as the words came out of his mouth, but it was too late to stop himself from admitting the truth. It wasn't the way Tucker envisioned coming out to this father, hoping for something a bit more personal and with less of an audience, but the news had broken just the same. The room went silent. Everyone but Ken froze, shocked at Tucker's abrupt revelation. He slowly put his fork and knife down on the table, looking Tucker in the eye.

"What?" he asked quietly.

"You heard me," Tucker said, holding his gaze. "One of those fairies you were just laughing at? Those queers? That's me. I'm gay, Dad."

Ken nodded once, then turned to look at Pam. She winced slightly,

CHAPTER 13

anticipating the verbal explosion she assumed would follow.

"I'm gonna pretend I didn't hear that," Ken said to her, smiling, before picking his cutlery back up and continuing to eat. Kiara's eyes widened, and she turned to look at Tucker in shock.

"Then I'm done here," Tucker said simply, taking his half-full plate and dropping it forcefully in the sink, shattering it to pieces. His heart felt like the plate in the sink, broken suddenly and with abrupt force, but he refused to let it show on his face. He wouldn't give his father the satisfaction of seeing how upset he was, no matter how badly it hurt.

"No, Tucker," Pam pleaded.

Ken said nothing, unfazed, and continued eating. Tucker stormed into his room, quickly shoving his clothes back into his suitcase. Kiara and David exchanged shocked looks from across the table and hastened to do the same, apologizing quietly to Pam as they passed her. Tucker advised them to go to his car as soon as they finished packing, and they apologized once again as they hurried through the house to the front door with their suitcases. Tucker followed, slamming his bedroom door behind him.

"Tucker, please don't go yet," Pam begged. She turned to Ken. "Honey, say something! You didn't mean it, right? You were just shocked."

"Mean what?" Ken asked, smiling at her again. Tucker nodded in understanding, knowing that this was the end of their relationship as father and son, and stormed out of the house without another word, slamming the front door as hard as he could behind him. He threw his suitcase in the trunk with the others and got into the driver's seat, starting the car without speaking. Kiara and David took their same seats and sat quietly, looking stunned by the altercation they'd witnessed. Pam came running out of the house to Tucker's car door, knocking on his window. Tucker rolled it down and looked at her, but didn't speak.

"Tucker, please stay," she begged again, tears running down her face. "He's just shocked is all, same as I was. He'll come around if you talk to him."

"I've forgiven you," Tucker said calmly. "But I told you I'm not doing this again. The fact that he chose to ignore me completely rather than discuss my coming-out told me everything I needed to know. I am who I am and

I love myself, so if Dad doesn't support that, then I guess he's not my dad anymore. I'll see you later, Mom."

Kiara audibly gasped in the backseat but said nothing, clamping a hand over her mouth. His mother backed up from his window, understanding that Tucker was firm in his decision, and sadly waved goodbye in the driveway as he drove away. Tucker turned the radio on to fill the silence as they drove back to Orlando that evening, but said nothing as he silently fumed. His mother's initial reaction had been cold, but his father's was dark and icy in comparison. At least his mother had acknowledged it when he'd told her, but the fact that his father completely ignored that crucial bit of information about his son's life was something Tucker wouldn't stand for. Tucker was furious at his reaction and replayed the conversation over and over in his head as he drove, his jaw clenched in anger and his grip tight on the steering wheel.

"I'm sorry, I have to say something," Kiara eventually said after they were almost an hour into their return trip to Orlando. "What your dad did was really fucked up, Tucker. I'm so sorry."

"Trust me, I know what you're going through," David chimed in, patting Tucker's arm twice. "I wish there was something I could do or say to make things better, but all I can really say is that the hurt will fade with time. I know it did for me, though I'll never forget or forgive what my parents did."

"At least you still have your mom," Kiara said, trying to sound positive. "You can't count her out just because of your dad's reaction. She came around, so maybe he will too."

Tucker listened, but didn't respond, and the two gave up trying to talk with him, instead chatting with each other about nothing in particular. The parking lot outside of Tucker's dorm was dark and empty by the time they returned, and Tucker bid his friends a quiet goodnight after handing them their suitcases.

"Tucker, you can't be alone right now!" Kiara protested.

"Yeah, let's hang out somewhere," David added.

"I'm good," Tucker said solemnly. "I'd rather be alone right now, but thank you. I'm sure things would've been a lot worse if you guys hadn't come with

CHAPTER 13

me, so thank you for that too. I'm sorry I ruined your Thanksgiving."

"You didn't ruin anything, Tucker," David said, putting a hand on his shoulder and making eye contact with him. Kiara nodded in agreement. Tucker smiled sadly and walked away, ignoring their protests. The building was eerily silent when he entered, and he pressed the elevator button, the doors opening immediately. The common area on his floor was deserted, and he left his suitcase in the middle of his room as he climbed into bed fully clothed.

His phone buzzed, and Tucker fished it out of his pocket, accidentally answering Micah's call with his thumb.

"Micah?" he asked, laying his head down on his pillow.

"Hey, Tuck," came Micah's voice from the other line. "Happy Thanksgiving."

Tucker laughed humorlessly, remembering the events of the last few hours. "Yeah, you too."

"I'll make it quick," Micah said, "but I needed to talk to you about yesterday."

"Micah, now's not a good time," Tucker sighed.

"I'll be fast, I promise," he assured him. "Can you come let me in? I'm outside."

"What do you mean, you're outside?" Tucker asked, moving closer to his window to look down into the parking lot. Sure enough, he saw Micah standing on the sidewalk, looking around with his phone to his ear. "Micah, what are you doing here?"

"Can you please just come let me in so we can talk?" he asked, ignoring Tucker's question.

Tucker sighed and agreed, ending the call and rushing down the stairs to the lobby. He opened the door to the parking lot and let Micah in, the two of them climbing the stairs again in silence. Once they were back in his dorm, Tucker closed the door and turned to where Micah stood in the middle of the room, looking anxious and his hands shoved in his pockets.

"What are you doing here, Micah?" Tucker asked again.

"I went to your house to talk to you, but your mom said you'd just left to come back here. So, I came here too. I needed to talk to you in-person and I couldn't wait."

"What is so important that you had to see me in-person?" Tucker asked, feeling irritable. He was perplexed by Micah's actions and still hadn't forgotten his outburst toward David from the day before; after the day he'd had, he wasn't in the mood for Micah's added drama.

"I think I want to be more, Tucker," Micah said, his voice wavering.

"More what?" Tucker asked impatiently.

"More than friends. I don't want to be just friends with you. Seeing you with that guy made me so fucking crazy yesterday, and I hated feeling like that!"

"Micah," Tucker sighed, running a hand through his hair, "I already told you that David's just a friend."

"I know," Micah murmured, moving to where Tucker stood. "I'm just saying that I want more than that."

The buildup of emotions from the last few days released in a flood of tears and Tucker began to cry, unbothered that he had an audience. Micah closed the space between them, pulling Tucker into a strong hug and held him there as he cried. Without warning, he pulled Tucker's face to his, placing a gentle kiss on his lips. Tucker pulled away and took a step back, feeling confused.

"I don't know if I do anymore, Micah," he said, wiping the tears from under his eyes. "I liked you so much, and you hurt me a lot when you said those things before I moved. I know we've talked about it and I forgave you, but that changed me. I'm not the same guy I was, and as much as I want to believe what you're saying, I don't know that I do."

"I mean it," Micah insisted, taking another step forward. "I think I love you, Tucker."

"No, you don't," Tucker said, sticking a hand out to keep the space between them. "Maybe I awakened something in you that you didn't know was there, but you don't love me. Not who I am now, at least. I'm sorry, Micah, I really am, but I don't want anything more right now."

Micah was silent for a moment and then sighed heavily.

"So what now?" he finally asked.

"I don't know," Tucker answered truthfully. "I'm still living here in Orlando and you're still in Weeki Wachee, so lean into these new feelings and figure yourself out, I guess. I'm not the only gay guy in town, so I'm sure you'll meet someone."

"Okay," Micah mumbled, defeated. "I'll see you later then, Tuck."

"Wait, don't go," Tucker said, staying where he was in front of the door. "It's late already. Stay here for the night. You can sleep in my roommate's bed and leave in the morning."

"After all that?" Micah asked. "I think I'm embarrassed enough already, but thanks."

"Micah, please. Today's been shitty enough and I couldn't handle you getting into a wreck or something because you drove back home so late. Please just stay, if you ever wanted to be my friend," Tucker pleaded.

"Fine," Micah said.

Tucker shut off the lights and the two of them got into their own respective beds without another word, both wanting to forget the events of the day, and praying for a new morning to start things over again.

Chapter 14

Tucker woke the next morning, and the events from Thanksgiving came flooding back to him as he stared at his ceiling, making him furious with his father all over again. His phone buzzed, distracting him, and he grabbed it, opening a text message from David. It was the video Tucker recorded of him snoring, and Tucker laughed in spite of his foul mood. There was a stirring to his right that startled him, momentarily forgetting that he'd asked Micah to stay the night before. He apparently hadn't woken him, and could see Micah's slow breathing on his back as he faced the wall away from Tucker's bed. His feelings hadn't changed overnight, but he still cared for Micah as a friend and knew it was the right decision over letting him drive back in an awful mood and in total darkness.

There was a knock at his door, so Tucker hopped down from his bed and trudged to open it, expecting Kiara to barge in. Instead, David stood in his doorway when he opened it, waving with his phone in his hand.

"Kiara told me how to sneak in," he explained, noticing Tucker's confused expression. Tucker wordlessly moved aside, allowing David to enter. "I just wanted to stop by and see how you were doing. I know what it's like, coming out and not getting the reaction you'd hoped for, and it really sucks."

"I don't really know how I'm doing," Tucker answered honestly. David nodded in understanding but said nothing, letting silence fill the room again.

"Micah stopped by last night," Tucker said and gestured toward his sleeping form in Mike's bed, unsure why he was telling this to David as the words came out of his mouth. David looked surprised, but offered a tight-lipped smile when Tucker turned to look at him again.

CHAPTER 14

"That's good, right?" he asked quietly, eyeing Micah to make sure he didn't wake him. "How did it go?"

"Well, he told me he loved me," Tucker said.

"That sounds like it's good," David replied.

"I told him I didn't."

David's eyebrows shot up in surprise.

"Oh," he said simply.

"Yeah, just seeing him again, and how he talked to you even though I told him we were just friends, it really opened my eyes and I didn't like what I saw," Tucker explained softly. "I don't know if he was always like that and I was just blind because I liked him, or if this was something new because he felt threatened or something, but I told him he needed to figure himself out. So that's that, I guess."

"Well," David said slowly, "I'm glad you made a decision you feel comfortable with."

"Me too," Tucker chuckled. "Now that I'm waking up, I'm getting hungry. You want to go grab breakfast? It'll just take me a minute to get ready."

"I can't," David said apologetically. "A guy I used to date is in town and texted me after we got back last night wanting to hang out, so I made plans with him already. Besides, I wouldn't want you to leave him here all alone. I just wanted to stop by first and check on you. Rain check?"

"Sure," Tucker said, forcing a smile on his face. "Was it that guy I met, Andrew?"

"No, a different ex. Andrew was more recent and less of a commitment than this guy, Elliot, was."

"Oh."

There was a sharp inhale from behind Tucker, and he turned and watched Micah sit up abruptly, squinting as he stared sleepily at the two of them. He threw the covers off and dropped down from the bed, wordlessly pulling his shoes back onto his feet. He muttered a half-hearted goodbye to Tucker as he moved by him, shoulder-checking David as he opened the door and let himself out without acknowledging him at all.

Tucker sighed, noticing the irritated look on David's face, but he quickly morphed back to a neutral expression before meeting Tucker's gaze again. He clapped a hand on Tucker's arm before turning and letting himself out as well, not bothering to say goodbye. Tucker went back to bed, crawling deep under the covers, and tried to go back to sleep so he could convince himself the conversation he just had with David was a dream, but had no luck. He felt like he was being held hostage by his own brain—wanting to be happy with simply being David's friend, but knowing that he wanted more from someone who plainly didn't want the same and unable to move on from these feelings.

Kiara texted him a little later to check in on him, and Tucker assured her he was okay before ignoring the rest of her texts. Having no schoolwork to distract himself with anymore, Tucker dragged a chair to the bathroom counter and began the ritual of putting makeup on—shaving, primer, glue, powder, foundation, highlight, contour, blush, eyes, lips, and lashes. Two hours later, his reflection had completely changed, and a haggard clown stared back at Tucker. He wiped his makeup off in frustration, unhappy with the way he looked, and tried again, remembering what he didn't like and trying to fix it. When he finished the second time, there was improvement, but he was still unhappy with the finished product and wiped his face off again. He continued this pattern until he checked his phone and saw it was after midnight, wiping his makeup off once more and crawling back into bed.

Though he was still upset, being productive and having a creative outlet had helped Tucker's mood lift a little. When he awoke the following day, he started again, hyper-focused on making each face he put on better than the last. David and Kiara both texted Tucker to check in, and he ignored them both as he worked on his craft. By the time the sun was setting, he felt confident that he had some semblance of an idea of what he was doing.

There was a sharp banging on his door that evening, and Tucker knew to step out of the way before even opening it as Kiara stormed in, shooting him an irritated look.

"Do I seem like the type to accept being ignored, Tucker?" Kiara asked, crossing her arms over her chest.

CHAPTER 14

"No," Tucker replied, smirking slightly. Though he still wasn't in the best mood, Kiara's melodrama always amused him, and he felt almost thankful for the intrusion.

"Then I don't know why you bother trying, because I'm not letting that happen after what I just witnessed on Thanksgiving. Put something presentable on. We're going out," Kiara snapped.

"I'm really not in the mood, Kiara," Tucker sighed.

"I really don't give a damn," Kiara countered. Tucker raised his eyebrows, feeling both entertained and shocked. "Change. Now."

Tucker did as she commanded, throwing on a black t-shirt and a pair of dark jeans, and followed her down to the parking lot when she was satisfied with his outfit. They got into Tucker's car and he followed her directions as they left campus, following a few side streets until they emerged in an outdoor shopping area called Waterford Lakes. There was a long street that served as its entrance, with a roundabout complete with a small fountain in the center that provided drivers directions to different areas—the movie theater, different chain restaurants, various department stores, and even a pet shop with adoptable cats and dogs.

Though he'd never been there before, he followed the signs without relying on his GPS for directions in the extensive shopping area and parked in front of a shoe store that Kiara gasped at when she saw it. She pulled him inside and pushed him into a seat, modeling different styles of shoes that he knew she'd never wear just to get a laugh out of him—bright green platform flip-flops, brown heelless high heels that looked vaguely like horse hooves, and clear vinyl boots that lit up when she walked, to name a few. When she grew bored with the ugliest fashion show she could muster, they drove halfway around the large oval that made up Waterford Lakes until they were parked again in front of an ice cream store. Kiara clapped with delight, linking arms with Tucker and dragging him towards the front door.

There were small tables for two set outside, and as they approached, Tucker's stomach dropped as he recognized Adrian sitting at one of the tables with another guy around his age. Though their hands were on their own sides of the table, Tucker noticed their knees touching. Tucker tried to ignore him, facing away as they walked toward the front door so he wouldn't be recognized, but had no such luck.

"Tucker?" he heard Adrian say and grimaced slightly before turning to look at him with fake surprise on his face.

"Hey, Adrian," Tucker greeted with a small smile. "Sorry, didn't mean to disturb your date."

"Oh no, it's not a date," Adrian said quickly. The look on the other man's face, however, showed Tucker that it was the first he was hearing of that.

"Hi, I'm Kiara," Kiara interjected, waving slightly at the two men at the table.

"This is my friend, Mateo," Adrian replied, gesturing toward the man with the growing sour expression on his face, who nodded curtly to Kiara and Tucker as he crossed his arms over his chest.

"Well, I won't keep you," Tucker said, moving closer to the door.

"Hey," Adrian said, placing a soft hand on Tucker's forearm, "text me sometime. I still want to hang out."

"Sure," Tucker replied shortly, looking at Adrian's friend and back at him with a quizzical look. "Nice meeting you," he added, offering Mateo a sympathetic smile before the two entered the ice cream shop. He turned and looked out the window as they waited in line to order and saw the two outside arguing, though he couldn't hear what they were saying, and mentally cheered for Mateo when he stood up and walked away, looking disgusted.

He couldn't deny that he found Adrian extremely attractive, but felt bad for Mateo, as it seemed obvious to Tucker that he was expecting something different from Adrian that evening.

"That was so awkward," Kiara muttered to Tucker with a giggle. Tucker chuckled too, nodding in agreement. The two got their ice cream cones to go—Tucker, with a mint chocolate chip cone, and Kiara with a raspberry cheesecake cone—and walked around the shopping plaza, stopping to look in windows as they passed.

"So that's the guy you slutted it up with on your birthday, right?" Kiara asked, licking her cone as they walked.

CHAPTER 14

"I did not 'slut it up' with anyone!" Tucker replied, laughing.

"If memory serves correctly—which it does—then I beg to differ!" Kiara countered, nudging him with her shoulder.

"Yes, that is the guy that I danced with on my birthday," Tucker answered, ignoring her comment. "Adrian's hot, but that was weird, right?"

"Extremely," Kiara agreed.

"Whatever, it's not like I'm invested in him right now," Tucker sighed, licking his ice cream. "What about you? Slutting it up with anyone at school?"

"Not at all," Kiara chuckled.

"Well, maybe I can help you find a guy," Tucker offered, which made Kiara laugh even harder.

"You can barely even talk to David, and you think you can help me find somebody?"

"I can too!" Tucker argued, though he knew she had a point. "What kind of guys are you into?"

"Well, don't limit yourself," Kiara said slowly, looking shy for the first time since he'd met her in August.

"Are you into girls, Kiara?" Tucker asked, an excited smile growing on his face.

"I'm... keeping my options open," she responded vaguely.

"What the hell does that mean?" Tucker pressed with a laugh.

"It means I like who I like and don't worry about what's in their pants," she responded frankly.

Tucker stopped and turned to her, tilting his head slightly. "Thanks for telling me, Ki," he said earnestly. "I'm sure it feels kind of weird to say, with everything that happened with your sister and your parents, so I'm honored that you trust me enough to tell me."

"It's not a secret," Kiara replied, blushing. "I just don't broadcast it like some people."

"Like me?" Tucker laughed.

"Well, not *not* like you," she said, joining in on his laughter.

The two finished their ice cream cones as they got closer to the shop again and drove back to campus, chatting and playfully insulting each other as the pair often did. Tucker closed the door to his dorm with an enhanced appreciation of his best friend at school, feeling grateful that they were each other's chosen confidant.

Tucker continued his practice over the next few weeks whenever he wasn't working. He picked up extra shifts to help pass the time and make more money, and spent his time alone working on his makeup. Mike had returned to their dorm the week after Thanksgiving, startling Tucker when he walked out of the bathroom, and packed up his half of the room the following day and a half to bring it home with him until the beginning of January when classes began again.

Kiara, who became wise to Tucker's ignored texts, began showing up at his door unexpectedly to force him to talk to her. Tucker was happy to have company after Mike left, but found that he enjoyed being alone as well now that he'd found a hobby. He'd worked on his makeup with Jamie here and there before, but was becoming obsessed with it now, painting his face almost every day of the week.

His friendship with David was fine, and they still chatted, but the bond they'd formed over Thanksgiving had ebbed away as real life set back in, and Tucker only spoke with him whenever they worked at the same time again. David had mentioned, to Tucker's secret delight, that the guy David met with the morning after he stopped by Tucker's dorm was only visiting Orlando again since moving away and there had been no further contact.

Tucker found himself scanning the crowds for Adrian again while he worked, ignoring the awkward interaction outside of the ice cream shop and eager to push David from his mind, but had no such luck finding him until the weekend before Christmas, when he showed up to the club right after Tucker, placing his hand on the small of Tucker's back as they waited in line to show the bouncer their IDs.

"Hey stranger," Adrian murmured in Tucker's ear, making him jump.

"Hey!" Tucker greeted him, smiling. "I've been looking for you the past few weeks. Where've you been?"

"You know, here and there," he replied vaguely.

CHAPTER 14

"Well, welcome back," Tucker said to Adrian, nodding to the bouncer in greeting as he handed him his ID. The bouncer, who'd introduced himself to Tucker after his first week there as Ned, nodded back to Tucker and eyed Adrian up and down as if he was frisking him with his eyes. He grabbed Adrian's ID and grunted as he handed it back, giving him non-verbal admission. Tucker thanked Ned, and the two headed into the club, Adrian wrapping an arm around Tucker's side.

"So, how come you never texted me back?" Adrian asked, raising his voice to be heard over the speakers.

"Because I'm not a booty call," Tucker replied, leaning closer to Adrian's ear to compensate for the music.

"I never said that!" Adrian said, looking perplexed.

"You didn't have to—the 3 AM texts said it all," he countered cooly.

"You're right, that definitely screams booty call now that you put it that way. I'm sorry," Adrian said sincerely. "I'd just think about you when I couldn't sleep sometimes, and so I'd text you. I didn't think about the time."

"Oh, yeah?" Tucker asked, a flattered smile forming on his lips. "What about your friend Mateo?"

"Yeah, honestly," Adrian nodded. "I told you, Mateo's just a friend. I'm interested in you."

"Well," Tucker said, taking Adrian's hand off of his side and holding it in his for a moment before letting it go, "start thinking about me during the normal hours of the day and maybe we'll hang out sometime."

"I can do that," he replied, grinning.

"We'll see," Tucker said. This time, it was his turn to eye Adrian up and down, and he felt powerful as he turned and walked away towards the bar. The other bartender on staff, Shane, was working that night and was leaning against the bar as he chatted loudly over the music with Jamie, who was doing the same on the other side. She wore a tall dark red wig and a matching tight red bodysuit with black boots that hugged her breasts and curves, which were accentuated with panels of black fabric on either side. Tucker approached her and gave her a playful nudge with his shoulder in greeting, which she returned forcefully.

"Just the bitch I was looking for," she said, making Tucker laugh. It'd now been four months of hearing Jamie talk the way she did, and her vulgarity still caught Tucker off guard at times.

"Yeah? Why's that?" Tucker asked.

"I got you a present," Jamie said, grinning excitedly as she drummed on the bar with her hands.

"Me? What for?" he asked.

"For Christmas, duh! You're my kid," Jamie replied, rolling her eyes.

"What is it?" Tucker asked, now excited.

"I got you a gig!" she cheered, looking proud of herself. Tucker's eyes widened in surprise, and his stomach did a somersault from both excitement and anxiety at the thought of performing onstage.

"Wow!" he said, unable to put into words what he felt.

"It's on Tuesday, so start thinking of songs," she advised. Tucker's eyes opened even wider, his eyebrows now in his hairline from being raised so high.

"Like, this Tuesday? As in December 22nd, Tuesday?" he asked, shocked.

"Yeah, girl, but don't stress," Jamie assured him. "People love a good Christmas show, so you should be able to make some cute tips."

Tucker blinked, still processing everything Jamie just told him. "I've got nothing to wear," was all he could manage to say.

"I'm sure I've got some old costumes I can find for you," she said. "Girl, I just got you your first gig! Get excited!"

"You're right," Tucker nodded, convincing himself as he spoke. "I am excited! This is great news! Thank you, Jamie, really."

"That's better," Jamie replied, looking satisfied. "Merry Christmas, kid."

Shane, who'd been standing there for the entire interaction, cleared his throat and pushed the tray full of shots toward Tucker.

"Oh, right!" Tucker said, grabbing the tray. "Duty calls. Bye, Jamie!"

"Bye, girl," Jamie called as he walked away.

Tucker spent the rest of the night thinking about the upcoming show, his mind spiraling as he considered songs to perform, makeup to wear, and how he'd handle his debut performance onstage, having never performed on a

CHAPTER 14

stage before. His phone rang as he handed Shane the second empty tray of the night, and took a quick break to step outside. It was his mother, he noted in surprise, and he answered the call against his better judgement.

"Hey, Mom," he answered.

"Hi honey," she greeted warmly. "Do you have a second to chat?"

"I'm at work, so I can't talk for long, but what's up? Everything okay?"

"Everything's fine," Pam assured him. "I need to talk to you about Christmas."

Tucker had been dreading having the conversation about holiday plans with his parents, having not spoken to his father since their argument on Thanksgiving. He knew very well that he had no other real options and would have to go home, but no part of him was interested in seeing his father if he hadn't changed his mind in the last month.

"What about it?" he asked, feigning ignorance.

"We want you to come home," she said. "It's Christmas—you should be with your family!"

"Mom, we've talked about this—" Tucker began, but was cut off by a rustling on the other end of the call.

"Tucker, it's your father," Ken interrupted, his tone gruff. "We need to talk, and I want you to come home for Christmas."

"If you feel the same way you did on Thanksgiving, there's not much to talk about," Tucker answered coldly.

"I don't know how to feel, damnit!" Ken exclaimed, clearing his throat and lowering his voice again. "You have to understand that this is all new for me and your mother."

"*You* have to understand that I am who I am and I'm not changing. I like the person I'm becoming and I won't just pretend I'm not whenever I'm home to make you happy. If that's not something that you can accept, then I'm not coming home," Tucker countered.

"Look, come home for Christmas and we can talk about it, okay?"

Tucker bit the inside of his cheek as he considered what his father said, but ultimately agreed to come home on Christmas Eve and Christmas Day, informing them he had to come back to Orlando that night for work the following weekend. His parents were hesitant, but ultimately agreed to his conditions, satisfying Tucker. The call ended, and Tucker finished the rest of his shift with a smile on his face, which wasn't hard when he was laughing as he watched Crystal Waters host her show.

He texted Kiara an update when he got home that evening, receiving multiple excited texts in all caps in response. Tucker thought about doing the same for David, but he thought better of it after realizing it'd be like rubbing salt in an open wound for him. That phone call with his parents had been a refreshing reminder that people could change—his mother had since he'd first come out to her, after all—and he had a small glimmer of hope for both his parents' acceptance again.

Chapter 15

"Girl, let's go!" Jamie's impatient voice came from outside her drag room door, followed by her pounding. It was the day of Tucker's first gig and he stood in Jamie's apartment, suddenly terrified. She'd invited him over to get ready for the show, gifting him a red velvet dress with white trim on the skirt and sleeves, and monitored his makeup as he painted, looking fairly impressed with his end result.

"You've been practicing!" she'd said, nodding in approval. "I'm still the most beautiful," she'd commented as she looked at herself in the mirror, "but you're getting there." She had left the room to let Tucker get dressed, and he now stood there in full drag—the dress Jamie'd gifted him, a pair of white heels, and the same black wig he'd worn on Halloween with a Santa hat bobby-pinned to it—analyzing himself in the vanity mirror. He felt his doubts rise—whether he looked good enough, whether he'd be a good enough performer, whether the audience would like him—but pushed them down by repeatedly thinking to himself that he was doing this for no one else but him. He took a deep breath, ignoring Jamie's pounding, and finally opened the door.

"Finally!" she groaned, a hand on her hip. She wore a short gold dress and a nude high heel with what Tucker knew was red velvet lingerie with white trim underneath, noting that it was like the dress he wore now, for her planned reveal during her number later that night. She turned and strutted to the kitchen, Tucker trying to emulate her effortless walk as he followed behind her. Crystal, wearing a tight green velvet gown glittering with different colored rhinestones like ornaments on a Christmas tree, and

Kitty, wearing a white bodysuit and pointed headpiece to make her look like a snowflake, waited for them in the kitchen looking calmer and more patient than Jamie sounded or Tucker felt.

"Okay, Miss Karma!" Crystal exclaimed when Tucker came into view. "Girl, you look good!"

"Really?" Tucker asked, smiling.

"Yeah, girl, that dress is cute!" Kitty said admiringly.

"Thanks, I got it from Jamie," he said.

"I made it," Jamie bragged.

"Of course you did," Kitty grumbled, rolling her eyes.

"Girl, I tried showing you how to sew a couple of weeks ago!" Crystal said, giving Kitty an exasperated look.

After an issue with Kitty's previous roommates (a couple that broke up almost every other day that finally called it quits and moved out of their shared apartment), Crystal and Jamie had offered to let Kitty move into what used to be their guest room. So far, Jamie had texted to complain about Kitty's cleaning habits (or lack thereof) four times within the three weeks they'd lived together, to Tucker's amusement.

"I know, but it's hard," Kitty whined.

"This is why she isn't my daughter," Jamie muttered to Crystal.

"She's not mine either!" Crystal said defensively. "Just because I suggested she move in here does *not* mean I'm her mother!"

"I don't need you two whores as mothers," Kitty scoffed.

"Then why are you trying to take my drag all the damn time, then?" Crystal asked her.

Tucker watched the queens squabble with each other, his eyes bouncing back and forth between them as they spoke like he was watching a game of tennis. He knew that they would forget this petty argument before they even got to the car, having watched plenty of other squabbles occur between the three queens in the last few months.

"Hey!" Jamie eventually yelled, slamming her palm down on the kitchen counter she was leaning on. Crystal and Kitty, who were now verbally picking apart each other's costumes and makeup, went silent. "Somebody

CHAPTER 15

get this bitch a shot," she instructed, throwing her head in Tucker's direction, "and let's go!"

Crystal and Kitty, both now feeling competitive with each other, raced to one of the cabinets to grab a shot glass and shoved each other out of the way as they both attempted to grab the same bottle of vodka Jamie had in the freezer.

"Bitch, careful with my gown!" Crystal barked at Kitty, finally grabbing the bottle and slamming the freezer door. Kitty wrapped her hand around the bottle right below Crystal's and the two walked the bottle back to their shot glasses, moving the bottle back and forth as they poured and getting vodka all over the counter by the time they filled the shots. Jamie snatched the shots and handed one to Tucker, throwing her head back as she swallowed her own. Tucker did the same, careful not to smudge his lipstick, and shuddered at the feeling as the vodka went down his throat and into his empty stomach. He'd been too nervous to eat for most of the day, so he could feel his cheeks flush almost immediately.

"Alright, let's move," Jamie instructed, turning and walking out the door. Tucker followed, and heard Kitty and Crystal behind him as they walked down the apartment complex's stairs toward Crystal's white Kia Soul, which looked like a small white cube. Kitty and Tucker squeezed into the back, careful to not let their wigs get messed up as they sat down, and Jamie sat up front with Crystal, and the four of them raced out of the parking lot toward Haven.

Tucker was surprised to see how many people were at the club right before Christmas and took deep breaths to calm his thumping heart as he scanned the room for any familiar faces. David was working the bar, wearing a Santa hat and red velvet pants with matching suspenders and no shirt, and Tucker noticed a few regular patrons he'd gotten to know as he'd worked around the dance floor in the past.

A trio of drag queens Tucker didn't recognize were huddled near the bar and leaned in to talk to one another after looking Tucker up and down, making him feel self-conscious. He waved anyway, trying to be as friendly as possible, but received no response from his peers.

"Just ignore those whores," Kitty advised, having watched the whole interaction happen. "Whatever they're saying is none of our business. Remember that. Plus, that queen's wig looks *horrible*." Tucker smiled at her in acknowledgement, but didn't respond. He knew she was right, but he hated feeling judged by people he'd never met, especially other drag queens.

Jamie took the group's lead and led them by the bar toward the dressing room, Tucker waving hello at David as he went. He could see the wheels turning in David's head before he registered it was Tucker, a big smile appearing on his face as he took off his hat and bowed slightly in greeting. Tucker laughed as he walked away, waving hello to other patrons he didn't know, like he saw the rest of the queens doing. The four squeezed into the dressing room, joining another queen dressed as a nutcracker who Jamie introduced as Daya Beaties. Crystal, who would be hosting the show, announced the lineup—Daya, then Tucker, followed by Kitty, then Jamie, and Crystal would close the show. Tucker's palms began to sweat, and he wiped them on his dress as he took deep breaths to calm himself. He handed a flash drive containing his music for the show to Crystal, who brought it to the DJ, and returned to tell them the show would start in five minutes.

Tucker followed the group as they went down a hallway he hadn't been down before and exited on another side of the building that wrapped around and connected to the dance floor. There were tall tables with ashtrays on them outside and a few people stood around smoking, complimenting the queens as they passed. He could hear Crystal on the microphone as the show started, cracking a few jokes and telling the audience to tip the bar staff extra during the holidays before breaking down the show's lineup for the night. Tucker heard music play and Daya dashed inside, ignoring the stage and dancing heavily on the floor around the audience. He could hear them cheering for her as she performed, and when he peeked inside, he saw Daya in a split on the floor, lipsyncing to the song like it was nothing. As her music ended, he heard Crystal on the microphone again, applauding Daya's performance.

"Alright, next up is a new face here in Orlando," Crystal advised the audience, "so I want y'all to make her feel extra welcome tonight. Please

CHAPTER 15

help me welcome to the stage, the newest member of the House of Kahlo, it's the lovely miss Karma Kahlo!"

Tucker heard the audience cheering loudly and felt his mouth go dry as his music started, but he fixed a smile on his face as he entered the building. He climbed the three stairs on the side of the stage, his heart pounding, and faced the crowd as the lights overhead blinded him. He'd chosen a familiar Christmas song that he knew he'd be able to recall if he got a sudden bout of stage fright, and began to lipsync and move around the stage as The Carpenters' "Merry Christmas, Darling" played. As the song progressed, he moved down the stage's built-in runway, picking parts of the song to direct to different audience members, and soon members of the crowd began to walk forward with dollar bills in their hands, smiling when Tucker took the money from them with a wink or a blown kiss.

He made his way down the stairs at the end of the runway, his heel catching on the first step and making him trip, but he caught himself with his other heel and steadied himself on the floor as the audience gasped. He turned and continued with the song as if nothing happened, even though he was mortified, making the crowd cheer and tip him more. Tucker twirled as he moved around the dance floor during the musical interlude, gaining more confidence as the song was almost at the end, and danced with the more enthusiastic members of the audience as he passed them. The song came to a close, and Tucker laughed and bowed as the audience cheered loudly again, grabbing his tips and blowing air kisses to the audience as he turned to walk out the door. Mid-turn, the front part of his heel connected with the stage and Tucker fell on his stomach, wheezing as the air was pushed out of him. Crystal hurried back to the stage and prompted the audience to cheer once more as Tucker quickly got back to his feet and hurried out the door, head down in embarrassment.

When he walked back to the smoking area, Jamie was howling with laughter, bent over and her hands on her knees. Tucker's face grew even hotter than it already was and he fought to keep embarrassed tears out of his eyes, turning his face away from Jamie and the other queens around him.

"I'm sorry, girl, I'm sorry," Jamie said as she laughed, noticing Tucker's expression, "it's not funny, but that was so damn funny! You just ate it!"

"Don't worry about it," Kitty assured Tucker, "I've fallen off the side of that stage in the middle of a number more times than I can count."

Crystal could be heard from inside announcing Kitty next, and she put a reassuring hand on Tucker's shoulder and offered a sympathetic look before moving around him and heading inside as the music started. Jamie's laughter finally subsided, and she wrapped Tucker in a big hug.

"I'm sorry, that wasn't funny and I shouldn't have laughed," she said when she pulled away. "But I'm sure you would've too if it was the other way around, so don't try it!"

Tucker rolled his eyes but smiled, knowing that Jamie was right and it probably looked hilarious from the outside.

"Go wait in the dressing room," Jamie instructed, "and I'll bring you a present after my number."

Tucker did as she said, walking back to the dressing room the way he came. Daya, now out of drag except for the makeup, wearing jeans and a bright pink shirt, was exiting as Tucker was about to enter and they offered each other awkward smiles as they passed. He sat at the mirror, analyzing his makeup, and reassessed his performance. Aside from the trip at the very end, Tucker thought he'd done a great job and had a lot of fun! He had been scared he'd mess the song up or his wig would fall off, but once he was on the stage he realized that the crowd was there to support the performers regardless of what they looked like. It was a freeing feeling, and Tucker already wanted to do it again.

He could very faintly hear Crystal's voice through the speakers as she finished up the show, and Jamie swung the dressing room door open as she entered, slamming it into Tucker.

"Ow, damn!" Tucker yelled, reaching to rub the middle of his back where the door connected.

"Sorry, girl," Jamie said as she entered, balancing two shots of a brown liquid in one hand and one clear shot in the other. She was still in her red lingerie, tips sticking out of both bra cups and her gold dress slung over her right shoulder. "Here, drink these," she instructed, handing the brown

CHAPTER 15

liquor to Tucker.

"What is it?" he asked, inspecting the glasses.

"Does it matter?" she retorted. "Just drink it, Mary!"

Tucker shrugged and took the first shot and almost spit it out immediately, forcing himself to swallow instead.

"Oh my god, what is that?" he asked, grimacing.

"Whiskey, girl! Hurry and take the other one," Jamie encouraged. "You're still underage and I'm not trying to go to jail because I gave some booze to your gay ass."

Tucker knew Jamie had a point and didn't want to get her in trouble—even though the shots were her idea—so he took a breath to brace himself and took the shot, throwing his head back as soon as he felt liquid touch his mouth and swallowing as quickly as possible. He coughed and shuddered at the sensation, and Jamie cheered. She quickly took her shot, swallowing the liquid like it was water, and reached for her bag, pulling out a clear plastic bag containing blue gummy candy shaped like sharks.

"You want one to get rid of the flavor?" she offered.

Tucker, still feeling the alcohol burning his throat, nodded and held his hand out. Jamie carefully pulled two out of the bag with her nails and placed them in Tucker's palm.

"This is *special* candy," Jamie advised, giving Tucker a pointed look he didn't quite understand. "I wouldn't drink any more after you eat that."

"What makes it so special?" Tucker asked.

"Girl!" Jamie said with exasperation, throwing her hands up dramatically. "Did you learn *nothing* in that little po-dunk town you're always talking about? There's weed in it, Mary!"

"Oh!" Tucker said, his eyes widening as her words registered. He inspected the candy in his hand, gingerly moving it around with his pointer finger like it might explode. It looked like regular candy to him, he reasoned, and they were celebrating his first gig… He popped the sharks in his mouth, chewing carefully, and swallowed. He sat for a moment, waiting for something to happen, and looked at Jamie, confused.

"I don't feel it," he wondered aloud.

"It takes a little while to kick in," Jamie advised, popping a shark in her mouth and putting the bag away as she chewed. "Come on," she said once she'd swallowed, patting Tucker's shoulder, "let's get you out of drag and get some water into your system."

Tucker had completely forgotten he was still in drag, laughing when he turned back to the mirror and seeing his reflection, and realized that the shots had at least started to work their way through his system. He felt fine, albeit a little warm for the humid December weather, but really noticed his vision alter when he stood up and his head began to swim. He carefully removed his wig, placing it on the counter, and pulled his dress off over his head. It got stuck around his arms, and he could hear Jamie laughing and taking a picture of him before she helped him get it off.

"You're killing me tonight," she chuckled. "I'm going to send that to you tomorrow when you're sober."

"I'm fine," he assured her, leaning on the counter for support as he kicked off his heels, making Jamie snicker. He reached for the small canvas bag he'd brought with him, pulling out a change of clothes and a packet of makeup wipes, and shoved his drag in the bag along with the tips he'd made. He pulled his multiple layers of tights off at once, not minding that Jamie was still sitting next to him, and threw them in the bag along with the foam pads he'd been wearing. He quickly threw on the pair of jean shorts and black tank top he'd packed before sitting back down at the mirror and putting a black hat on to hide his disheveled hair, ripping off his fake eyelashes and throwing them carelessly into his bag to Jamie's dismay.

"I'm not giving you another pair of those if you ruin them," she warned him.

Tucker ignored her, opening the pack of makeup wipes and scrubbing his face until it was devoid of all makeup aside from his red lipstick-stained lips and a smudge of eyeliner. He looked to Jamie for approval, who laughed and gave him a thumbs-up.

"Where are the girls?" Tucker asked, finally noticing Crystal and Kitty had never come to the cramped dressing room.

"Probably out there partying," Jamie replied, scrolling on her phone. "You

CHAPTER 15

want to go out there too?"

"Hell yeah," Tucker grinned. He felt warm and giddy, and wanted to talk with his friends.

Jamie led the way back through the club towards the dance floor, and Tucker stopped when he saw David and hurried to the bar.

"David!" Tucker said excitedly.

"Oh, Tucker, there you are! There was a really pretty queen here earlier named Karma that I really wanted you to meet!" David said, grinning.

"Did you see me perform?" Tucker asked.

"I sure did! I shut the whole place down and told everyone I had to go watch my friend," he replied. "Just kidding—there was no one here, so I just walked to the doorway and watched," he added.

"It was so fun!" Tucker exclaimed.

"Except for that part at the end, huh?" he asked, visibly trying to stop himself from smiling.

"You saw that too, huh?" Tucker laughed, no longer feeling embarrassed. "I don't care anymore; it was only an accident and now people will definitely remember me."

"An excellent way to think about it," David agreed. "You want a water or anything while you're here?"

Upon hearing the word 'water', Tucker suddenly realized how dry his mouth felt. He nodded enthusiastically, and David handed him a small plastic cup filled with iced water.

"Shots!" Tucker called, grabbing the cup and drinking the water as fast as he could. When he finished, he noticed David was smiling but had a questioning look on his face.

"Were you this drunk when you were performing?" he asked.

"I'm not drunk at all," Tucker disagreed, shaking his head.

"Sure you aren't," David said, winking. "Just be careful, okay?"

"I will," Tucker promised with a smile. "I just had an edible, so I'm not going to drink anymore tonight."

David's eyes widened, and he clasped his face in mock surprise. "An edible?" he gasped dramatically. "Those are *illegal*, Tucker!"

"What can I say—I'm a bad boy," Tucker shrugged. "You into that?"

Before David could respond to Tucker's flirting, Jamie appeared next to him.

"Girl, there you are!" she said, giving Tucker a soft shove. "I thought I lost you in the crowd out there! I've been looking for you!"

"I did not tell David I had an edible," Tucker advised Jamie, making David turn away from them as he laughed.

"Oh, I'm sure," Jamie replied sarcastically. "You wanted to see the girls, so let's go see the girls!"

"The girls!" Tucker said excitedly, remembering Crystal and Kitty.

"Come back later and I'll get you more water," David advised Tucker, shooting Jamie an amused look. She blew him a kiss, and pulled Tucker away from the bar, who waved goodbye at David as he was escorted onto the dance floor. He was sure he was feeling the effects of the edible now, he thought, assessing his feelings of euphoria and lack of balance as he was led to where the two queens were dancing. They cheered when they saw him and he hugged them both, dancing with them until he started to sweat. He excused himself and stumbled back to the bar, feeling like the ground below him was shifting as he walked.

"Hey, are you okay?" David asked, looking concerned as Tucker leaned on the bar.

"Yeah, just hot," Tucker answered, wiping his moist forehead with the back of his hand.

"Here," he said, filling up another cup of ice water and handing it to Tucker, "pace yourself. You look really pale."

"I'm fine," Tucker assured him, sipping the water.

"Did you drive here?" David asked.

"No, Crystal drove us here," he responded, taking another sip. His heart was beating faster than normal, and Tucker thought it was from the dancing, but now that he was standing still he became alarmed. David gave Tucker a look of concern, and Tucker's stomach churned in response. He stepped away from the bar and hurried to the bathrooms on the other side of the room, barely making it to a stall before he vomited loudly into the toilet, his

CHAPTER 15

throat burning from the bile.

When he felt sure that he was finished, he spat for good measure and flushed the toilet. He took a sip of water from the bathroom sink as he washed his hands, swishing it around in his mouth to get rid of the taste. He quickly assessed himself in the mirror, noting redness around his eyes from tearing up while vomiting and how pale his face looked, and tried to walk in a straight line as he exited the bathroom. He still didn't feel sober, but he didn't feel as drunk as before, he thought thankfully.

Tucker tried to walk confidently back to the bar, slightly wobbling as he moved, and David was waiting for him with his half-finished cup of water.

"Are you okay?" David asked again, looking more concerned than before.

"Yeah, just a little messed up," Tucker said, feeling embarrassed that David was seeing him in his current state. He drank the rest of the water, relishing the cool feeling as it slid down his throat. David turned to help someone who'd approached the bar, and Tucker noticed Crystal, Jamie, and Kitty walking towards him.

"Girl, you keep disappearing!" Jamie said impatiently as he turned towards them.

"We're going to change and then we'll meet you back out there, okay?" Crystal instructed.

"I think I'm going to sit for a minute," Tucker told them. "I'm not feeling great."

"You'll be fine," Kitty promised, rubbing his shoulder as they passed him.

"You sure you're okay?" David said from behind Tucker, having heard the conversation.

"I don't know," Tucker answered truthfully. "I've never had an edible before and I've barely ever drank before, so is this normal?"

"It depends on the person," he replied. "I get off soon—do you want me to drive you home?"

Tucker shook his head, kicking himself for trying to plan ahead earlier in the day.

"I left my stuff at Jamie's, so I have to wait for them to be done so I can go get it," he sighed.

"Well, there's no way you're driving tonight, so do you want to just crash on my couch if you're ready to go now?" David offered. Tucker nodded, and David offered him a sympathetic half-smile.

Tucker moved to one of the black couches that were pushed up against the wall, ignoring the two men aggressively making out next to him. He texted Jamie to tell her what was going on and asked her to grab his bag in the dressing room, and she simply responded, 'k'. David approached twenty minutes later, offering Tucker his hand to help pull him off of the couch, and wrapped a guiding arm around Tucker's shoulders as he led him out of the club to where his car was parked. It was a short drive to his apartment, and David played Christmas music as they drove to make Tucker feel a bit more cheery.

Physically, Tucker did not feel well and mentally vowed not to drink and do edibles at the same time ever again. Mentally and emotionally, Tucker was thrilled. David was being kind and warm, which he always was, but was touching Tucker more than usual, he noted. He was afraid to get his hopes up, but couldn't keep his heart from soaring when David began to sing along to a Christmas ballad that was playing on the radio, looking at Tucker and smiling whenever they stopped.

By the time they were in David's apartment building's elevator, Tucker was beginning to sober up and could walk without fumbling for the most part, allowing David to lead the way down the hall to his apartment, unlocking the door and holding it open for Tucker as he entered. The apartment was fairly small—there was a sleek-looking kitchen area directly to the right with a black granite countertop island and two matching stools pulled up to it, directly in front of Tucker was the living room that had a small gray couch against a wall and a television mounted on the wall across from it, and a bathroom and a room Tucker presumed was David's bedroom to the left.

"Nice place," Tucker complimented.

"Thanks," David said. "It's a little small, but it does the trick while I'm in school. Come in, get comfortable."

David went to the shiny metal fridge, pulling out two bottles of water, and

CHAPTER 15

sat on the couch, patting the cushion next to him as a sign for Tucker to join him. Tucker obliged, and their knees touched as they sat together in silence. He glanced down, noticing that David was still shirtless, and pulled his eyes back up as fast as he could in case David saw. David also seemed to remember that he was still shirtless and excused himself to his room, returning in a white t-shirt and gray sweatpants.

"So how are you feeling?" he asked as he dropped back on the couch next to Tucker.

"I'm starting to feel better," Tucker answered. "Thank you for letting me crash on your couch tonight. I'm sorry."

"No need to be sorry!" David assured him, placing a hand on Tucker's shoulder. Tucker glanced at his hand, then quickly looked away and took a long sip of water. "Besides, when a friend needs help, you help them."

"That's very noble of you," Tucker said, turning to David and smiling. "Are you like a knight in shining armor for all of your friends?"

"If necessary," David shrugged, looking around the room as he spoke. "But lately it seems like you've been the only one that needs it."

"David?" Tucker asked. David looked at him, and Tucker leaned forward, their faces touching. Before their lips met, Tucker felt a hand on his chest and leaned back, confused.

"Tucker, we've talked about this," David murmured solemnly, looking disappointed.

"We did?" Tucker asked, only feeling more confused.

"Yeah, on your birthday. Remember, you were flirting at the bar and I told you I was flattered but wasn't looking for anything other than friends? You told me you were fine with that," David explained.

Tucker said nothing, turning his body forward so no part of them touched. He searched his memories, trying to recall what David was talking about, but remembered almost nothing from that night.

"You don't remember," David muttered, a look of realization dawning on his face.

"I... I'm so sorry," Tucker stammered, getting to his feet. "I blacked out that night and I don't remember and I'm still drunk right now and I'm so sorry, David. Excuse me."

He walked around the couch, careful not to brush against David's legs, and ignored David's repeated affirmations that it was okay as he locked himself in the bathroom. Tears immediately formed and fell down Tucker's cheeks and he sat on the bathroom floor, hugging his legs. How could he have been so stupid, thinking David liked him? He brought his fist down on his knee, angry with himself for ruining a perfectly wonderful friendship. There was no way David would want to be his friend after this, he thought miserably.

"Tucker?" David called from outside the bathroom door, knocking lightly. "It's okay, really. You don't have to stay in there."

Tucker didn't move, sniffling as he wiped his tears away. Black streaks smeared across his eyes and the back of his hand from the leftover eyeliner, but he didn't care.

"Tucker?" David repeated, knocking lightly again. "Please come out. I promise I'm not mad or upset with you. You didn't know."

Tucker stood, but still didn't open the door. He turned to the mirror and wiped his face again, trying to get the black off when he realized he looked like a rabid raccoon.

"I'm just going to stay in here a few more minutes," Tucker finally said, watching his reflection mouth the words as they came out of his mouth. "I'll be fine, don't worry," he lied, fighting to keep his voice steady.

"Okay," David said from the other side, sounding unsure. "I'm going to go to bed, but I put a blanket on the couch for you. Holler if you need anything, okay?"

Hearing David's concerned voice made Tucker begin to cry again, to his dismay.

"Yup," was all he managed to get out, his mouth quivering as he fought for control of his emotions. He heard David's bedroom door close and counted to one hundred before carefully opening the bathroom door, peeking out to make sure David wasn't there. When he decided the coast was clear, he crept to the front door, opening it and closing it behind him as quietly as possible. There was no way he could stay with David after embarrassing himself like that, he thought to himself as he raced down the hall to the elevator, riding

CHAPTER 15

it down to the lobby and hurrying out the building's front doors. He pulled his phone out of his pocket, opening his contacts and pressing call.

"Hey," Tucker said when the call was answered, "it's a long story, but can you come pick me up?"

Chapter 16

Barely ten minutes after the call ended, a sleek black sports car pulled up to where Tucker sat against the wall outside of David's apartment building. The window rolled down and Adrian sat in the driver's seat, looking cool and calm as always with a smirk on his lips

"It's after one in the morning," he called to Tucker. "Look who's doing the booty calling now."

Despite his foul mood, Tucker couldn't help but smile at Adrian's teasing. He unsteadily got to his feet, still feeling the effects of one or both of the substances he'd consumed that night, and got in Adrian's car. It smelled like leather and the seat squeaked as he sat down.

"Hey," Adrian said, taking his hand and rubbing his thumb along the back of Tucker's palm.

"Hi," Tucker smiled, blushing.

He mentally chastised himself for succumbing to yet another guy after what had just happened in David's apartment, but reasoned this was healthy to get David out of his mind. Adrian sped off, turning twice before pulling into his apartment building about a block away. He took Tucker's hand and led the way to his apartment, which was on the first floor. He opened the door for Tucker, following closely behind and locking it once they were inside.

Adrian lived in a large studio apartment, with a queen-sized bed and a dresser in one corner, a desk with papers strewn across it in another, and a black leather couch similar to the one at Haven sat in-between, facing a giant flat-screen TV on the wall. Tucker looked to his left and noticed a

CHAPTER 16

kitchen setup, but didn't get to look too closely before Adrian took his hand again and brought him to the couch, where he continued to hold it as they sat together closely.

"So what's going on?" he asked. "You okay?"

"Yeah, just a little drunk," Tucker sighed. "It's been a long, weird night. I took some shots and tried edibles at the same time, which is an awful idea, so I was going to stay at a friend's house to sleep it off, but I had to leave. So that's when I called you."

"Yeah, sounds like it's been rough," Adrian said, giving him a sympathetic look. "You want to go to bed?"

"I don't want to be rude, but yes," he replied, sounding relieved. "I'm exhausted."

"Well come on," Adrian said, smirking, as he pulled Tucker off the couch and to his bed. He had soft white sheets on the bed and a fluffy maroon comforter on top and gently moved them aside to allow for their entry. Adrian began unbuttoning the white shirt he was wearing, the fabric semi-transparent, and brought Tucker's hands up to his shirt with one of his. Tucker began helping him unbutton the bottom half of the shirt, and Adrian shrugged it off to reveal his wide shoulders and broad, hairy chest. Tucker stared in awe and Adrian smirked again at his reaction, taking one of Tucker's hands and placing it on his chest. Tucker's fingers curled around the hair, moving from one pec to another before lowering to Adrian's stomach, which had a thick line of hair descending from his chest to below his navel and into his pants. Adrian tugged at the bottom of Tucker's tank top and pulled it up and over Tucker's head, taking a moment to run his hands down Tucker's chest and stomach and brushed against his crotch as he lowered it again. Tucker looked down at Adrian's hand, and then into his eyes, and Adrian roughly pulled Tucker against him, their lips crashing together.

Adrian's hands roamed over Tucker's body, brushing against his nipples and down his back before resting on his waistband, sticking his fingers in Tucker's pants as he worked on the shorts' metal button and moaned into Tucker's mouth. Tucker ran his hands through Adrian's hair and against his chest before doing the same to Adrian's jeans, making quick work of the buttons and dropping them to the floor. Adrian finally undid Tucker's shorts as well, and the two stood there with pants around their ankles and tongues in each other's mouths until Adrian broke the kiss, pulling Tucker into the bed.

The two rolled around, kissing and touching each other as their bodies pressed together as tightly as possible, rocking together like waves in a storm and creating a heated friction between the two. Adrian began playing with the waistband on Tucker's underwear, slowly pulling it down as he licked and nipped at Tucker's neck, but Tucker pulled away, breaking the spell.

"I'm sorry, Adrian, but I'm really not in the right head space to fool around tonight," Tucker said apologetically, running his hand through Adrian's chest hair. "Would it be okay if we just went to sleep tonight and messed around some other time? I'm so tired and I still don't feel good."

"What, are you serious?" Adrian asked, a confused smile on his face.

"I really want to, just not tonight is all," Tucker explained.

Adrian pulled away further, his smile disappearing as his mouth formed a tight line.

"You *are* serious," he murmured, staring into Tucker's eyes. "You mean to tell me that I've been coming on to you for months, trying to get you to come home with me, and when I finally do you don't even want to fool around now?"

"I'm sorry," Tucker said, alarmed by Adrian's sudden change in attitude. Adrian chuckled, though there was no humor in his tone, and he got out of bed, scooping up Tucker's clothes.

"So am I," he said coldly, "for wasting my damn time. You should go."

"What?" Tucker asked, bewildered. "Go? It's so late! I'm not saying I don't want to fool around, just not tonight! Come on, Adrian, please don't do this."

"Well I *do* want to tonight," Adrian retorted, shaking Tucker's clothes in his hand to emphasize his point. Tucker quickly got out of Adrian's bed and dressed while Adrian sat in his underwear on the edge of his bed with his arms crossed, his face cold and impassive.

"This is fucking unbelievable," Adrian muttered, his voice full of malice,

CHAPTER 16

as Tucker dressed. "I can't believe I wasted so much time on you. Why did I put so much effort into this bullshit? Look at you, you're not even worth it! You're just some fucking flabby kid that doesn't know good dick when he sees it."

Tucker, now dressed, pulled his shoes on and opened his mouth to say something, and Adrian lifted his hand to stop him before he even spoke. Tucker felt tears forming again, so he turned and rushed out the front door, slamming it behind him. He found his way to the front of the building and exited its front doors. He had no idea where to go next and felt panicked. His phone read 2:13 AM and Tucker realized, to his dismay, that its battery was at 5%. Tucker frantically opened his texts and began to text Kiara before realizing he had no idea where he was, and deleted the message he'd started in defeat.

He looked around, trying to get an idea of where he was, but everything that wasn't directly next to a streetlight was pitch black. His heart slammed against his chest and a nervous sweat formed on Tucker's forehead as he started walking, picking a direction and hoping for the best. He'd sobered up a bit more after the altercation with Adrian, but had still been drunk enough on the car ride over that he couldn't remember how he got from David's apartment to where he was now. He walked to the end of a street, thought better of it, and turned and walked the other way back towards Adrian's apartment building in defeat. He pulled out his phone again and quickly began calling Jamie, desperate to get in touch with someone before his phone died. The phone rang and eventually went to voicemail, and Tucker hung up in frustration.

He had never felt more stupid. Why did he think calling Adrian would be a good idea, knowing their only interactions had been flirting and what it would lead to at Adrian's place? *I'd hoped Adrian wasn't a dick*, he thought to himself bitterly. He leaned against the wall, feeling lightheaded, and slowly slid to the ground, putting his palms to his eyes and letting his frustrated tears wet them. A woman in scrubs, presumably a nurse, walked by him and into the apartment building without a second glance as he looked up at her, making Tucker cry more.

"Have I already hit rock bottom at nineteen years old?" he whispered to himself. Hearing the words aloud seemed to snap Tucker out of the spiral he was in and he pushed himself back up to his feet, determined to get somewhere safe to finally sleep off whatever was left in his system. He turned to his left, making the decision to follow his instincts and hoping they wouldn't lead to his demise, and started walking down the dark sidewalk toward whatever was waiting for him ahead.

Chapter 17

Tucker made it across two intersections before panic set in again, and he started to second-guess himself. Why did he think he could trust his instincts to lead him to safety in a town he'd been in four months, and was now in a part of it he'd never been before? He had the fleeting thought of turning around once more, considering apologizing and succumbing to Adrian's wishes if only to have a bed to sleep in for the night, but felt the cold dread in his stomach at the thought of seeing Adrian after what had just happened, and quickly pushed it from his mind.

Having no other options in mind, Tucker pulled his phone out once more, quietly cursing to himself when it alerted him that its battery was down to 2%. His fingers flew across the screen as he pulled up David's number and called, praying that he would answer and come help him. To his dismay, it went to voicemail, but Tucker stayed on the line, having no other choice, and left a message.

"Hi David, it's Tucker," he sniffled into the phone, trying to hide the fact that he'd been crying from his voice. "Um, if you get this, could you come get me? I'm so sorry I left, but now I'm on the streets and I have nowhere else to go and I need your help. I think I'm still kind of near where you live, and right now I'm near a gas station and a Chinese restaurant. I'll stay here in case you get this soon, but my phone's about to die so if you call back and can't get me, that's why. I'm really sorry again, David. Bye."

As soon as Tucker ended the call, his phone made a sad beeping noise, and the screen went black, now officially out of power. Tucker sat in the middle of the sidewalk, staying true to what he said in his voicemail and remaining where he was in case, by some miracle, David woke up from a deep sleep, listened to Tucker's voicemail, decided he didn't hate Tucker for trying to kiss him, and came to find him. The quiet was eerie, and the only sounds Tucker could hear were the far-off chirping of bugs in the dark brush along the sidewalk and the buzzing of the streetlights overhead.

He began to hum, at first nothing in particular, but it eventually changed into the melody from the song he'd performed earlier that evening, which already felt like a lifetime ago. He had felt so good about himself then, and now he hated himself more than anything for getting into this situation. Why couldn't he have just stayed at the club with the queens? Why didn't he just tell Jamie he wasn't really interested in drinking? Why couldn't he have just told Micah that he loved him back, dispelling David from his mind and eliminating boys from the growing list of issues Tucker had to deal with?

The thought of Micah was bittersweet—imagining all the good things that could have been between them, but also imagining all the arguments they would have inevitably gotten into when distance became an issue or if Tucker stayed friends with David.

David, Tucker thought, making him sigh in defeat. He wanted so badly for David to like him back that he had ruined a great friendship with a wonderful guy by drunkenly flirting with him—not once, but *twice*. In his defense, Tucker reminded himself, David was giving off signals of attraction that multiple people caught on to since they met on Tucker's first day at UCF. He remembered the way David winked at him as they talked, similar to how he had at the club hours ago, and how he had given Tucker his phone number. *But I was obviously wrong*, he thought to himself bitterly, his mind replaying David's disappointed face as he pushed Tucker away from him over and over again.

Tucker laid on his back, staring up at the night sky to count the stars, and realized he couldn't see them with all the city lights shining. It was the first time he'd noticed that, he realized, having never had that issue while he grew up in Weeki Wachee. Granted, he had lots of other issues back home that he didn't have in Orlando, like living with his family and having virtually no other queer people in town to commune with, but in that moment he felt a

CHAPTER 17

quick pang of homesickness for the town's familiarity and its view of the stars.

He didn't know how long he'd been staring at the empty night sky and humming to himself when he heard gravel crunching near his head, and he looked directly into a car's lit headlight when he turned his head, blinding himself. He cursed quietly as he sat up quickly, bracing himself as the lightheaded feeling briefly washed over him again.

"Tucker?" someone said. Tucker's ears were ringing as he sat there blinking the spots out of his eyes. He felt hands on his shoulders lift him up to his feet and found himself looking into David's face when he could finally see again.

"You found me," Tucker muttered, feeling a mix of bewilderment and relief at his familiar face.

"Thank god you described where you were," David sighed, ushering Tucker to the passenger side door. He opened it and gently pushed Tucker in, closing it once his legs were inside and coming around the other side.

"Thank you for coming to get me," Tucker said, unable to stop the tears from falling down his cheeks once more. He was feeling so many emotions that he couldn't tell any longer if they were tears of relief, tears of embarrassment, or tears of sadness. "I'm sorry I keep crying tonight, and I'm sorry I tried to kiss you."

David reversed the car and got back onto the road, speeding down the desolate streets back to his apartment.

"I told you it was fine," he said, his tone almost too even as if he was working hard to control it and not scream at Tucker.

"It's not fine," Tucker protested. "I wouldn't have if I remembered—"

"Exactly, and you didn't, so it's fine," David interrupted.

Tucker could tell that David was upset with him and knew that he had every right to be. David had welcomed him into his home as a guest and Tucker repaid him by trying to kiss him, then left in the middle of the night and later left a mysterious voicemail asking him to come get him from an unknown location. Tucker would've been upset too, if the situation were reversed!

"How did you find me?" Tucker asked.

"I've lived here for a few years, and there's only one Chinese restaurant around here next to a gas station that I know of, so you gave me a pretty good idea in the voicemail," David explained, his voice curt. "You're just so damn lucky I checked the time and saw you called when my body woke me up."

David whipped into the parking lot and into his spot, turning the car off and exiting the vehicle before Tucker even got his seatbelt off. Tucker quickly followed after him, trying to catch up and only barely making it into the elevator with David before the doors closed.

"If you're mad at me, please just yell," Tucker mumbled, feeling ashamed of himself. "You have every right to be."

"I'm not mad," David replied, staring straight ahead.

A bell chimed as the elevator doors opened, and David led the way back to his apartment. Tucker remained silent as they walked through the hall, only speaking again when David was unlocking his door.

"I can tell you're mad," Tucker said. "I deserve it, so just let it out. Please."

David opened the door, and they entered, Tucker looking at David as he locked it again from the inside. David turned around, his jaw clenched and his brows furrowed, and he inhaled sharply.

"I'm not mad, Tucker," he repeated. "I'm upset. I was so fucking worried about you! I told you it was fine and thought you were asleep on the couch, and then I wake up in the middle of the night and see you left a voicemail an hour ago saying you're out on the streets somewhere all alone! What the hell were you thinking, Tucker? Are you stupid? Because that was a pretty fucking stupid thing to do, and even you should know that!"

Tucker kept eye contact with David as he spoke, even though he wanted to look anywhere else. Even after everything that'd happened, David still wanted to be his friend, and Tucker felt undeserving of that.

"It's late and I'm exhausted, so let's both go to bed and we're going to talk about what the hell happened in the morning," David said, looking at Tucker sharply.

Tucker nodded and walked to the couch, but David grabbed his shoulders

CHAPTER 17

and steered him towards his bedroom. Tucker looked at David, confused.

"You've left the apartment once already, and I'm not doing this shit again," David said, no amount of humor in his face or tone. They got into David's bed, Tucker not even bothering to undress, and tried to go to sleep.

"Thank you for saving me," Tucker murmured into the dark. He thought David was asleep and hadn't heard him, but he felt David roll on his side to face away from Tucker before he finally responded with in a gruff voice, "Don't ever do that again. I won't come find you next time if you leave again."

Tucker nodded, even though he knew David couldn't see what he was doing, and stared at David's ceiling until he drifted off to sleep. He had jarring, stressful dreams that night, of a monster twisting into the shapes of Jamie, Micah, Kiara, and Adrian as Tucker was hunted in a dark forest. Each face taunted him in a different way—Jamie chided him that he'd never be a good performer, Micah pleaded with Tucker to come to him and love him, Kiara repeated over and over again that David liked Tucker, and Adrian, which was when the monster was closest to catching Tucker, simply whispered, "come to bed, Tucker". Each time it would get close enough to whisper to Tucker, he'd wake up with a start and try to sleep again, only starting the dream over again and never truly falling into a peaceful slumber.

Chapter 18

Tucker jolted awake the next morning, feeling mentally and physically exhausted, and noticed David was gone. He laid in David's full-sized bed, wishing that everything that'd occurred the night before had been a part of his nightmares instead of reality, fearing the repercussions he'd now have to face.

Tucker ventured out from the bedroom and found David sipping coffee quietly on the couch, reading a book on his phone. Tucker sat silently on one of the stools close by, not wanting to get too close to David after what he'd done the night before. He felt like he was back in high school again, sitting in the principal's office in anticipation of a reprimand while the principal acted like Tucker wasn't even there until he was ready to speak. David didn't even glance at Tucker until he finished the chapter he was reading and finally locked his phone as he shifted his attention to Tucker's worried face.

"Hey," Tucker said sheepishly, desperate to break the tense silence.

"Hey," David responded, his tone still sharp from the night before. "Want some coffee?"

He nodded, and David brushed by Tucker as he moved to the kitchen, keeping his back to him as he pulled out another mug and filled it with steaming coffee. Tucker wasn't usually one to drink coffee, but was desperate for caffeine to wake him up.

"I know I've said it already, but I'm so sorry for what I put you through last night and I'm really grateful that you came to get me," Tucker blurted out as David handed him the mug.

"I know you're sorry," David said evenly, sitting back down on the couch.

CHAPTER 18

"Now let's talk about what the hell happened."

Tucker sighed. He'd known the conversation was coming, but still felt reluctance and shame wash over him anyway.

"What happened was I was drunk and emotional and really, really stupid," Tucker said simply.

"I'm aware of that," David replied. "But I want to know what happened."

"When I tried to kiss you and you stopped me and told me what we'd talked about on my birthday, I was so upset at myself for doing that to you and for more than likely ruining our friendship over some drunk attraction," Tucker explained. "I know you said it was fine, but I also know how nice you are and I figured you were just saying that to make me feel better, so I left so you wouldn't be uncomfortable in your own home and called this guy Adrian to come get me."

"That guy from the bar?" David interjected.

"Yeah," Tucker sighed sadly. "Which was such a stupid thing to do. He told me I could stay at his place for the night and when I told him I wanted to go to bed, I guess he thought that was code for sex. We fooled around a little, but I stopped him before things went too far and he got so mad at me for leading him on—which I wasn't! I just didn't want to that night because I felt awful and just wanted to go to sleep. But he didn't care and kicked me out. I tried to call Jamie and only got her voicemail, so I had no other choice but to call you right before my phone died. I didn't want you to have to be involved any more than you already were, with everything that'd just happened, but I had no one else to call, so thank you for saving me."

David said nothing, his facial expression hard, as he analyzed Tucker's face and processed his words. He ran a hand through his disheveled hair, patches sticking up in different directions from where his head was on his pillow, and shook his head in exasperation, momentarily unable to speak.

"I don't even know where to begin," he finally said.

"I know," Tucker mumbled, feeling ashamed.

"Yeah, Tucker, I'm a nice person most of the time, but I don't just say stuff for no reason," David stated. "When I said it was fine, I meant it. I know you were drunk and you didn't mean it, and I know now that you blacked out on your birthday, so I understood.

"But then you just leave with some guy you barely know to make yourself feel better without even letting me know? Just to go fool around?" he continued, sounding more agitated the more he spoke. "Tucker, you could have died! He could've killed you, or raped you, or robbed you, and nobody would have had any idea what happened because you just decided to leave. I would have never forgiven myself if you left here while I was sleeping and something awful happened to you. I can't believe you'd be so fucking selfish!"

"I know," Tucker repeated softly.

"What if I hadn't woken up? What would you have done then?" David challenged, staring at Tucker intensely.

"I don't know," he answered honestly. "I didn't want to, but I had nowhere else to go, so I might have just gone back to Adrian's and let him have his way so I could sleep. I don't even know if he would've let me back in if I'd tried. I really don't know what I would've done, David. I'm just really thankful I didn't have to find out."

David's jaw clenched and his eyes narrowed, but Tucker couldn't tell if he was thinking or preparing to hit Tucker. He braced himself for whatever came next, but David simply stood up and went to his room, returning moments later with shoes on.

"Come on," he commanded, turning and walking out the front door.

"Where are we going?" Tucker asked, bewildered, and followed quickly when David kept walking. He closed the front door behind him and jogged to catch up with David, who made quick strides down the hall and threw the door to the stairwell open. He took two stairs at a time down to the first floor with ease, Tucker on his heels, and marched out into the parking lot, unlocking his car and sliding into the driver's seat.

"Where are we going?" Tucker repeated once he was safely in the car with his seatbelt on.

David remained silent, throwing the gearshift in reverse and flying out of the parking lot. Tucker surveyed his surroundings as they flew down the road, trying to remember where he was the night before now that there was

CHAPTER 18

daylight. He'd plugged his phone into David's car charger, and it pinged lightly to alert Tucker that it was on again. David slowed and pulled to the side of the street, putting the car in park. Tucker looked around, confused, but saw no reason why they'd stopped.

"This is where I found you last night," David finally explained. "Do you remember which way you came from?"

"Why?" Tucker asked cautiously.

"Please, just answer the question," David said.

Tucker pointed straight ahead, and David nodded, putting the gear back into drive and heading in that direction, following it for two more lights before turning right and parking outside of a tall, modern-looking building.

"What was that guy's name again? Adrian, you said?" David asked, opening his door and stepping out.

"David, what are you doing?" Tucker asked, his heart rate rising.

"Tucker," he said firmly, leaning in to make eye contact, "was that his name?"

"Yes," Tucker answered quietly, scared of the quiet rage he was seeing from David for the first time since they'd met.

"Stay here," David instructed, slamming his door. Tucker watched David, still in his pajamas, enter the building's lobby and check the directory on the wall to the right, his finger scrolling down until it stopped on something Tucker couldn't see. He watched helplessly as David walked around a corner and out of Tucker's view, and quickly unlocked his phone, frantically calling Kiara.

"Hey!" Kiara greeted him when she answered.

"Kiara, I need to talk to you right now," Tucker whispered urgently.

"Okay," she said cautiously, "I'm about to get on a plane to Washington, but I can talk for a minute. Are you alright?"

"Yeah, I'm fine," Tucker assured her. "Listen—last night I got really messed up at the club and David let me sleep on his couch, but I tried to kiss him and he stopped me, and apparently we'd already had a conversation about that on my birthday, *which I didn't remember!*"

"What?!" Kiara yelled into her phone.

"Listen!" Tucker shushed her. "So me, being drunk and emotional, thought it'd be best to leave, so I did in the middle of the night and went home with that guy from the club, Adrian. But then, when I told him I was too tired to have sex, he kicked me out and David had to come pick me up off the street in the middle of the night! And now we're at Adrian's apartment, and I think David's going to fight him or something! What do I do?"

"Wait, back up," Kiara instructed. "Did you just say you left in the middle of the night with some random guy you barely know and went back to his place without telling anyone where you were?"

"Yes, but focus!" Tucker replied.

"No, *you* focus!" Kiara retorted. "What the hell were you thinking, Tucker? He could've been a murderer!"

"Kiara, relax, I'm fine," he assured her. "What do I do about David right now? Should I go in there?"

"You're not fine—you're stupid! How could you be so fucking selfish? You could have died!" she said, ignoring his question.

"God, Kiara, focus!" Tucker pleaded.

"I'm plenty focused. Maybe you should stop focusing on trying to hop on some guy's dick for a second and focus on your priorities, like keeping yourself safe!" she argued.

"What the hell is that supposed to mean?" he asked, taken aback.

"If it—"

Tucker could hear an announcement playing through the airport speakers on Kiara's phone, silencing her momentarily.

"I have to go, Tucker," she said shortly, obviously irritated.

"Wait, no, I'm sorry!" he said quickly. "Please, help me! What do I do?"

"Do nothing," Kiara instructed, her tone firm. "It sounds like you've done enough, so let David handle it."

"But this is my fault!" Tucker countered.

"David's a big boy. He can handle himself," she said. "Really, I have to go now."

"Okay, fine," he sighed. "Thanks for talking. Have a safe flight."

"I'll text you later, you idiot," Kiara replied, hanging up.

CHAPTER 18

Tucker sat there, fiddling with his seatbelt, and toyed with the idea of sneaking inside to see what was going on, but didn't want to risk making David any more upset with him than he already was. The car was so silent that Tucker could hear a faint ringing in his ears, making him uncomfortable. He opened his social media apps to distract himself, giving up after a few minutes of uninterested scrolling, and huffed impatiently to himself.

He had no idea what was going on inside of the building, but assumed that David would yell at Adrian or try to fight him, and he squirmed uncomfortably at the thought of David getting hurt because of Tucker's stupid decisions. What if Adrian called the cops and David got arrested? Or what if David got seriously injured, and it was all Tucker's fault? He'd never be able to forgive himself, Tucker vowed, biting his lower lip anxiously. He turned on the radio, switching from station to station as they played cheery holiday music, but felt that he wasn't in the Christmas spirit after the events of the last twenty-four hours and turned the radio off again, preferring the silence.

He laid his head back on the seat, closing his eyes and focusing on his breathing, and counted to five as he breathed in and out to mellow himself. He could feel himself spiraling again, this time from a lack of sleep and high levels of anxiety, and was determined to gain control of his own mind once more. He laid his palms flat on his thighs and breathed, in and out again and again, until his eyelids felt heavy, and he gave in to sleep once more, this time quiet and dreamless, bringing Tucker a few moments of peace for the first time since he arrived at Jamie's apartment the day before.

Chapter 19

Tucker woke with a start as David's door slammed shut. He sat in the driver's seat, staring forward with his hands on the steering wheel, and Tucker noticed there was blood on the tips of his swollen purple knuckles and speckled across the right shoulder of his white shirt.

"David, what happened?" Tucker asked, alarmed.

"Doesn't matter," David murmured, turning slowly to look at Tucker. His bottom lip was cut and there was a red mark right under David's eye that was already beginning to bruise. Tucker gasped when he saw David's wounds, all grogginess from his nap now gone.

"Yes, it does!" Tucker argued. "What happened? Are you okay?"

"I'm fine," David said. "I don't want to talk about it."

"Come on, David, just talk to me," Tucker pleaded.

"I'm sure you can piece it together," he replied tersely.

"I'm sure I can too, but I'm trying to talk to you about it," Tucker retorted.

David exhaled sharply through his nose in annoyance at Tucker's persistence, but didn't look away from his challenging stare.

"I told him that what he did to you wasn't right," he said. "The guy actually laughed at me when I said it, like I was the one being ridiculous and not him for kicking you out while you were still drunk in the middle of the night. One thing led to another, and he pushed me, so I hit him and we got into a fight. Happy?"

"David, you didn't have to do that," Tucker breathed.

"I know I didn't, but I did and it's over," David replied, not bothering to hide the agitation in his voice. He threw the gearshift into drive and turned

CHAPTER 19

in the street, heading back to his apartment.

Tucker sat quietly as they drove, getting the hint that David wasn't interested in talking. He didn't know what to think of David's actions. On one hand, Tucker thought it was really brave and noble of David to come to his aid like that and call Adrian out for what he did. On the other, though, he felt mortified that David got into a fight because of him, and a little scared of the rage he was seeing from David for the first time. He'd always been so positive and joyous whenever they'd talked, and he didn't even get the way he was now when he was fighting with Micah at the beach during Thanksgiving break, so his anger was something new for Tucker.

Tucker could almost hear Kiara in his mind telling him that this was yet another sign that David liked him, he realized bitterly, and quickly pushed the idea aside before his emotions latched on. David was only a friend, he reminded himself pointedly, and Tucker was happy David even considered him that after what had happened between them.

When they were back in David's apartment, he quickly checked out his wounds in the bathroom mirror and washed the blood from his hands and lip before telling Tucker to shower, advising him he'd bring him to Jamie's after. Tucker did as he was told, David definitely not seeming like he was in the mood to be argued with, and relished the soothing sensation of the hot water hitting his scalp and rolling down the rest of his body. Soon the bathroom filled with steam, and Tucker exited dressed and feeling refreshed. David was waiting for him on the couch and wordlessly strode to the front door when Tucker pulled his shoes on.

"Ready?" David asked evenly, pulling the door open.

"I think so!" Tucker said cheerfully, trying desperately to lighten the mood. He could feel how tense David was from how he was moving and felt saddened knowing that it was his fault.

He pulled up Jamie's address in his phone's GPS once they were in David's car again, and they drove on the busy highway in a tense silence until Tucker couldn't stand it any longer.

"David, why did you go to Adrian's today?" Tucker asked.

"What that guy did to you wasn't right," David replied. "You're just a kid—he took advantage of you."

"A kid?" Tucker repeated. "David, you're only two years older than me. I already turned nineteen, so I'm not even toeing the legal line anymore. I'm not just a kid."

"Whatever, you know what I mean," he said.

"No, seriously, you need to hear that," Tucker said. "I know you're not into me, and that's totally fine, but I'm not just a kid if you're worried about my age or something."

"God, Tucker, can you drop it? You're new in town, you were drunk, and what he did wasn't okay. I didn't want him to get away with doing that to you."

"But what if he gets you in trouble? What if he calls the cops?" Tucker pressed.

"He's not going to call the cops," David said dismissively. "He pushed me first, so I was only defending myself. And he hit me back, so we're even."

Tucker sighed, giving up on getting through the tough exterior David had put up and resigned to sitting in silence for the rest of the trip. Following the robotic voice coming from Tucker's phone, David turned into Jamie's apartment complex and pulled into an empty spot next to Tucker's parked car.

"Well," Tucker said, feeling awkward, "thanks for the ride. Sorry again for causing so much trouble. I won't bother you with anything like that again."

"Wait," David said as Tucker opened his car door. He reached into the seat behind him and pulled out a plastic gift bag covered in little cartoon Christmas trees and filled with bright red tissue paper. "I meant to give you this last night at your show, but things went a little differently than I assumed they would and I almost forgot."

He placed the bag in Tucker's lap, who sat in his seat stunned. Tucker had only bought presents for his parents—and had done the bare minimum there, getting them gift cards—and hadn't imagined anyone would get gifts for him.

"Just don't open it now," David advised, his lips faintly rising in a half-smile. "It's always awkward to watch someone open a gift."

CHAPTER 19

"Thank you," Tucker breathed. "I'm sorry, I didn't get you anything."

"Don't worry about it," David said. "I didn't expect you to. Don't worry, it's not anything big. I just like to do things for my friends."

"Well, thank you," Tucker repeated, smiling. "Merry Christmas, David."

"Yeah, you too, Tucker," he replied, his smile growing a little more.

Tucker unbuckled his seat belt and exited the car before he could do or say anything to ruin the positive moment they were ending on, quickly crossing the parking lot and running up the stairs to Jamie's apartment. He knocked on the door, and Jamie swung it open moments later, squinting at the sun.

"Hey, girl," she whispered.

"Hey," Tucker said, slipping inside. The apartment was dark, the only light coming in from the windows as it peeked around the curtains. "Are you okay?"

"No, I'm dying," Jamie muttered. "I drank too much and now my body is trying to kill me."

"I'll be quick, then," Tucker promised.

"Your stuff is in the drag room. Merry Christmas. I'm going back to bed," Jamie said, trudging back to her room and closing the door behind her. Tucker crept quietly to the drag room, grabbing his canvas bag that he'd had at the club and his belongings he'd left before the show, and closed the front door quietly behind him as he left.

His mind kept wandering to David's gift, which was sitting in the passenger seat, as he drove back to his dorm, but forbade himself from opening it until he'd packed his suitcase and was ready to go to his parents'. Once he was back in the school parking lot, which was now mostly deserted as everyone went home for the holidays, he grabbed his bags and bounded up the stairwell to his room, throwing everything on his bed when he entered.

He pulled a small suitcase out of his closet and quickly packed a few different outfits, his toiletries, and his parents' gift cards, confidently zipping it closed and grabbing David's nearby gift. The bag felt a little heavy, but not indicative of whatever was inside, Tucker noted, as he sat down on the floor with it. He gingerly pulled the tissue paper out of the bag and set it aside, reaching in once more and grasping something fairly flat with a sharp corner that pressed into Tucker's palm. He pulled it out and realized that he was holding a picture frame, turning it over to see what it held.

Underneath the glass front was a photo of David and Tucker that he didn't recognize. They were standing at Haven's bar, and it looked like David had taken the picture, he thought confusedly. He held the frame a little closer, trying to take in the details captured in the picture taken inside the dark club. Tucker was leaning on the bar, grinning, and David, who was also smiling, had turned to take a picture of the two of them from the other side of it.

"My birthday," Tucker murmured to himself as the realization hit him. It made sense now why he didn't remember the picture—he didn't remember much of anything from that night.

Tucker placed the framed photo upright on his dresser, smiling at the two in the picture. He felt sad, he realized, looking at their captured grins. Things had been so different at the beginning of the semester, and he was certain that whatever friendship had been building with David wouldn't be the same after what'd happened the past two days, whether David wanted to admit it or not.

He pulled his phone out, eager to text Kiara and let her know about the gift, but felt another pang of guilt and put his phone back in his pocket. Talking about David with Kiara had been one of the reasons he'd felt confident enough to kiss him the night prior and knew that bringing the gift up would only fuel that fire once again. He instead fired off a quick text to her, hoping that she'd had a safe trip, and put his phone next to the frame on the dresser. He hopped onto his bed, legs dangling over the side, and looked around the half-empty dorm room, embracing the silence. The halls were technically supposed to be closed while campus was shut down in-between semesters, but Tucker hadn't encountered any issues so far and found no reason to leave while he continued to work in town.

He spent the rest of his day trying to keep himself busy and occupied so his mind wouldn't wander to David or anything else he didn't want to think about, and focused on cleaning his side of the room, organizing his makeup brushes, and other small tasks he'd been avoiding. Happy to be back

CHAPTER 19

in his own bed that night and only slightly dreading visiting his family the following day, he fell asleep quickly.

When Tucker arrived at his parents' house the following afternoon, there was an awkward tension between the three of them as they greeted each other outside of the tinsel-decorated house, but they all sat in the living room to talk at his mother's behest.

"Your father and I have been doing some reading," his mother began once they were all seated, "and we want you to know that we're doing our best to learn and grow. We love you, Tucker, and we just want you to be happy."

Tucker's father nodded, but did not say anything. His mother jabbed his side with her elbow, causing him to grunt in surprise.

"Ken, isn't there something you want to say?" Pam asked, looking at Ken pointedly.

"Not at the moment, no," he replied gruffly. He half-turned toward Tucker, but would not fully look at him as he spoke. "I don't get it, Tucker. Why would you want to be like this?"

"Jesus, Dad, what part of what I said on Thanksgiving did you not understand?" Tucker exclaimed, exasperated at his father's continued ignorance. "I didn't choose anything! This is how I am! Are you stupid—"

"Tucker, that's enough," Pam interrupted, her tone fierce as she turned her pointed stare toward him. "You may be in a disagreement right now, but he is still your father."

"You can't just disagree with who I am—it's not up for debate," Tucker countered, returning her stare with a pointed look of his own.

"Please, enough," she replied, her tone softening.

Ken stood up, walked to the kitchen, and grabbed a beer from the fridge. He cracked the can open, took a hearty slurp, and walked out the front door. "Going to get some firewood," was all he said before the door closed behind him, and Pam sighed with disappointment.

"I appreciate what you're trying to do, Mom," Tucker said. "I'm still the same person you've always known—I just happen to like men instead of women. I guess he just can't accept that."

"I know, honey," Pam reassured him. "I'm just sorry I didn't when you first told me. I'll keep working on him and he'll come around. I promise."

"I know, mom," Tucker said quickly, trying to stop his mother from crying. "You and I are good now, so let's focus on that and move on, okay?" Pam sniffled but nodded with a smile.

Tucker's father returned a half an hour later, not speaking to Tucker but acknowledging him with a slight nod as he passed him, which Tucker took as slight improvement over ignoring his existence completely. He still hadn't forgiven his father for his reaction on Thanksgiving, and wasn't about to give him a free pass for his ignorance, but reasoned that a cautious neutrality wasn't the worst thing that could happen for the two of them during the holiday, if only for the sake of his mother.

The rest of Christmas Eve was spent as it always was for Tucker's family—decorating the Christmas tree while every classic holiday movie they could find on TV played in the background, and eating fast food while they drove around the town and looked at the decorations after dark. The decorations in the major parts of town remained the same over the years—putting a Santa hat on a dolphin statue that stood atop a small fountain, small inflatable snowmen in various parking lots with signs advertising store sales taped to their hands, and most notably, a large dinosaur statue that doubled as a mechanic's garage was covered in lights and tinsel—seeing these same decorations only strengthened his family's tradition, and they enjoyed the soft lights that covered the houses in the different neighborhoods they drove through.

His parents sent Tucker to bed early when they returned home, claiming Santa would be visiting soon, so they could spend the rest of the night doing any late-night gift wrapping without interruption. Tucker laughed and obliged, knowing that they were all fully aware Tucker no longer believed in Santa. He scrolled on his phone as he laid in bed, texting Brooke and the twins to wish them an early Merry Christmas and going through old photos for funny holiday pictures he'd taken in years prior, and came across the video he'd taken of David snoring the last time they were at his parents'.

Tucker sighed sadly, imagining his heart drooping like a cartoon, and his finger hovered over the delete button. He still found the video funny

CHAPTER 19

and had good memories associated with it, but with those memories came romantic feelings for David and the recollection of how happy Tucker'd been getting to share a bed with him. Tucker took a deep breath and pressed delete, the video disappearing with a little clunking sound. He set his phone down next to him and stared at the ceiling, feeling bittersweet about his decision, until his lids closed and he fell asleep.

Christmas morning came and went in a flash, with Tucker and his parents sitting around the tree as they exchanged presents, and he was pleased with the holiday experience he was having with his family, which was the complete opposite of the last time he visited. Kiara had texted him to wish him a Merry Christmas, and he returned the sentiment, feeling pangs of jealousy when she started sending him pictures of the snow she was experiencing with her parents while he was stuck in Florida, sweating.

He helped his mother prepare their dinner, which was much less involved than Thanksgiving. The three of them sat around the table, which was covered in a dark green tablecloth and had little snowmen statues holding it down, and ate in a pleasant silence until they were all too full to move or speak, only groaning in satisfaction. Once Tucker felt that he could stand again, he packed his gifts—a few new outfits, a pair of running shoes, and an insulated water bottle to keep his drinks cool as he walked around campus—hugged his mother goodbye (his father offered a curt nod and offered a lame excuse about needing to use the bathroom), and drove back to Orlando.

Tucker slowly drove around the parking lot outside of his dorm once he was back on UCF's campus, making sure the coast was clear and there was no staff that would catch him entering the hall, before parking in a spot hidden behind a large bush and rushing up to his room.

He laid in his now-familiar twin bed and stared at the white stucco ceiling, letting his mind wander. He thought back to his performance earlier that week, grinning when he imagined himself back onstage in front of the cheering audience, and silently vowed to ask Jamie about getting another gig whenever he saw her next. His thoughts shifted to school, and his smile faded.

After completing a full semester, he still had no idea what he was interested in or what he should major in, and the pressure of talking to other students who knew exactly what they wanted to do didn't help with his decision. He committed to spend his energy correctly in the spring semester and focus on his studies rather than boys. His mind wandered back to David again at the thought of boys, and Tucker felt almost breathless. *Good things come in threes*, he reasoned to himself, and vowed once more to not read into anything David might say or do, despite anything his friends said, and not let David hold this unknown power over him.

Tucker smiled, feeling more optimistic about his future at UCF now that he'd set some goals for himself, and got out of bed to write them down on a piece of paper. He taped it to the wall next to his pillow, and admired his handiwork. His newest poster, which he repeated in his head like a mantra, now read:

1. *Focus on school.*
2. *Focus on drag.*
3. *Focus on anything else but boys.*

Chapter 20

The next few days after Christmas were quiet for Tucker. Campus remained closed, so he stayed holed up in his room, bingeing TV shows he'd been meaning to get around to and re-reading his beat-up copy of one of his desert island book picks, *The Perks of Being a Wallflower*. Kiara flew back to town on December 30th and had volunteered/demanded Tucker pick her up from the airport in an out-of-the-blue phone call that morning.

"I need you to do me a favor," she'd said when he answered the call, which had woken him up from a deep sleep.

"Who did you kill and where are we burying the body?" Tucker asked, rubbing the sleep from his eyes.

"You, if you don't listen!" Kiara laughed. "I'm flying back to Orlando today and I need you to pick me up for the airport at noon."

"I thought you weren't flying back until next week?"

"Yeah, well, plans have changed."

"Are you okay?" Tucker asked, quickly becoming concerned. "Do you want to talk about it?"

"I'm fine, and not right now. I have to pack, so I'll see you at the airport?"

"You can count on me," Tucker replied.

"Thanks, Tucker," Kiara said, sighing with relief.

"Fly safe," he said as Kiara ended the call.

Tucker stared at his phone, his brows furrowed with concern. Kiara could be spontaneous when she wanted to be, but she always stuck with the plan once she had one, so a sudden change in itinerary like this was completely out of the ordinary for her.

He got out of bed, now wide awake despite his original intentions of sleeping in while he still could before classes began again, and quickly showered and dressed to be sure he would be ready to leave in time. Feeling too antsy to sit around, Tucker left early for the airport, parking with plenty of time to spare.

He stopped at a coffee shop inside the airport on his way to Kiara's terminal and bought them both coffees from a particularly attractive barista named Zachariah, a guy around his age with warm brown skin and a dazzling smile surrounded on either side by deep dimples in his cheeks, predicting she'd need it after this sudden change of plans. Gripping the two steaming cups, Tucker found an open seat in a row of vinyl chairs that were all connected and separated by the metal armrests on either side, and sat to wait for Kiara's plane to arrive within the next half hour.

Tucker felt his phone buzzing in his pocket, so he balanced both coffees in one hand while the other fished his phone out, blindly answering the call, in case it was Kiara.

"Hey, girl," Jamie greeted him.

"Oh, hey!" Tucker said. "How are you?"

"You know, the usual—gorgeous, glamourous, amazing, humble," Jamie replied. Tucker could imagine her checking herself out in her vanity mirror while she spoke, which made him grin. "Are you working the New Year's Eve show tomorrow?"

"No, I'm actually off, so I won't be there."

"Well, why the hell not, Mary? Come see the show! Tip your mother!"

"Okay, fine!" Tucker laughed. "Can I come by your apartment first to hang out with you and the girls?"

"Sure, if you want. But after last time, you're driving yourself! I will not be responsible for your drunk ass again."

"You're the one that got me messed up in the first place! Remember the edibles you gave me?" Tucker pointed out. An older woman sitting two seats away looked at him with alarm, and he shrunk a little in his seat, his cheeks warm with embarrassment.

"Tucker, you're a minor. I would *never* give you alcohol—or god forbid,

CHAPTER 20

drugs! Those are illegal!" Jamie cried with fake shock. "And if you ever tell anyone otherwise, I'll set what little drag you have on fire. Capisce?"

The monitor in front of Kiara's terminal changed its display, indicating that her plane had arrived and would be disembarking soon. Tucker smiled, eager to see his friend again after being away for almost two weeks.

"Understood. Listen, I'm at the airport picking up my friend right now, so I have to go. I'll text you tomorrow when I'm on my way over, okay?"

"Sounds good. Bye, girl."

Tucker shoved his phone back in his pocket and took a long drink from his coffee cup, cringing as the scalding beverage hit his mouth and blistered his tongue. One of the airport's staff members, a bored-looking brunette in her late forties that bore a nametag labeled Karen, opened the terminal doors and people began flowing out from the plane. He watched as an older man slowly made his way through the doorway and into the airport, meeting the woman who'd heard Tucker on the phone earlier and pulling her into a long hug, the two laughing as they swayed back and forth.

Finally, Kiara emerged from the crowd of people disembarking, sporting a velvet pink jumpsuit and a matching backpack, and rushed to Tucker, pulling him into a hug.

"I am so glad to see you," she said, her voice muffled in his shoulder.

"Me too," Tucker laughed, his arms outstretched so he didn't spill coffee all over her. He handed one of the cups to her when she pulled away, which she took graciously and drank.

"Oh my god, you're a genius," she said once she'd stopped drinking. She wrapped her arm around his torso, leading him toward the baggage claim area.

"Not that I'm complaining," Tucker said once they'd found her bags and loaded them into Tucker's car, "but why are you back so soon? What happened?"

"Ugh, family drama," Kiara said, checking her eye makeup in the visor mirror above her seat as Tucker drove. "It was awful, Tucker. My parents didn't even invite my sister over for Christmas! I knew they weren't speaking, but I thought they'd at least pretend to make nice during the holidays, especially with me coming back home after moving away for school."

"And I'm assuming you called them out on it?"

"I sure as hell did!" Kiara said, snapping the visor closed and turning to look at Tucker. "It's completely unfair! They're acting like bigots, so Leticia has to suffer for it? They're both college professors, for god's sake, so you'd think they'd be a little more educated on what it *actually* means to be queer by now!"

"So what happened? They kick you out too or something?"

"I wish they would have tried! Michael and Virginia would have never heard from me again, I can guarantee you that. No, they tried to act like everything was normal, and I made sure to bring Leticia up every day so that they were uncomfortable. As they should be, cutting ties with their daughter over who she is, what she can't help—I was *furious* with them, Tucker. It's like they were kicking her out all over again. They're so smart—Dad teaches chemical engineering and Mom teaches veterinary medicine, both at Washington State—but they were just being so fucking *stupid*! Finally, I couldn't stand it anymore and I changed my plane ticket."

"And they just let you? They preferred you left rather than talk about your sister?"

"Now you see why I'm so mad!" Kiara yelled. "The whole situation was just so ass-backwards. I felt like I was in *The Twilight Zone* or something."

"Yeah, no wonder you're upset! I would be too if I were you!" Tucker said. "Did you get in contact with your sister, at least?"

"Oh, yeah, we talk all the time. She totally called it, but I was hoping she'd be wrong this time. She acts like she's fine with how it all went down now, but I know that's not true."

"As long as you're there for her, that's all you can do."

"I know," Kiara sighed. "So, anyway, that's how things went for me. How was your Christmas? Any luck with the whole David situation?"

Tucker snorted, shooting her a skeptical look. "No, absolutely no luck with the David situation. He gave me a Christmas present the last time I saw him—you know, after I tried to kiss him, then *ran away in the middle of the night* and he had to come get me, then later went back and fought

CHAPTER 20

Adrian—so I'm even more confused now than ever. I shouldn't be, I guess, because he made things crystal-clear when I tried to make a move, but then he gave me a present. Who does that?

"A really, really nice guy and a good friend, that's who," Tucker said before Kiara could respond. "Christmas was... fine. Things are better with Mom, Dad barely acknowledged me, so it kind of evened everything out."

What Tucker had failed to mention, though, is that he'd felt so bad about everything that'd happened with David before Christmas that he'd bought him a late Christmas/apology gift, which was currently bagged up and hidden under his seat—David's three desert island movies: *Love, Actually, Mamma Mia!,* and *Legally Blonde.* He didn't know when he'd have the chance to give it to him, but he knew he'd feel better when he did.

"I hope you've learned your lesson with Adrian, you idiot," Kiara grumbled.

"Trust me, I definitely have. I'm so sorry I snapped at you when I told you what was going on—you were completely right and I was selfish."

The two continued catching up as Tucker drove them back to campus, helping Kiara bring her bags back to her dorm once they'd parked. They said their goodbyes outside of Kiara's lobby as she lugged her large black suitcase through the doorway, and Tucker followed the now-familiar path back to his building.

He'd just exited the stairway on his floor when his phone buzzed, and he answered the call quickly when he saw it was Kiara calling.

"Ki', is everything okay?"

"Want to have a sleepover?" Kiara asked from the other line. "This whole situation with my parents really pissed me off, but it also made me really upset and I could use some company."

"I'll be right over," Tucker promised, ending the call. He changed into sweatpants and a t-shirt, grabbed his pillow, comforter, and phone charger from his room, balling it all up into one large bundle, and made the quick trip back to Kiara's dorm.

She met him at the lobby doors, a sad smile on her face, and led them back up to her softly lit dorm room, where they spent the rest of their day watching movies Kiara picked and painting their nails—dark blue for

Tucker, fuchsia for Kiara—two best friends content just to be in each other's company again.

***

Tucker arrived at Jamie's the next day, Kiara in tow, as the sun was setting behind the apartment building. Crystal answered the door, a look of surprise on her face as she flashed her brilliant white smile.

"Well, hey, Miss Karma!"

"Hey, Crystal," Tucker chuckled, giving Crystal a quick hug. "This is my friend, Kiara."

"Hi, I'm Crystal Waters," Crystal greeted, extending a yellow-clawed hand to Kiara, who shook it before flipping it over to admire her nails.

"I love this yellow, Crystal!" Kiara said.

"I like her already," Crystal said to Tucker, winking at Kiara. She ushered the two of them inside, and they could hear Jamie and Kitty arguing from the drag room. "We're getting ready, so come on back."

The three of them followed the noise, gingerly opening the drag room door and peering inside.

"I'm telling you, bitch, I didn't steal your damn flash drive!" Jamie snapped, her hair pulled back in a ponytail and wearing a dark green silk robe.

"Well, you used it last week, so you should know where it is!" Kitty retorted, who stood across the room shirtless in a pair of pink sweatpants.

"And I gave it back to you after the show! Maybe if your room wasn't a damn mess all the time, you could find it!"

"Ladies, we have company!" Crystal loudly interrupted, earning nasty looks from both queens.

"Hey," Jamie greeted them blandly. Kitty offered a tightlipped smile, and Tucker laughed at their dramatics.

"This is my friend, Kiara. That's my drag mother, Jamie, and this is Kitty," Tucker said, pointing to each person.

"Hey, girl," Jamie said to Kiara. "You want to do drag too? If Tucker

CHAPTER 20

brought you over for that, sorry, but I'm done having kids."

"No, not me. Can girls do drag?" Kiara asked, looking between Jamie and Tucker. "I just thought it was a thing for gay guys."

"Miss Thing, anybody can do drag!" Crystal said, waving her hand as if to dispel Kiara's question like a cloud of smoke.

"Cool," Kiara smiled.

After the introductions were done and everyone went back to what they were doing, Tucker followed Crystal back to her room while Jamie and Kitty continued to argue.

"What's their problem, Crystal? I heard something about a flash drive?" Tucker asked.

"Girl, that's just the tip of the iceberg. They argue about *everything*," Crystal sighed, turning the light on in her room. Crystal had the master bedroom, which was cream-colored and had palm leaf wallpaper along the walls; there were two soft pink chairs to the left side of the room and a large queen bed in the middle with a matching palm leaf bedspread. To the right was a large metal clothes rack, where all of Crystal's drag hung, two large plastic crates full of various types of heels, and Styrofoam wig heads hung from the walls, each sporting a different colored and styled wig.

Kiara gasped dramatically as she entered, her hands flying to her mouth in surprise. "It looks just like Blanche's room in *The Golden Girls*!"

"She likes my nails *and* knows her references! Karma, you have good taste in friends," Crystal said. "Kiara, come try on a wig. I want to show you how anyone can be a queen!"

Tucker sat in one of the soft pink chairs, laughing as Crystal pulled a wig cap over Kiara's hair and placed a bright yellow wig that matched Crystal's nails on her head.

"See?" Crystal said, turning Kiara toward the vanity mirror tucked in the corner by the clothes rack. "Slap on some makeup, five pairs of tights, and some heels, and you're a drag queen! Isn't it fun?"

"I need to buy so many wigs right now," Kiara breathed, a huge smile on her face as she analyzed herself in the mirror. Crystal turned toward Tucker, looking amused, and he quickly pulled out his phone and snapped a picture while Kiara wasn't looking.

"Okay, girl, don't go stealing my hair now," Crystal eventually said, pulling the wig off of Kiara and placing it back on the wig head. "I'm wearing that tonight, so you'll see it again soon."

Kiara sat in the chair next to Tucker and watched as Crystal painted, careful strokes and light patting from a variety of makeup brushes that resulted in the gorgeous, stage-ready mug of Crystal Waters over an hour later. She put the finishing touches on her makeup, swiping a bright red lipstick in the middle of her lips and pressing them together, forming a perfect pouty lip when she pulled them apart again.

"And *that*, darlings, is how we do drag in the Waters family," Crystal said, eyeing them in her mirror.

"Do you have any kids, Crystal?" Tucker asked.

"Not here in Orlando," she replied, pressing one more layer of banana-colored powder on the apples of her cheeks to bring out her highlight. "I'm from Atlanta, so I've got a lot of drag family there. My late mother, Sophie Waters, was there until she passed five years ago, and I've got a few kids—Sara Sota, Addie Tude, Stormi Waters, to name a few—but I moved down here almost eight years ago now and said my tubes were tied, dear! Now I'm just the fun auntie for new queens, like you."

"She bringing out the whole family tree again?" Jamie joked as she entered Crystal's room, her makeup fully done.

"No, I'm just talking to *your* daughter about being a successful drag mother, whore!" Crystal retorted, tossing a makeup brush towards Jamie, who laughed as she ducked.

"Crystal boring y'all in here?" Jamie asked Tucker and Kiara, ignoring Crystal's remark.

"Not at all!" Kiara said. "I've always thought drag queens were so fun and glamorous, so I loved getting to watch Crystal get ready."

"I'm about to tuck, so you might not want to watch me get ready anymore," Crystal laughed. Tucker tapped Kiara on the arm, and the two stood, moving to the kitchen and closing Crystal's door behind them.

Having now been to their apartment a few times, Tucker felt comfortable

CHAPTER 20

enough there to not ask for things and went to the fridge, taking out two water bottles and tossing one to Kiara. Kitty came out of her room, makeup done and fully dressed in a white and red sequined jumpsuit with a matching red wig braided down her back, and joined them.

"You find your flash drive, Kitty?" Tucker asked, hoping it was an innocent question and wouldn't set her off all over again.

"Yeah, no thanks to *your* mother!" Kitty said, rolling her eyes. "It was in my makeup bag."

"I told you I didn't have it, bitch!" Jamie yelled from the drag room.

"Nobody's talking to you, you ugly cow!" Kitty yelled back. Kiara's eyes widened, and Kitty laughed at her reaction. "It's all in good fun, I promise."

"It's not going to be so fun when I snap the heels off of all your ugly-ass shoes!" Jamie said, joining them in the kitchen in a skimpy silver strapless dress covered in rhinestones. Her hair was pulled up even tighter than before, and she bore a ponytail that matched her natural hair color and stretched down to her knees.

"Try it, I dare you," Kitty warned, pouring two shots of vodka and passing one to Jamie, who threw her head back as she swallowed it.

Kiara turned to Tucker, a confused look on her face, and Tucker just shrugged and smiled. Their words were venomous, but Tucker had grown fairly accustomed to how cutthroat the queens were to each other without any real malice behind what they said. Now Tucker found it entertaining to watch.

Once Crystal joined them, wearing the same bright yellow wig Kiara'd tried on earlier and a sparkling one-sleeved black sequined mini dress that accentuated her long legs, the group departed for the club. True to what Jamie said, Tucker and Kiara drove in his car, while the queens piled into Crystal's.

There was some traffic on the highway as they neared downtown, so it was already after 11:00 by the time Tucker and Kiara parked in the gravel lot at Haven that evening. They headed inside, Tucker grabbing David's gift before locking his car, and weaved their way through the crowded lobby once they got through security. As always, the music was pumping through the club, the vibrations prevalent in the mirrors on the walls.

The inside of the club was just as busy as the lobby, and Shane and David were both working the bar that evening, each taking one side of the bar to assist the long lines of patrons that had formed. Tucker and Kiara joined David's line, moving to the music as they waited for their turn. When they were next, they approached the bar while David wasn't looking, and bore an obvious look of surprise when he made eye contact with Tucker.

"Hey!" he said, sounding just as surprised as he looked.

"Hey. I know you're busy, so I'll be quick," Tucker shouted over the music. "Can we just get two waters?"

"Sure thing," David replied, turning to fill up two plastic cups. He placed them on the bar with two small black napkins underneath, which Kiara took.

"Thanks," Tucker said, tipping David a five-dollar bill.

"Oh, no, you don't have—"

"I know, but I want to. You're working your ass off tonight, so let me tip you since I'm not buying a real drink."

"Thanks, Tucker," David said, offering him a small smile.

"And this is for you," Tucker said, placing the small green paper bag on the bar. "Merry Christmas." He turned, stepping out of line and leading Kiara to the dance floor.

"That was so smooth!" Kiara yelled in his ear.

"I thought I was going to throw up. I was so nervous," Tucker laughed, taking his water from Kiara's hand. He quickly drank, throwing the empty cup in a nearby trash can, and the two maneuvered through the dance floor until they found some space under the disco ball in the middle of the room. They danced to two songs, jumping around and flailing their arms, before the drag show started, hosted by Crystal.

She introduced the first queen, someone Tucker hadn't seen perform before named Farrah Nuff, who Tucker and Kiara tipped as she made her way around the room lipsyncing an R&B song that Tucker didn't recognize, but Kiara obviously did as she mouthed the words along with Farrah. The next queen was Kitty, who unleashed a multitude of flips and splits to a remixed Cher song, and was showered with dollar bills by the end of her number.

Jamie was after Kitty, who performed a burlesque number and was practically naked by the end of the song, sporting two silver pasties on her breasts and a matching silver thong, which made Kiara scream and jump up and down as she stripped, throwing handfuls of dollar bills at Jamie. With five minutes left before midnight, Crystal closed the show, performing Pink's "Raise Your Glass", complete with a shot from the bar before lipsyncing the beginning of the bridge—*Aw, shit, my glass is empty. That sucks!*—which earned enormous cheers from the audience.

The number finished with a minute to spare, and the whole club counted down to midnight together. The excitement of what was to come in the New Year was palpable throughout the building, and Tucker could feel it too, a fluttering feeling in his gut. When the clock struck midnight, bringing in the New Year, the crowd cheered, music blared, and everyone found someone to kiss. Tucker and Kiara turned to each other, shrugged, and quickly kissed, giggling once it was over.

"Yeah, I am *so* gay," Tucker laughed, earning a light punch in the arm from Kiara, which made them both laugh. Tucker's phone buzzed in his pocket, and he quickly checked it to be sure it wasn't an emergency. It was a text from David, who Tucker could see was no longer at the bar.

DAVID: Just opened your present—I love it! Thanks a lot, Tuck. Merry Christmas.

Tucker smiled at David's message, closed out of it, and put his phone away. It was a new year now, he reasoned, and he wouldn't be succumbing to Last Year Tucker's bad habits—*focus on school, focus on drag, focus on anything else but boys*. A new song began to play and Kiara grabbed Tucker's hands, forcing him to jump around and dance with her, which they did the rest of the night, both thankful for the other's company as they rang in the New

Year.

III

Part Three: Spring

Chapter 21

In the weeks leading up to the spring semester's start in the early weeks of January, Tucker was proud of the work he'd put into bettering himself. After New Year's Day passed, he'd asked to regularly pick more shifts up at the club and now worked Wednesday through Monday nights, putting whatever money he didn't need immediately in a savings account his mom opened for him years ago that had remained untouched.

The first few nights back at work, Tucker was scared that Adrian would show up, but there had been no sign of him since their last meeting at his apartment before Christmas. Tucker was focused on his work, making sure he was smiling and chatting with the patrons he met, winking back at the older men playfully flirting with him, and not stopping to talk with David at the bar every chance he got.

David had seemed aloof since their last meeting as well, barely acknowledging Tucker whenever they worked together, but Tucker reminded himself that it was for the best if he planned to stick to his goals. *Focus on school, focus on drag, focus on anything else but boys,* he thought whenever he could feel himself wanting to talk to David or text him. So far, it had worked to Tucker's benefit. He was making more money each night and wasn't experiencing the same pangs of sadness and loneliness whenever he saw David at work or had a passing thought of him.

He'd talked to Jamie about doing more shows at Haven, but was disappointed when she told him the Christmas show was a one-time thing because of another performer dropping out of the show last-minute. She assured him, though, that she would call him if there was ever another opening.

He'd hoped for a better answer, but reminded himself that he was still what the other performers referred to as a "baby queen", and that his time would eventually come if he continued to put in the work. He'd continued to paint when he had free time, pleased enough with his makeup to post on a new social media account he'd created for Karma Kahlo, and Kiara had even stopped by his room a few times to do her makeup with him. He was secretly pleased with himself when her finished drag look didn't come out as well as his, but commended her bold choices and laughed when she threw a makeup brush at him in response.

He'd also remained firm in his decision to focus more on school, and enrolled in more classes than he had the previous semester—English Composition 2, Math For Non-Majors, World History, American Government, Computer Sciences, and American Literature—determined to redeem himself from his tumultuous academic experiences from the previous semester. Within the first week of attending the classes, all held in auditorium-style rooms so large that his professors all wore microphones to ensure they could be heard, he'd realized just how big of a challenge he'd signed up for. He had already been assigned two papers, four assigned readings, and a test all due by the end of the second week of the semester, and Tucker had never felt so stressed.

When the semester began and Mike didn't show up, Tucker had asked the Resident Assistant for his building, an overly perky redhead named Denise, if she knew what happened to him.

"Oh, you didn't know?" Denise asked.

"No, that's why I'm asking you," Tucker said, feeling annoyed. "Is he okay?"

"Oh, he's fine!" she assured him. "He just dropped out is all. So his portion of your room will remain empty for now, and if we get a surplus of new students within the next couple of weeks, we'll assign one to your room."

"Dropped out?" Tucker asked in disbelief.

"Believe me—it happens all the time," Denise said with a chuckle.

"Okay, well, thanks for letting me know," Tucker said with a wary look. He went back to his room, scrolling through all of his text messages until he found one from Mike from the beginning of the semester, and called the

CHAPTER 21

number. He hadn't saved Mike's number because he didn't think he'd need it, but was kicking himself for not doing it sooner now that he needed to contact him. The phone rang multiple times, and Tucker was about to end the call right as Mike answered.

"Mike, hey, it's Tucker from school," Tucker said, relieved to hear for himself that Mike was alive and presumably fine.

"Oh, hey! What's going on, man?" Mike asked, sounding good-natured as usual.

"You tell me!" Tucker said with a laugh. "School's started and you aren't here. The RA said you dropped out?"

"Yeah, that's true," he confirmed. "I tried for a semester, but I just really wasn't happy in school. When I told my parents during the break, they told me I didn't have to go back if I didn't want to and my dad offered me a job at his roofing company! Isn't that awesome?"

"Totally," Tucker lied. "Okay, well, I won't keep you. I just wanted to make sure you were alive."

"Thanks, Tucker," Mike said appreciatively. "You're a cool guy. I'm really glad I met you."

"Thanks, Mike," Tucker said, smiling at his compliment. "You are too. Good luck with the roofing business."

For the first few days after the call, Tucker felt weird touching Mike's side of the room. He felt like Mike would come through the door at any moment to reclaim his space, but eventually accepted that he now had the room to himself and promptly redecorated; pushing furniture around to open the room up more and lowering Mike's bed until it was desk-height.

Tucker was now in the middle of his second week of classes and sat at his makeshift desk, multiple textbooks open for different classes, scrambling to make sense of his different assignments. He hadn't been able to talk to Kiara much since classes began again, and it'd been radio silence from David aside from when they had to talk to each other at work. *Focus on school, focus on drag, focus on anything else but boys,* he reminded himself.

He stopped, putting the pencil he'd been flicking around in his hand down, and had the fleeting thought—*is this worth it?* He still had no idea what he wanted to major in, or what he wanted to do with his life, so was the stress he was already feeling worth it to him? He could follow in Mike's footsteps and just drop out, he reasoned, but what would he do instead? Mike had a backup plan, but Tucker had nothing aside from his job and his schoolwork. He sighed, resigned to his fate for the next four years, and picked his pencil up again, scanning one of the textbooks on his bed until he found the paragraph he was looking for, underlining details about the three branches of government that he'd need to study for his test on Friday.

He took a look at his phone and dropped it in shock, shooting out of his chair and racing to his closet, changing into his usual work uniform of a form-fitting black t-shirt and a pair of tight jean shorts.

"Shit, shit, shit, I'm so late," he whispered to himself frantically. Once he slipped his sneakers on, he sprinted out of his room and down the stairs to the lobby, throwing the door to the parking lot open and running to his car.

He started the engine before he even closed his door and shot out of the parking lot, barely making it out of campus and onto one of the main connecting roads before the traffic light turned red. He turned sharply to get into the right lane that merged onto the highway, waving his hand behind him in apology as a car honked indignantly.

"Okay, you're fine," Tucker said to himself, trying to calm down as he rocketed down the highway towards Haven. "You're an hour late, but maybe they won't notice!"

"Who am I kidding? Of course they're going to notice," Tucker groaned in response to his own words.

A car in front of him was going too slow for his liking, so he swerved in and out of lanes until he was in front of it, cursing softly to himself the whole time and keeping an eye on his rear-view mirrors for police cars. After what seemed like an eternity to Tucker, he saw the exit sign he needed to take and pulled off of the highway, willing every traffic light to stay green so he could get to the club as fast as possible.

The first light he encountered was red, and he pounded on his steering wheel in frustration at both the light's awful timing and his own mistake. This wasn't the first time that he'd been careless with his timing since classes

CHAPTER 21

began in the new semester, and he was furious with himself for letting it happen again. When it finally turned green, Tucker turned and was fortunate enough to catch the remaining two green lights he needed before he could pull into the club's packed parking lot and into the first spot he found. He threw the door open and ran as fast as he could across the gravel parking lot, praying that Shane, the newly appointed bar manager, wasn't the one working that night.

Chapter 22

Tucker rounded the corner and weaved in and out of groups standing idly by as they huddled around each other in the cold evening weather, chatting and smoking by tall ashtrays, and waved to Ned as he jogged passed the bouncer. To Tucker's dismay, Shane was the bartender on duty that night, and was working double-time to get drink orders from the patrons crowding the bar on all sides. Tucker wordlessly grabbed a tray that was sitting on the back corner of the bar and hurried to the dance floor, hoping to make up for lost time.

Though the parking lot was packed, the club itself wasn't busy, so Tucker found himself watching the small groups on the dance floor and standing around helplessly while Shane worked through the people gathered around him at the bar. Jamie and Kitty were milling around the dance floor, chatting with random patrons in matching gold and silver sequined mini-dresses that Tucker'd heard Jamie previously refer to as "tipping dresses", Kitty sporting a blonde wig and Jamie donning a sleek black ponytail that brushed her lower back, and made their way over to him when they ran out of people to talk to. Tucker finally understood why she called them tipping dresses as he witnessed patrons hand them dollars just for walking around in drag and made a mental note to incorporate that into his night whenever he got his next gig.

"Hey, girl," Jamie greeted, dropping a dollar on his tray for a shot, throwing her head back and swallowing the liquid.

"Hey, stranger," Kitty said as she approached, following Jamie's lead and buying a shot, throwing her head back in a more exaggerated way than Jamie

CHAPTER 22

and grimacing as she swallowed the alcohol.

"Hey Kitty, how are you?" Tucker asked, chuckling at her dramatic reaction to the shot.

"You know, looking beautiful, living my life," Kitty replied, playing with her wig, which was teased into a large ball of blonde clumps of hair.

"When do you plan to start looking beautiful, after we leave?" Jamie asked, smirking at her own joke.

"Bitch, don't start," Kitty laughed, pointing a warning finger at Jamie.

"Do you have a show tonight? I must have my days mixed up," Tucker wondered aloud, getting the queens' attentions again.

"No, the manager asked us to come in to help promote our show nights. Feels kind of pointless, but hey, they're paying my ass to be here, so whatever," Jamie replied flippantly, gesturing to the small crowd.

"Want to go smoke?" Kitty offered, looking at Jamie.

"I thought you'd never ask," she replied, waving goodbye to Tucker as the two sauntered off toward the smoking area outside.

After a half an hour of attempted sales, Tucker heard his name being called and turned to see Shane motioning him to come to the now-empty bar. Tucker sighed, bracing himself for whatever happened next, and fixed a cheerful look on his face as he walked to the bar.

"Hey, Shane," Tucker said, keeping his tone light and friendly. "Not too many people buying shots out there tonight."

"Tucker, where were you?" Shane asked, visibly irritated. "This is the third time in two weeks you've been late!"

"I'm so sorry," Tucker apologized frantically. "School started last week and I've just been so busy with homework and lost track of time. I swear, it won't happen again."

"Well, I'm glad you're not denying it," Shane said, eyeing Tucker, "but I can only give you so much grace. I'm taking you off of the schedule for a couple of weeks so you can figure your life out."

"What?" Tucker yelped. He'd expected a reprimand, but was shocked to hear his punishment. "Please, give me one more chance!"

"Trust me," Shane said, "me not firing you today is giving you one more chance. We all like working with you, Tucker, but you have to be at work for that to happen. I'll let you know when you're back on the schedule, alright?"

Tucker squared his jaw, fighting the embarrassed tears forming in his eyes, and nodded silently, not trusting his voice to remain level.

"Here, pass me the tray," Shane instructed, holding out his hand. Tucker handed it over, not making eye contact. "Go home, do your homework, and we'll see you again soon, okay?"

"Sure thing," Tucker mumbled, looking at the ground as he turned and walked away. Thick tears rolled slowly down his cheeks as he hurried through the mirror-lined hallway and out the front doors to where his car was parked in the gravel lot. He sat in the driver's seat, not even bothering to turn the engine on, and let the tears fall freely. He hated that he was an emotional crier, and knew these were not tears of sadness, but of embarrassment, shame, and self-judgement. He mentally kicked himself for not setting an alarm, remembering bitterly how sure he was that he'd be able to just remember when he had work and when he needed to leave.

Tucker took a deep breath, wiping his face with his hands, and started the car. He felt odd driving home from Haven so early in the evening, but tried to spin his suspension positively as he drove. At least he'd be able to have more time for homework and studying, and maybe he'd even get to hang out with Kiara again soon. *Focus on school, focus on drag, focus on anything else but boys,* he reminded himself for the millionth time.

When he got back to his dorm, he devoted the next three hours to homework at his makeshift desk, alternating between studying for his American Government test on Friday, researching credible sources to use for his papers, and flipping through chapters of Charlotte Brontë's *Jane Eyre* without comprehending what he was reading. Tucker checked his phone for the time and was shocked to see it was well after midnight, which was later than he'd planned to work on his assignments. He sighed in defeat and pressed on, turning to his laptop and opening up one of his soon-to-be-due papers.

Tucker didn't know when he fell asleep, but woke with a start when his alarm started to blare from his phone's speaker, his face tearing away from

CHAPTER 22

the bare mattress it'd become suctioned to in his sleep. He silenced it, quickly stretching as he stood up before heading to the bathroom. As he showered, his mind swirled with thoughts of his upcoming assignments, facts he tried desperately to retain for his test the next day, snippets of *Jane Eyre* that he could recall but made no sense of, all in a horrific mental tornado of impending academic doom that made Tucker sit on the beige-tiled shower floor with his head between his legs as he attempted to calm his pounding heart and hyperactive breathing.

I think I'm having a panic attack, Tucker thought to himself in alarm. His chest felt constricted, and though he was breathing fast and deep, it felt like he couldn't get any air into his lungs. He had no idea how long he sat on the floor, letting the water rush over him, but was eventually able to calm down enough to stand and collect himself. He shut off the shower, feeling shaken, and quickly dressed. He began to pack his materials back into his backpack for class, but seeing them made his heart pound once again, and he placed everything back on the bare mattress he used as a desk. Tucker felt a pressure on his chest, unsure of what to do—should he attend his classes, or use the time to work on his assignments?

Tucker brought his things over to his bed, ultimately deciding to take the day off from classes and use it for homework, and fired off emails to each of his professors, apologizing for missing class and claiming he was violently ill. He took a moment to lay back and relax before diving back into his work, staring at his ceiling as he focused on keeping his breathing slow and under control. He grabbed his phone and called Kiara, desperate to talk with someone, but her phone went to voicemail and Tucker hung up without leaving a message. His phone pinged with a text alert shortly after, and he smiled when he saw it was from Kiara.

KIARA: Sorry, heading to class. You good?

TUCKER: Honestly, not really. School's made me so stressed already. Can we hang out soon and decompress?

KIARA: Maybe, but my schedule's looking pretty packed right now. My classes this semester are no joke!

TUCKER: Same here. I think I just had a panic attack thinking about everything that's due tomorrow...

KIARA: Tell me about it! I'm stressing too.

TUCKER: No, I seriously think I just had a panic attack.

Kiara didn't respond right away, and after a few minutes of waiting, Tucker gave up on another reply. Tucker sighed and placed his phone down on its screen so he wouldn't get distracted, and worked more on his papers, finishing his first one for his English Composition 2 class and shifting his attention to his research paper for World History.

After a few hours of writing, Tucker decided to take a break and checked his phone for any updates from Kiara. He hadn't received any more texts, but had received multiple notifications from the account he'd made online for drag. Confused by the sudden burst of attention online, he opened the app and scanned the new comments on his pictures. They were from accounts he didn't recognize, and were all hurtful messages calling him disgusting, making fun of his makeup, and even a few telling him to kill himself.

Who were these people, and why were they attacking him? What had he done to anger these strangers? He checked the alerts he had for his direct messages, and was shocked to see they'd messaged him directly as well, rephrasing and repeating the same things they'd written under his pictures. Tucker quickly deleted them, stunned by the negative attention he'd received for no real reason. He took a screenshot of the comments and texted them to Jamie for advice, not knowing how to handle the situation. Sure, he'd encountered a few homophobes growing up and tried his hardest not to

CHAPTER 22

let what they said bother him, but he'd never been harassed online like this before and was bewildered by it.

Tucker rubbed his eyes with his hands and ran them through his hair, willing himself to focus on the important issues at hand, which were his homework assignments. He took a big breath to prepare himself, and dove back into his work, fingers flying over the keyboard as he rushed to finish another assignment. He felt his stomach rumble, realizing he hadn't eaten yet, but ignored it as he continued, desperate to finish his work. With little confidence, Tucker finalized his second paper after a few more hours and shut his laptop, turning to the thick novel he'd been assigned and groaning when he realized he still had over half of it to read before his class the next day.

Tucker laid in bed the rest of the day, unmoving as he scanned page after page of *Jane Eyre* without really paying attention to the story until he was over two-thirds of the way finished. He stopped, startled when he turned to the window and saw that it was already dark outside, and switched his novel out for his American Government textbook. Tucker vaguely understood politics, but was having an awful time retaining information so far in the course and was determined to pass his upcoming test. He scanned the four chapters they'd covered so far in the two weeks of classes, paying close attention to passages he'd underlined and quizzing himself under his breath as he covered the definitions of terms explained within the textbook with his hand. He quickly became frustrated, not getting many terms correct, and slammed the book shut.

Mentally exhausted from a day full of homework, Tucker put his study materials back into his backpack and left his room, heading down the stairs and out the door toward Knightro's. The night sky was clear and the winter air was chilling as Tucker made the short trek to the dining hall, crossing his arms in a futile attempt to retain some body heat. There had been few changes in the menu since the previous semester, so Tucker grabbed his now-familiar meal of a burger and salad and found a small table away from where large groups of students were gathered and laughing. He stared down at his food while he ate, trying to block out the other people in the building as he quizzed himself again in his head.

After his plates were cleared, and with little success mentally answering his own questions, Tucker dumped them in the designated dish area and walked glumly back to his room. Now that the evening air was finally cold, students were enticed to stay outside longer as they chatted or did homework together. Tucker vaguely recognized a small cluster of students from his Math for Non-Majors class on his walk, but said nothing as he walked by. When he got back to his room, Tucker couldn't bring himself to take his textbook out again and opted for a good night's sleep instead, praying that everything he was trying to learn would cement in his brain overnight. He crawled into bed, sighing in contentment as he laid on his side and curled his legs to get comfortable, and stared at the sign he kept taped to the wall as he fell asleep. *Focus on school, focus on drag, focus on anything else but boys...*

Chapter 23

By the time Tucker was finished with his classes late Friday afternoon, he'd wished he'd skipped the day altogether. He'd nervously turned in both of his papers and was able to mumble through a discussion about *Jane Eyre* without it being too obvious that he hadn't finished the novel, but had completely forgotten about the readings he'd also been assigned in World History on top of his research assignment and one in Computer Sciences, making both lectures extremely confusing for Tucker as they referenced the reading heavily. His last class of the day was American Government, and he exited the building that afternoon with his stomach in knots. Out of the thirty questions on the test, he'd felt confident about two of his answers, and prayed that he'd guessed correctly on the others.

Though the sun was high in the cloudless sky, the air was chilled and seemed to cut through every thick layer of clothing Tucker had on, and he stuck his hands deep in his pockets as he walked across campus towards Knightro's to fill himself with anything vaguely comforting. As he crossed the small wooden bridge that led to the back entrance of the Student Union, he caught the eye of his Astronomy professor from the previous semester, Professor Thomas. She was walking in his direction dressed in a very fashionable-looking black coat and a thick crimson scarf tossed over her shoulder, and smiled at him as they approached each other.

"Mister Peterson," Professor Thomas greeted warmly, stepping to the side to allow other students to pass by.

"Professor Thomas! It's nice to see you," Tucker smiled, following her lead and stepping aside.

"Likewise," she said, her eyes crinkling behind her glasses as she smiled. "How is your semester going so far?"

"It's so much harder than the last one," Tucker answered truthfully. "I would gladly trade most of my classes to take yours again."

"I'm flattered," Professor Thomas chuckled, pushing the thick black frames higher up on her slender nose. "I know you're a very bright student, so I'm sure you're just being hard on yourself."

"Thank you, but I doubt it," Tucker said with a laugh.

"I wouldn't be so sure," she said knowingly. "I see it happen all the time. Things are often worse in your head than they actually are."

"Maybe you're right," Tucker said thoughtfully.

"Well, I hate to run, but I have to make my way back to my classroom," Professor Thomas said, readjusting the dark brown messenger bag that hung off of her shoulder. "It was lovely to see you again. Take care and good luck with this semester. Try not to be so hard on yourself!"

"Oh, sorry!" Tucker apologized. "I hope I didn't make you late. I hope you have a good semester as well."

Professor Thomas offered Tucker another warm smile before moving around him towards one of the large buildings behind him. Tucker continued his trek towards Knightro's, now feeling a little warmer despite the biting wind that whipped across his face as he walked. *Maybe she has a point*, he thought brightly. *Maybe I'm just being hard on myself. I'm sure I didn't do that bad on my assignments!*

His mood improving with every step, Tucker felt a small smile form on his lips, and wore it the rest of his journey to Knightro's. Once inside, his face flushed as it met the heat being pumped through the building, and grabbed a bowl of thick tomato soup that had tortellini floating in it, and some bite-sized shortbread cookies, before finding a table near a large window. Tucker stared out into the courtyard facing the window as he slurped his soup, enjoying the satisfying feeling of the hot liquid traveling down his throat and into his stomach. There were few times during the year that Florida had cold weather, and Tucker tried to fit every stereotypical winter food, activity, and article of clothing into those days whenever possible. He ate

CHAPTER 23

and people-watched quietly until his dishes were empty and his stomach was full, before heading back out into the cold.

He decided to text Kiara once he was back in his dorm, getting comfortable in his bed and wrapping the blanket around himself like a soft, poofy cocoon as he waited for her response. She didn't reply right away as she usually did, but Tucker didn't let it deter him, reminding himself that she was probably still in one of her classes. He checked his text message chain with Jamie, wondering if he'd missed a reply from her, but was disheartened to see she'd never responded to the text he'd sent previously about the mysterious comments on his drag pictures. He thought about texting David, but quickly decided against it.

"Focus on school, focus on drag, focus on anything else but boys," he reminded himself in a pointed whisper.

Tucker resigned to absentmindedly watching videos on his phone, jumping from cooking videos to cute animal interactions to fashion how-to videos as they automatically played one after another. When he became bored with those, he checked his texts again and became frustrated to see Kiara had yet to reply an hour after he'd texted her. He doubted she was in class on a Friday evening, so he felt ignored by one of his only friends at school. Tucker inhaled deeply, trying to dispel the negative feelings with his exhale, and decided to check his grades online to see if his quiz had been graded yet. It'd only been a few hours since Tucker had left the classroom, but the professor advised the class that he would have their grades by that night. He held his breath as he logged in to his account on the school's website, navigating to the desired course and clicking on the grades tab, and exhaled sharply as he scanned through his assignments and found the grade he was looking for.

Tucker had earned a 10% on his American Government quiz, plummeting his overall grade in the course down to an F. Tucker quickly locked his phone screen and pushed it away from him, forcing himself to breathe deeply in an attempt to remain calm. He stared at the room's carpet, unblinking, as he came to terms with the reality of the situation. He was now failing a class, which was something he'd never done before, and knew how hard it would be to raise it back to a passing grade of C or better. His mind reeled, trying to formulate any sort of plan to fix the situation, but remained blank with no solutions.

Tucker threw off the blanket and dropped to the floor, pacing back and forth as he nervously ran his hands through his hair. It was too late to drop the course, so he was stuck in the class, and knew already that his professor didn't offer any form of extra credit to help bring his grade up. Tucker's phone rang, interrupting his thoughts, and he shoved the blanket around on the bed as he searched for it, his hand wrapping around it on its third ring.

"David?"

"Hey, Tucker," David said on the other end. Tucker could hear music pumping in the background and knew David was working.

"Hey, is everything okay?" Tucker asked cautiously. "Aren't you at work right now?"

"Yeah, I am," David responded.

"Okay," he said slowly, "so what's up?"

David didn't answer, but Tucker could still hear the music playing and knew the call hadn't disconnected. His eyebrows furrowed in confusion.

"David?" Tucker said.

"Yeah, sorry, I'm here," David replied.

"So what's up?" Tucker repeated. "I haven't heard from you in a while, so this is a little surprising. Are you sure you're okay?"

"Yeah, I'm fine," he said. David paused again, and Tucker stayed silent as he waited for David to continue.

"Shane wanted me to call you," David finally explained.

"He did?" Tucker asked, his spirits raising slightly. He'd been waiting for Shane's call, eager to go back to work, but had had no idea when he'd hear from him. "When can I come back?"

"That's why I'm calling," David said. "That guy Adrian just showed up, and he got really pissed when he saw me and demanded a manager."

"Oh shit, did you get in trouble?" Tucker asked, suddenly concerned.

"Some, yeah," he replied. "Shane wasn't too happy to hear I fought one of our patrons at his own apartment."

CHAPTER 23

"Yeah, that doesn't sound very good," Tucker agreed.

"But Adrian said…," David began, trailing off and emitting a quiet groan that Tucker barely heard.

"Said what?" Tucker asked, his heart pounding. *Did David get fired because of my mistake?*, Tucker thought, horrified.

"He said that it was because of you, and told Shane how you showed up at his place drunk," David explained. "I tried to tell Shane that it wasn't true, but he didn't listen to me."

"What?" Tucker asked, shocked. "I didn't show up at his place! He came and got me, and was well aware that I was messed up!"

"I know," he said.

"So, what, am I off the schedule even longer now?" Tucker asked nervously.

"No," David sighed, "Shane said that was the final straw and made me call you, since I was the one to hire you, and tell you… you're fired, Tucker. I'm really sorry."

Tucker's mouth opened in surprise, and his heart plummeted into his stomach. "I'm fired?" he repeated softly, thick tears immediately pooling and falling down his face.

"I'm so, so sorry, Tucker," David murmured. "I tried to tell Shane, I really did. It wasn't your fault."

Tucker stood in the middle of the room with his phone to his ear, crying softly and saying nothing.

"Please don't cry," David said sadly. "I can hear it. I'm so sorry, I don't want to make you cry. Please, let's talk some more when I get off of work tonight."

"I have to go, David," Tucker said quickly, ending the call. He sat down on the floor, crossing his legs and propping his arms on them as he cried into his hands. He let the tears flow, their frequency only rising as his mind wandered miserably back to his hopeless future in his American Government class. He felt hopeless and alone, and allowed himself to wallow in self-pity until he was out of tears and his eyes dried up.

He sniffled, wiping his face and rising to his feet, and walked to the sink to splash cold water on his face in an attempt to reduce the red puffiness around his eyes. Tucker's phone rang as he stood in front of the sink, but he ignored it. His good mood had dropped within minutes and he couldn't bear anything else that could possibly worsen it at the moment. It eventually stopped, and pinged a minute later, alerting Tucker that whoever had called had left a voicemail. Curiosity got the better of him, and after drying his face, Tucker went to his phone and checked his notifications. It'd been Jamie who had tried to reach him, he realized, and Tucker put his phone on speaker as he played the voicemail.

"Hey, girl, it's me," Jamie's recorded voice played throughout his room. "Listen, I got your text, and I wanted to talk to you. If you want to keep doing drag, then you're going to have to toughen up, Mary. Opinions are just like assholes—everyone's got one, and they're typically full of shit. I've seen plenty of hateful shit like that in my inbox before, but you just have to ignore it and get over it. I'll talk to you later."

There was a click, and Jamie's voicemail ended. Tucker's eyes narrowed with annoyance as he stared at his phone, his mouth turned down in a scowl. After being ignored, Jamie called him to tell him to get over it? Tucker thought about calling her back, but didn't feel like talking with anyone, much less arguing with his drag mother. He turned the phone's volume down to silent and locked it, shoving it in his pocket so he wouldn't be bothered. Like a rollercoaster, Tucker's emotions had started high that evening before dropping unexpectedly into feelings of hopelessness, and were now launched into corkscrews of frustration and anger.

He slipped his shoes back on, not bothering to grab a coat, and shoved his bedroom door open as he stomped through the empty common area, down the stairs, and out the lobby's front door back into the cold night air with no destination in mind. He crossed his arms, both out of frustration and in an attempt to keep warm, and followed the sidewalk to the main walkway that connected around campus. He silently turned right toward the school's theatre, his mind replaying Jamie saying "get over it", David saying "you're fired", and the mental image of his failed quiz grade in a sadistic loop over and over again as he walked. He stopped once he passed the theatre and encountered a gate protecting an ongoing construction project, and turned

CHAPTER 23

around as he continued his aimless journey around UCF's campus.

Chapter 24

Tucker's breath puffed in front of him in a semi-transparent cloud as he walked, putting his mixed feelings into every aggressive step he took. Though it couldn't have been much later than eight o'clock, the sky was completely dark and lamps stationed along the walkway emitted a pale yellow light that Tucker followed. His feet moved without any indication of where he was headed, and Tucker found himself back in the courtyard in front of Knightro's. It was mostly empty now, as most students had already eaten their dinner and were off partying or doing whatever else usually happened on Friday nights that Tucker was unaware of, and he sat at one of the abandoned tables.

The metal tabletop felt even colder than the air, shocking Tucker as he laid his bare arms on it and put his head down. He heard a door open and slam shut, accompanied by a mix of different voices, but did not bother to pay any attention to them until he heard a vaguely familiar voice.

"Tucker?"

He picked his head up, and noticed a group of three standing in front of the doors to Knightro's facing him. It took a moment for his brain to register their shadowed faces in the limited amount of light, but finally realized that it was Darcy, Addie, and Gray from the Queer Alliance.

"Hey, guys," he said with a half-hearted smile. Darcy was the first to move toward him, and the other two followed behind her as they all joined Tucker at the table.

"I thought that was you!" Darcy said with a smile as she sat down. "How's it going? I haven't seen you around since the end of last semester."

CHAPTER 24

"It's... been going," Tucker responded vaguely, not feeling like recounting the evening's events. "This semester has been much tougher than I thought so far. Sorry I haven't been able to stop by more."

"Trust me, we get it," Gray chimed in. "This is my second year and I'm still trying to get the hang of juggling all of my course work."

"Have you tried using a planner?" Addie asked Gray.

"Yeah, but then I forget to check my planner and I'm screwed," Gray replied, throwing their hands up in exasperation.

"Are you doing okay?" Darcy asked, looking at Tucker. "I know we don't know each other super well so I hope it isn't weird for me to say, but you're just giving off this vibe right now and I feel like something's wrong."

"Yeah, you look stressed," Addie affirmed, nodding her head as she studied Tucker's face.

Tucker sighed, shaking his head in defeat. "It's been a rough day," he explained.

"Want to talk about it?" Gray asked. "I'm not doing anything right now, so I've got plenty of time to listen."

Darcy and Addie nodded in support, looking at Tucker with concerned faces.

"Really, I don't want to bother you guys," Tucker protested. "You're all in good moods—I don't want to bring you down!"

"Emotions don't scare me!" Darcy said challengingly.

"Well," Tucker huffed, "first, I failed a test and now I have an F in American Government. My professor doesn't have any extra credit assignments, so I doubt I'll be able to pass the class and now it's too late to drop it. Then, I got a call from David and he fired me because of some bullshit that happened over winter break.

"It's a long story," he added, noticing the alarm on their faces. "On top of that," he continued, "I got some awful messages online telling me to kill myself and a bunch of other stuff, and my drag mother basically just told me to get over it. I can't get my friend on the phone to talk about it and I haven't seen her in weeks, so it's just a lot of stuff piled up."

"I'm really sorry," Addie said apologetically. "I wish I had something more helpful to say, but that really sucks."

"Yeah," Tucker said with a humorless chuckle.

"I don't know about Addie, because she's a genius," Darcy said, making Addie bump her shoulder affectionately, "but I know I've been there before."

"Me too," Gray nodded. "My very first semester here, I thought it'd be a great idea to get all of my tough courses out of the way at once and I almost failed three of my classes. I was so close to dropping out, but thankfully I was able to turn it around enough to just barely pass everything. I'll never do that again, trust me."

"How, though?" Tucker asked. "It's so easy for your grade to drop, but so hard for it to climb back up again. I feel like I won't be able to get back up to passing before the end of the semester."

"Honestly, it was a lot of luck," Gray said, shrugging. "I studied and tried really hard, but I also made sure I talked to my professors so they knew I was trying. I think it helped me in the end."

"For me," Darcy added, "I made sure that I did every assignment, but put the most focus into the big stuff—tests, papers, whatever it is in your class that has the most impact on your grade. Plus your final exam pulls a lot of weight as well, so I promise that you can probably still turn things around."

"I promise you can *probably* turn things around," Addie repeated, laughing at Darcy.

"Listen, I can't see the future! I'm just trying to be helpful!" Darcy laughed, bumping into Addie playfully.

"Ugh, couples," Gray said, rolling their eyes jokingly and making Tucker laugh.

"We were going to get a late dinner at Knightro's," Addie said. "Do you want to come eat with us, Tucker?"

"Thanks for the invite, but I already ate," Tucker said. "You guys go ahead. Thank you for talking with me, though. That really does make me feel a little better."

"It's only the second week! Don't give up just yet!" Darcy said, patting Tucker on the arm for encouragement.

"You sure you don't want to come?" Gray invited as the three of them

CHAPTER 24

stood up to leave.

"Thanks, but I'm good," Tucker replied with a smile. "I'm freezing, so I think I'm going to head back to my dorm. Hopefully, I'll be able to stop by again soon."

"Yeah, don't be a stranger!" Darcy said. "And let us know when you have another drag show. David told us about your last one when our meetings started again last week and we'd love to come!"

"I'll definitely let you know," Tucker laughed.

The three of them said their goodbyes before turning towards the dining hall and hurrying inside, talking loudly about how hungry they were and what they heard was being served for dinner. Tucker watched them enter the building before rising and leaving the courtyard as well, shoving his hands in his pockets as he trudged back to his dorm. Whatever pent-up emotional energy had been fueling him before was now gone, and he felt emotionally and physically exhausted as he slowly made his way up the stairs toward his room.

He kicked off his shoes and pulled himself up onto his bed once he was inside, once again wrapping himself in his blanket cocoon for a sense of comfort and warmth. He pulled his phone out of his pocket as he laid on his side, unlocking the screen and opening an email he'd received while he was out. To his surprise, it was from his American Government professor, and Tucker scanned the email with suspense. It read:

Mr. Peterson,

I hope this email will find you well. I wanted to write to you now that I've posted grades from our most recent test. As I am sure you have seen by now, your results were less than ideal and I am sure you are feeling alarmed at your current letter grade. I wanted to write to you, as I am for other students who scored similarly, to advise you it is not the end of the world. I remember how I felt when I received a poor grade when I was a student, like my academic career was over before it had even started, and I assure you that is not the case.

As we discussed when going over my syllabus on the first day of classes, I do not offer any extra credit assignments. I do this because, in my experiences, when students see that there is a way to boost their grades, they do not try as hard on my assignments, knowing that there is a safety net of sorts. However, I wanted to let you know that, though there are five planned tests this semester, only four of them will count toward your final grade. I include a fifth test for instances like these, to allow students another chance to redeem themselves, and I will replace that fifth test's score with your lowest one prior, as long as it surpasses what you have already scored. The dates for these are included in the syllabus, but let me know if you have any questions. Chin up, Mr. Peterson, and don't let this deter you from continuing to try your hardest during my class this semester. Enjoy your weekend.

Best,

Professor Lee

    Tucker held his phone in his hand, stunned, once he'd finished reading the email. His first thought was that he was frustrated that his professor would withhold that information from his students, but he quickly moved on from that to feeling like there was hope for his grades yet. Tucker sat up, feeling the evening's emotion burden that was sitting on his chest lighten with this news, and reread the email to make sure he had understood his professor correctly.

    Tucker smiled after reading the email for the second time, already feeling better. He momentarily forgot about his other issues, choosing to focus on this piece of good news to raise his spirits. He sent a quick reply, thanking his professor for the opportunity to bring his grade up and letting him know that things can and will get better, and promising him that he would continue to try his hardest on all of his assignments. He reached down into the top drawer of his dresser, pulling out a few pieces of milk chocolate candy, and popped them into his mouth as a small form of celebration.

    Tucker's phone lit up, and when Tucker saw it was David calling again,

CHAPTER 24

he let the call go to voicemail. It felt bittersweet, but Tucker was finally beginning to lose romantic interest in David. Though his feelings should have stopped a long time ago when David told Tucker that he just wanted to be friends, he'd had such trouble trying to move on from his crush on him until the Spring semester had started. Between being busy with school and not initiating any contact with him, thoughts of David now rarely crossed Tucker's mind, and his firing earlier that evening had nailed what he hoped was the final nail in the coffin for his romantic feelings towards him.

When his phone went dark after David's call ended and immediately lit up again with another call from him, Tucker sighed and picked up his phone, staring at its screen and debating whether he should answer it or not. Against what he knew was his better judgement, Tucker accepted the call and placed the phone up against his ear.

"Hey, David."

Chapter 25

"Tucker, hey!" David said from the other end of the call. Tucker could still hear the music playing through the club, but it sounded muted, like he'd stepped outside this time before making his call.

"What's up? Aren't you still working?" Tucker asked.

"Shane let me off early," David said. Tucker could hear the wind whipping across the phone's microphone as David walked, muffling his words.

"On a Friday night?" Tucker asked incredulously.

"I kept trying to get you your job back and told him that whole thing with Adrian wasn't your fault, but he didn't want to listen. I guess it was slow enough tonight, because he told me he could handle things and to go home. I think he just got tired of listening to me."

"Thanks, David, I appreciate it," Tucker said glumly. As if the news hadn't been upsetting enough the first time David told him that day, hearing how adamant Shane was about not giving Tucker his job back was like rubbing coarse salt in an open wound.

"I feel like this is all my fault," David said, sighing.

"Don't worry about it, it wasn't your fault," Tucker assured him. *Though it was your idea to go over to Adrian's apartment and fight him, not mine*, he thought to himself.

"It is, partly!" David argued.

"What's done is done, David," Tucker said firmly.

"Well, I want to make it up to you," he pressed. "If you're not doing anything tonight, can you come over? I cook when I'm upset, so let me make you some dinner or something to say I'm sorry. I feel awful about this."

CHAPTER 25

"You want to make me dinner?" Tucker asked confusedly.

"Yeah, is that weird?" David asked.

A part of Tucker wanted to accept David's offer immediately, eager for the chance to spend time with him again in what he imagined would be a pretty romantic setting. Friends don't typically cook friends dinner, he reasoned. But another, more logical part of Tucker remained guarded. Was this him just falling back into old habits, reading too much into innocent situations? Did he want to risk being vulnerable with David again, knowing how much he let himself get hurt the last time he tried? Tucker bit his lip as he considered his answer, weighing his options in his mind as if they were on an imaginary balance beam that could show him the right answer with a tip of its scales.

"No, it's not weird," Tucker finally answered, his voice quiet. "Yeah, I can come over in a little bit."

"Okay, great," David said, sounding relieved. "I'm on my way back now, so give me, like, half an hour? I'll text you my address."

"See you then," Tucker said, ending the call. He put his phone in his pocket and walked to the mirror above his sink, staring at his reflection. Tucker didn't know what he was feeling after that phone call, like he was afraid to get excited about the potential the evening ahead of him held. He certainly didn't need the evening to have any potential, and reasoned that he really would be just fine if he and David were nothing more than just friends, but that didn't mean the attraction he felt for David weren't there.

Now that he had talked to David again, he realized that his mantra had been useless after all, and the torch Tucker held for him burned bright as ever. Tucker twisted the sink's right knob and let cold water flow out of the faucet, pooling some in his hands and splashing his face to wake himself up. He spluttered as some water got up his nose, grabbing a nearby towel and drying his face.

Tucker sighed, running a damp hand through his hair nervously as he analyzed the waterlogged version of himself in the mirror. He turned, not wanting to look at himself any longer, and moved to his closet, rifling through coats and sweatshirts hanging on the clothes rack until he settled on a navy blue sweatshirt and a pair of faded gray jeans. He changed quickly, moving back to the mirror to make sure he looked okay. He leaned against the counter, fishing his phone out of his pocket as it buzzed, and opened a text from David containing his address and the go-ahead to start driving over. Tucker grabbed his keys, shoved a stick of gum in his mouth, and headed out the door.

His phone rang again as he sat down in his car's driver's seat, and he connected his phone to the car's bluetooth before answering the call.

"Hey, stranger," Tucker greeted.

"Hey yourself, stranger!" Kiara countered playfully.

"What's up?" Tucker laughed.

"Not much, just calling to tell you to get your ass down to the courtyard so we can finally hang out," she replied.

"Oh, sorry, Ki', I can't," Tucker said apologetically.

"Why not?" Kiara asked.

"It's a long story, but David invited me over, so I'm driving to his place right now," he said.

"Wait, you're doing what? I thought you were finally getting over him!" Kiara asked, her tone pointed.

Tucker knew Kiara was trying to protect him, but he didn't feel like explaining himself to his friend after being ignored recently and became irritated as he navigated the busy Orlando streets after leaving the campus.

"I don't know what's happening, Kiara. I'm just going with it right now," he snapped. "I've been trying to hang out with you for weeks now, so don't get upset at me for not being available now that you finally remembered to talk to me."

"Woah," Kiara said firmly, and Tucker imagined her putting a finger up dramatically to no one as she spoke. "That is not what this is about, so don't pull that shit with me, Tucker. I'm sorry I haven't been able to hang out lately, but I've been a little preoccupied with all of my course work!"

"Well, you could have said that instead of just not talking to me," Tucker retorted.

"You're right, and I'm sorry," Kiara replied, her tone still pointed, "but

CHAPTER 25

that's not what we're talking about right now. David has told you *twice* now that he's not interested in you, so why are you doing this to yourself? It's like you're a glutton for punishment!"

"I don't know!" Tucker yelled. "It's been a shitty day, and he seemed really upset after he fired me, so I'm going over because he asked me to. I don't know what's happening, and I'm trying not to read too much into anything, but I can't help that I like him, Kiara!"

"Wait, he fired you?" Kiara asked, her tone softening immediately. "What the hell happened?"

Tucker sighed, glancing at the GPS on his phone as he turned on to a side street as it instructed.

"Basically, Adrian came to the club and complained about everything that happened a few weeks ago and blamed it all on me. I've been late a few times because of how much homework I've had and Shane said that was the last straw, so he made David call and fire me since he was the one that hired me."

"Tucker, I'm so sorry! I didn't know," Kiara apologized quickly.

"I know, it's fine," Tucker assured her, his irritation subsiding. "I'm sorry, I didn't mean to take my frustration out on you like that. It's just been a hard, confusing day and I don't really know what's going on now. I can't explain why I still like him and why I'm doing this to myself because I don't really know. Believe me, I tried, but once he called me today and acted the way he did, it's like all of my hard work just washed away and I was back where I started."

"Well, for what it's worth, I still don't think this is a good idea," Kiara grumbled.

"You're probably right," Tucker laughed.

"I usually am, aren't I?"

"Yeah, but where's the fun in that?" Tucker replied. "I swear to you, if he calls me his friend again tonight, that's it. I won't have to see him anymore now that I don't work at the club, so I will live a David-free life. If something were to happen tonight, that'd be nice, but I don't *need* anything to happen and I'll be just fine without him."

"I'm holding you to that," Kiara said, and Tucker knew she meant it.

"Good, I'm counting on it!" he laughed again.

"Okay, I'll let you go, then. I promise we'll hang out soon. Study date?"

"Sounds great," he said with a smile. "Hope you know more about American Government than I do, because I'm failing at the moment."

"Wait, what?" Kiara asked in shock. "Oh my god, Tucker!"

"Okay, gotta go, bye!" Tucker said quickly, ending the call. He chuckled to himself, feeling rejuvenated after talking with his friend after weeks without proper contact. He switched back to the radio and flipped through the pre-programmed stations until he found one he liked, moving to the music in the seat as he drove.

The traffic was light as he approached David's apartment building, memories of the awful night he'd spent there the month prior flashing in his brain as he recognized different buildings in the area. Tucker pulled into a parking spot designated for visitors and put his car in park, but did not turn off the engine.

He sat there, hands gripping the steering wheel, and stared out the windshield at the building in front of him. Kiara's words of reason from their recent conversation rang in his mind, and feelings of doubt and regret began to bubble up from within him.

"It's going to be fine," Tucker reassured himself. "I already said it—if tonight leads to nothing, then that'll be the end of it. This is not a big deal."

He took one more glance at himself in the small rearview mirror above him, then shut off the car and stepped out. He checked his phone as he entered the building's lobby to confirm what floor he had to go to, and after a quick elevator ride, he strode down the hall with false confidence until he was standing in front of David's door. Tucker took a deep breath and exhaled, knocked three times, and waited for David. He heard a door open behind him and glanced at a woman exiting her apartment with a little black Pomeranian, both paying him no attention, and faced forward again once he heard David's door squeak open.

David stood in the doorway in a form-fitting black t-shirt and jeans, a worn red dish towel thrown over his shoulder and a smile on his face.

"Hey, you made it!" he beamed.

CHAPTER 25

"Here I am," Tucker smiled nervously. "Completely sober this time," he added quickly.

"Please, come in," David invited warmly, ushering Tucker inside and closing the door behind him.

Chapter 26

Tucker was hit with the strong scent of different herbs and spices as he entered David's apartment, and his eyes followed David as he moved back to the small kitchen, which was in chaos. There were bags of flour and sugar on the counter amidst small containers of rosemary, thyme, and other herbs, and an abandoned metal mixing bowl surrounded by empty wrappers and egg shells. There was a covered saucepan emitting steam and a small frying pan on the stove that David stood in front of, stirring something Tucker couldn't see around with a wooden spoon.

"Sorry, the kitchen is kind of a mess at the moment," David said, glancing at Tucker apologetically.

"No, not at all!" Tucker lied.

"You don't have to stand in the doorway—go sit down and get comfortable! I'm just about done with everything," David advised.

Tucker moved to one of the barstools near the kitchen and sat quietly, watching David work.

"So what have you prepared for us tonight, Chef David?" Tucker asked.

"I think calling me 'chef' is a bit of a stretch," David laughed as he stirred the sauce. "Pasta's my comfort food, so I'm just making some spinach and cheese ravioli that I had in the fridge for emergencies and a garlic butter sauce to go with it. Oh, and there're cookies in the oven."

"Wow, you did all of that in the time that I was driving over?" Tucker asked incredulously.

"Don't get too impressed—it was all really easy," he replied, looking over his shoulder at Tucker with a smile.

CHAPTER 26

"I haven't had a meal that wasn't from Knightro's or a fast-food restaurant in over a month, so I'm blown away," Tucker laughed.

Their eye contact lingered for a moment before David turned his attention back to the food, and Tucker felt the familiar sensation of butterflies in his stomach. Remembering his promise to Kiara that tonight would be the last night he'd let himself have feelings for David, Tucker embraced the feeling instead of pushing it away. If tonight was going to be the end of any romantic potential between the two, Tucker was determined to lean into his feelings and live in the moment.

David reached into a nearby cabinet and retrieved two white porcelain bowls, spooning ravioli into each and drizzling the garlic butter sauce on top. Though Tucker had eaten earlier that evening, his mouth watered at the sight and his stomach grumbled in agreement. David carried the bowls around the island countertop and placed one in front of Tucker before sitting on the other barstool with his own. He passed Tucker a fork, and the two silently dug into their dishes.

Tucker groaned in delight, nodding as he savoured the combination of herbs in the rich sauce mingling with the soft and salty pasta. David watched him and laughed, his own mouth full too.

"So, have you always enjoyed cooking?" Tucker asked once he'd swallowed his food.

"Yeah, it was something my mom and I would do together when I was younger, and I picked it up again once I was living on my own," David replied.

"Have you talked to your parents at all?" Tucker questioned. "I know you said around Thanksgiving that you weren't on good terms, but I didn't know if things had hopefully changed for the better since then."

"You remembered that?" David asked, looking surprised.

"Yeah, of course I did!" he answered, smiling slightly.

"That was so long ago, I'm a little surprised is all," David said. "But, to answer your question, no, we still haven't talked. I don't know if we ever will again, to be honest with you. They're really old-school Catholics, so they think I'm shaming them and going to hell and all that bullshit."

"Wow, that must be really hard," Tucker muttered. "I'm really sorry, David. They don't know half of what they're missing out on by not knowing you."

"Thanks, Tuck," David said, smiling at him before turning his attention back to his pasta. "What about you—how's everything with your parents?"

"Getting better, actually," Tucker replied before taking another large bite out of his ravioli. "Kiara planted the seed of acceptance in my mom when we were home for Thanksgiving, so we all sat down and kind of hashed things out when I went home for Christmas. Dad still doesn't really understand, but at least he isn't ignoring me or my sexuality like he was when I told him."

"That's awesome!" David said through a full mouth of food, making Tucker chuckle. He nodded in agreement, chewing his food.

The two returned to eating in a comfortable silence as they finished the contents of their bowls, David swiftly taking Tucker's out of his hands once he was done and placing them in the sink. David's oven beeped, and he pulled out a steaming tray of sugar cookies that were just slightly golden-brown, which was exactly how Tucker preferred them.

"Those smell so good, but I'm so full now," Tucker groaned.

"They're not going anywhere," David laughed. "They have to cool, so why don't we move to the couch and just chat for a minute until they're bearable enough to eat."

Tucker nodded in agreement and followed David's lead, both plopping on the small couch and groaning with pleasure as they stretched their legs out and relaxed. He couldn't help but notice their legs were touching, and he was brought back to his memories of the last time they were in that exact position. He cleared his throat and turned to look at David, who mimicked Tucker and did the same.

"So," Tucker said, looking at David expectantly.

"So?" David repeated, smiling.

"I don't know, you were the one who said we should sit here and chat!" Tucker laughed.

"Okay, fine, let's chat," David said, sitting more upright. "I want to talk about earlier tonight."

"David, really, we don't have to—"

CHAPTER 26

"I want to," David interrupted firmly. "I know I've said this already, but I'm so sorry for what happened, Tucker. I never meant for this to happen and would have never gone to that guy's apartment if I knew it'd get you fired."

"I know," Tucker said softly.

"And when Shane made me call you to tell you," David continued, "and you started crying… something just clicked for me. I was so upset with myself, and with Shane for making me do it, and Adrian for finding a way to screw you over even worse than he already did."

Tucker listened quietly, feeling stunned and confused by David's confession. He said nothing, mentally urging David to continue.

"I just don't want anything like that to ever happen to you again," he said, looking into Tucker's eyes searchingly.

"That's because you're a good friend," Tucker said, putting on a slight smile to try to ease David's obvious guilt. "You're the knight in shining armor, remember?"

"That's the thing, Tucker, I'm not always like that," David replied, sounding mystified. "I'm a good friend, but I've done more for you this year than I've done for any of my other friends. I just have this feeling when I'm with you, like I want to protect you, and that's why I went to Adrian's that day. That's why I went home with you and Kiara on Thanksgiving, and why I showed up at your dorm after we got back to check on you, and why I asked you over here tonight. I thought it was just me wanting to be a good friend, but it finally clicked tonight that it's not just that. I like you a lot, Tucker, and I'm sorry I hurt you. I'm sorry this is out of nowhere, but I needed to tell you."

Tucker stared back into David's eyes, speechless. His mind raced, trying to comprehend what David had just told him. After everything that had happened so far that year, after turning Tucker down twice, David had feelings for him now? He should have felt elated at David's news, but Tucker remained guarded.

"Are you sure you aren't just feeling guilty, David? I thought you just saw me as a kid," Tucker murmured, breaking eye contact and looking down at the couch cushion he was sitting on. He wanted what David said to be true, but he couldn't bear to put himself out there and be let down again. What if, subconsciously, he was just trying to do damage control since he was the one that upset him?

Tucker felt a hand on his chin as David lifted his head up again, a concerned look on his face.

"Of course I feel guilty, Tucker, but that isn't it," he murmured.

David's hand moved to Tucker's cheek and leaned in, pressing his soft lips against Tucker's for a moment before pulling away again. He smiled, and Tucker's heart soared with joy. He leaned forward and kissed David again, pulling away with a smile of his own on his face.

"Okay, I believe you," Tucker said, blushing.

"Good," David chuckled, taking Tucker's hand and lacing their fingers together. "I know you're not just a kid, Tucker. I was just upset and feeling overprotective when I said it, but I know that you're an adult. I've just been single for a long time and told myself that I wouldn't look for romance anymore, which is why it took so long for things to click."

"So, what does this mean?" Tucker asked carefully, looking from their intertwined hands to David's face.

"Well, I like you, and you seem to still like me, so I think this means I should take you out on a date soon and we see where this goes," he replied. "What do you think?"

"I'd like that," Tucker said with a grin.

"Good," David said, matching Tucker's grin.

The two sat on David's couch for another couple of hours, only getting up to use the bathroom or to grab a cookie once they'd cooled off. They talked about everything from their favorite colors and foods, to their biggest fears and job aspirations (Tucker had no idea what he wanted to do with his life, and David was interested in a career in journalism).

David began to yawn more and more consistently as they chatted, and Tucker took it as a sign to leave. They softly kissed again at David's door before he left, and David made Tucker promise to text him once he was back safely in his dorm, which Tucker agreed to with a laugh. David had been

CHAPTER 26

attentive before, but this side of him was something new to Tucker that he'd have to get used to, but already enjoyed immensely.

Tucker called Kiara as soon as he closed the car door, eager to fill her in on the evening's events. She answered on the first ring, as she usually did, and greeted him with one word.

"Spill," she instructed.

"Are you sitting down?" Tucker asked, grinning, as he pulled back onto the road towards campus.

"Yes, now tell me what happened!" Kiara demanded impatiently.

"Okay, so he made us dinner, he told me he liked me, and we kissed," Tucker blurted, feeling giddy as he recounted the evening.

Kiara screeched, her shrill scream blasting through Tucker's car speakers and making him wince.

"Tell. Me. Everything!" she finally said.

Tucker filled in the details of the story as he drove, interrupted every other sentence by Kiara squealing or gasping dramatically. She made Tucker pause when he got to David's kiss in his story, demanding details about his kissing abilities, and Tucker confirmed he was a great kisser, his face beet-red.

"Tucker, this is amazing! I'm so happy for you!" she said once he'd finished his tale.

"I have to admit, it feels pretty surreal," he laughed. "I'm just going to take things one day at a time so I don't get too ahead of myself, you know?"

"Brilliant plan in theory, but I know you and I don't believe for one second you can be so chill about this," Kiara replied.

"I can too!" Tucker argued. "I'm super chill!"

"You're probably planning your wedding as we speak!" she teased.

Tucker pulled into the parking lot behind his dorm building and into an empty spot, throwing the car in park and shutting the engine off.

"Oh my god, you're the worst," he laughed. "I just got back to campus, so I'm gonna go. I just wanted to fill you in, so I'm sure we'll talk more about this later."

"You bet your ass we will!" she promised. "We've been talking about David since August, so you better keep it up now that you've got him locked down."

"He is not 'locked down'. He just said he liked me," Tucker said.

"Whatever. We'll talk about it," Kiara said.

"Goodbye, Kiara," Tucker laughed, hanging up before she could push any further.

He bounded up the stairs to his floor, a newfound spring in his step and a smile fixed on his face, and pulled out his phone to text David once he was changed out of his clothes and in bed.

TUCKER: Hey, I just got back to my room. Thanks again for dinner and a great evening. :)

Though David seemed exhausted when Tucker had left and he was sure David would be asleep by the time Tucker got home, he replied immediately.

DAVID: Thanks for coming over. I'll have to cook you a proper meal soon. I'm headed to bed, but wanted to make sure you got home first. Goodnight, Tuck.

TUCKER: Goodnight, David. Let me know when you're free and want to hang out again.

DAVID: You know I will. :)

DAVID: And just because I want to say it again: I really like you, Tucker.

TUCKER: I really like you too, David. Goodnight.

Tucker read David's final text with a huge grin over and over again, his stomach filled with butterflies. He finally locked his screen and put his phone aside, rolling over to face his handmade sign like he always did as he fell asleep. He read the three lines in his head and rolled over to slide out of

CHAPTER 26

bed. He pulled a pen out of his backpack and hopped back into bed, reaching over and crossing out the third sentence. Satisfied with his changes, Tucker placed the pen on his dresser and resumed his nightly ritual, reading his newly updated sign until he fell asleep. *Focus on school, focus on drag...*

Chapter 27

Tucker wasn't able to see David all weekend because he was working, but the two kept in constant contact over text from the moment Tucker woke up, blushing as he read David's text wishing him a good morning. He spent the weekend continuing to catch up on assigned readings and homework assignments, but the workload now seemed less daunting while he was able to talk to David.

Tucker felt slightly ashamed to admit it to himself, as he'd spent a lot of time and mental energy trying to be as independent and self-sufficient as possible lately, but David helped keep him calm and collected just by talking with him. His classes seemed easier to comprehend the following Monday, and Tucker wondered how much he'd been hindering himself the entire time as he walked back to his dorm. David, wearing a navy blue cardigan over a tight white t-shirt and khaki pants, lounged with his feet up on a bench in the courtyard, scrolling on his phone, and grinned when he looked up and saw Tucker looking at him.

"Are you stalking me now?" Tucker joked as he approached him.

"So what if I am?" David challenged with a grin.

"Yeah, that'd be fine," he laughed, joining David on the bench.

"I was waiting for you because I wanted to see if you were free tonight to go on an actual date with me," David explained, sitting upright to look at Tucker. "I wanted to ask you in person."

"I'm definitely free," Tucker said with a smile, his cheeks flushing.

"Okay, cool," David said, sounding relieved.

"I have to do some homework first—do you want to come up?" Tucker

CHAPTER 27

offered, jerking his head towards his building.

"Won't I distract you though?" David asked.

"Oh, you absolutely will, but I'm fine with that," Tucker nodded enthusiastically, making David laugh. Tucker stood, extending his hand, and David grabbed it as he stood up, holding on to it as they walked into his building.

Tucker rushed into his room, quickly wiping the counter down and kicking his laundry deeper into his closet so that his room appeared tidy before he opened the door again and allowed David to enter. He hopped up and sat on Tucker's bed, legs dangling over the side, and watched Tucker as he unpacked his backpack and worked on a packet he'd been assigned in his English Composition class earlier that day. Tucker could almost feel David's eyes in the back of his head and rushed through the packet to finish it as quickly as possible without too many errors. He could hear David chuckle quietly as he shoved the paperwork back into his backpack, eager to not have to think about homework and enjoy David's presence.

"You didn't have to rush," David said. "I'm fine just going on my phone while you work. School's important, Tucker."

"Yeah, but it was busywork anyway," Tucker said dismissively, making David smile again. "So where are we going on this date tonight?"

"I was thinking something simple—dinner and a movie? Maybe dessert afterwards?" he offered.

"Sounds perfect," Tucker replied with a smile of his own. "Let me get changed and I'll be ready to go."

Tucker grabbed a pair of dark blue jeans and a black sweatshirt that had UCF embroidered in gold thread on the front, moving to the bathroom to change. He pushed his hair around with his hands in the mirror until he was satisfied with its shape, then turned to David and gave him a thumbs-up.

David grinned, hopped down from Tucker's bed, and the two went out the door. Tucker followed David to where he parked in a nearby lot closer to the gym, which was in the front of the school, and slid into the passenger seat.

David drove off of campus, occasionally looking over at Tucker with a smile on his face, and pulled into a small plaza two streets away, parking in front of Giovanna's, where Tucker had been once before with David and Kiara right before Thanksgiving.

The restaurant was almost completely empty when they entered, and a short Italian woman with gray hair pulled up into a giant bun on her head greeted them warmly before shepherding them off to a booth, handing them both menus before telling them exactly what they should order. David nodded and accepted the woman's advice, handing the menus back to her without even opening it.

"That's the owner's wife, Giovanna," David advised quietly once she was out of earshot. Tucker nodded knowingly, remembering the older man with the thick Italian accent who'd waited on them the last time they were there.

Though they'd been around each other countless times since meeting in August, Tucker still felt strangely nervous as the two sat at their table awaiting their meals. The cards were all on the table now and both knew how the other felt about them, but Tucker felt that things were different now—things were *real* now. He took a deep breath, casting what he reasoned were first date jitters to the side, and grabbed David's hand, running his thumb across David's palm.

Soon, Giovanna returned with large bowls filled with pasta, smaller bowls piled high with salad, small plates of baked chicken over greens, and a basket of steaming breadsticks. Both of their eyes widened as Giovanna put dish after dish on their table before smiling warmly at them both and walking away, and they chuckled together at the sheer amount of food the woman delivered to them.

They ate as much as they could before David paid the check, both thanking Giovanna profusely as they exited the restaurant. David drove them another ten minutes to a much larger shopping plaza, where they bought tickets to the next available movie and sat together holding hands as they watched the movie about a football team, slightly regretting their choice.

"Was it just me, or was that movie kind of terrible?" David asked as they left the theater later that evening.

"It was awful," Tucker confirmed with a laugh.

"We'll have to try this again with an actual plan next time," David vowed,

CHAPTER 27

taking Tucker's hand in his.

"I'd love that," Tucker replied, blushing.

Too full for dessert, David drove Tucker back to his dorm, where the two exchanged a long, deep kiss in David's car before Tucker got out, lips red and his face flushed. He went to bed that night feeling giddy, a smile fixed on his face as he recounted his first real date with David over again in his head.

This was the trend as the months went by—David hanging out with Tucker after his classes were finished in his dorm while he did homework or studied, the two going on dates to different restaurants around town or other spots David thought of, like mini-golfing at a Congo River-themed attraction or walking around the outdoor farmer's market and sampling different food trucks. On their sixth date in March—watching the fireworks show happening inside the Magic Kingdom at Walt Disney World from one of Disney's resorts open to the public—Tucker turned to David and took his hand, causing David to tear his eyes away from the sky to look at Tucker with a smile.

"Do you want to be my boyfriend?" Tucker blurted, surprising himself. He'd barely formed the thought before his mouth opened and said it out loud.

David's close-lipped smile grew into a toothy grin. "Of course I do, Tucker. I sure hope you want to be mine, because I've been calling you my boyfriend for weeks."

Tucker matched David's grin, and the two kissed for a moment before turning their attention back to the fireworks, Tucker leaning his head on David's shoulder.

* * *

As the semester continued, Tucker barely stayed afloat in most of his classes, and was still working hard to get his grade in American Government back up to passing. He'd taken the fifth test his professor offered as redemption for his worst grade, but had only earned a C on it and wasn't able to boost his overall grade as much as he'd hoped for. Whenever he wasn't distracting himself around David, Tucker was scrambling to study as much as possible and work on every single assignment days before they were due.

He and Kiara made plans to study separately together every Wednesday evening in her dorm room, content with just being around each other while they worked. As finals approached at the end of April, they roped David into their plans and the three now met at David's apartment to work. On the evening of the last Study Day that the school provided for students right before finals began, Kiara sat on a barstool and took over the kitchen counter with her textbooks while David and Tucker sat side-by-side on his couch with their own books, all three working silently.

Tucker slammed his World History textbook closed with a grunt of frustration, shoving it back into his backpack and earning a raised eyebrow in acknowledgement from David as he looked up from the passage he was reading.

"You okay?" David asked.

"No," Tucker said glumly. "My first final is *tomorrow* and I don't feel confident on any of them. I just want to give up and let this semester finally crash and burn."

"But you've been working so hard!" David protested. "Yes, there's been some setbacks, but you can still pass everything if you do well on these exams."

"Just because I can doesn't mean I will," he grumbled.

"Not with that attitude, you won't!" Kiara chimed in, turning on her stool to face the two. "You're panicking, and that's only going to make things harder for you. Try to relax, Tucker."

"Literally all of my grades are on the verge of falling below passing, so it's a little hard to stay calm, Ki!" Tucker snapped. David rubbed Tucker's back in a slow circle, and Tucker took a deep breath. "Sorry, I didn't mean to snap at you. I'm just stressed."

"I know," Kiara said. "We all are, trust me! You think I'm ready for my Statistics exam? Hell no! But I'm just going to keep going over everything

CHAPTER 27

as much as I can, and that's what you need to do too. Repetition is the key."

"Kiara's right," David said, nodding in agreement. "Take a minute to cool off and then try again. All you can do is try to prepare as much as you can."

"Fine," Tucker huffed. "I'm going to just go on a quick walk around the building, and then I'll go back and try again, okay?"

"Okay," David replied, giving Tucker a reassuring smile.

Tucker stood, carefully stepping around David's textbooks strewn on the floor all around him, and walked out the door, taking the stairs down to the lobby two at a time. He knew Kiara and David were right, but it didn't make it any easier to hear. Tucker was terrified of failing, and the thought of having to redo all of his classes made his heart thud as he stepped out the building's front doors. The air was hot and thick with humidity, and a light layer of sweat immediately materialized on his forehead.

His phone buzzed in his pocket, and Tucker was surprised to see that it was Jamie calling. He'd been so busy with school and David that he hadn't done drag in over a month and hadn't heard from Jamie since he was fired from Haven in February.

"I thought you died, bitch!" she said when Tucker answered.

"You could have texted me!" Tucker retorted with a laugh, now used to her harsh way of speaking. "Phones work both ways, you know."

"Whatever, I've been busy," Jamie replied dismissively. "Where've you been? I haven't seen you in a while."

"I've been busy too. School's really tough this semester," he said. "And you haven't seen me because I got fired from the club ages ago, girl. You'd know if you texted me!"

"You got fired?" Jamie gasped. "What'd you do, steal a couple of dollars?"

"No!" Tucker replied, laughing. "I'd been late a few times, which was my fault, but there was some shit that happened with one of the patrons and he complained to my manager, so I got fired even though it wasn't my fault."

"Damn, that sucks, girl," she sighed. "But, that should make this even better! I got you a gig!"

"What? When?" Tucker asked, startled. He'd been so focused on school that drag had been pushed to the back of his mind and the bottom of his priorities list until the semester was finished. He didn't have time for a gig!

"The second week of May. I'll text you the details," Jamie advised. "Get excited, girl! Your mother just got you a paid gig!"

Tucker quickly recalled his calendar for the next few weeks in his mind, feeling relieved when he realized he'd be done with finals by then.

"Yeah, that's great news! Thank you," Tucker replied, unable to feign the enthusiasm Jamie seemed to be looking for.

"You're welcome," she said, sounding satisfied. "I hope you've been practicing, because I'm not helping you this time! You're on your own, girl."

"I'll be fine," Tucker lied, hoping he sounded convincing. He hadn't even thought about his limited drag wardrobe in months and had no idea what he'd wear.

"We'll see," Jamie replied skeptically. "I'll let you go, since you're so *busy* now. I'll text you about the show."

"Thanks again, Jamie," Tucker said earnestly. "It's going to be fun!"

Jamie ended the call, and Tucker smiled as he put his phone away. Though she was blunt, and could be harsh at times, talking with Jamie almost always put Tucker in a good mood. She was tough, but he could tell it was out of love. He wiped the sweat from his forehead and reentered David's building, greeted by him with a quick kiss, feeling refreshed and ready to try studying again.

Chapter 28

As always, Kiara had been right, Tucker noted begrudgingly. In the two weeks since they'd met with David at his apartment, Tucker had completed all of his final exams and had somehow not failed any of them. Some were easier, like the essay Tucker had to write for his English Composition class and the presentation he put together on the similarities in imagery between three short stories he'd read for his American Literature class, but some of his exams left him feeling nauseous and sweaty as he'd turned them in for grading.

Though he'd passed his final exams, there was still a chance they wouldn't be enough to bring his grades up to passing. Tucker sat on David's couch with his laptop on the Saturday after finals were over, refreshing his grades over and over as he awaited his updated final grades that were to be posted that day.

While Tucker was exuding stress and worry, David seemed to be in the complete opposite mood as he made them brunch in the kitchen. He whistled absentmindedly as he cracked eggs into a sizzling pan, turning to flip pancakes he'd poured earlier in another, and took a long sip of coffee from his steaming mug on the counter next to him.

"How are you in such a good mood right now?" Tucker asked, eyes still glued to his computer screen.

"I don't know, I just am," David shrugged, taking another sip of coffee. "It's the weekend, I'm hanging out with my boyfriend and making us brunch, and the semester is finally over. Today's a good day!"

"Yeah, but aren't you stressed about your grades?" Tucker pressed.

"A little, but what's done is done at this point. No sense in worrying about it," David said, shrugging again before turning back to the stove.

"Easy for you to say," Tucker grumbled, hitting refresh again.

"I can still hear you," David laughed, still facing away from Tucker.

"It is!" Tucker insisted, smiling despite the stress he was feeling. "You weren't the one teetering on the edge of failing all semester."

"You're going to be fine, Tuck," David said, turning around to look Tucker in the eyes as he spoke. "Even if the worst does happen, the world will not end. Everything will be fine. Okay?"

"Okay," Tucker sighed. He rose and moved to the kitchen, where David wrapped him in a comforting hug. "How are you so good at talking me down when I'm freaking out?" Tucker asked, his voice muffled in David's shirt.

"I've had plenty of practice," David replied, laughing when Tucker smacked his chest in indignation.

"You're such an ass," Tucker laughed, pulling away and moving back to the couch. He clicked refresh on the grades page again and gasped loudly.

"What?" David asked, concerned.

"Grades are out," Tucker said gravely. "I don't know if I can look."

"Yes, you can," David urged. "It's like ripping off a band-aid—just do it fast and get it over with."

Tucker inhaled deeply, trying desperately to calm his rapidly beating hard. He selected his first course, Math For Non-Majors, and let out a sigh of relief when he saw he'd be passing with a B. He moved on to English Composition, and then quickly to American Literature, exhaling when he knew he'd be passing both of those classes with Bs as well. Wincing, he checked World History next, and felt satisfied knowing he'd pass with a mid-level C. After that was Computer Sciences, which he hadn't been worried about, and nodded with approval at his high B. Finally, Tucker moved on to American Government, and with the delicacy of someone trying to deactivate a bomb, he carefully clicked on the grades tab. He loudly whooped and jumped to his feet, pleased with the C he'd received, even if it was at the bare-minimum of a 70%.

CHAPTER 28

"You passed?" David asked excitedly.

"I passed!" Tucker cheered, throwing his arms in the air and grinning gleefully. "I can't believe it—I really thought I was going to fail!"

"Oh, you did? I hadn't noticed," David said sarcastically, grinning.

"Oh my god, shut up!" Tucker laughed. He eyed the sizzling pans on the stove behind David, and his mouth began to water. "Now that I don't feel like I'm going to stress-puke, I'm hungry."

"Well, come to the counter, then!" David instructed, divvying up the pans' contents onto two white plates. He laid one in front of each barstool, grabbed some butter and syrup from the fridge, then came around the counter to sit with Tucker. The two smothered their pancakes in syrup and dug in.

"Hey, so I have something to tell you," David said once they'd finished brunch.

"What, are you pregnant?" Tucker asked, taking a sip of coffee from David's mug.

"No, asshole," David laughed, snatching his mug back. "I talked to Shane about you the other day."

"Oh?"

"Yeah," he continued. "Now that school's over, I know you're not going to be as busy anymore, so I talked him into giving you your job back for the summer."

"Wait, really?" Tucker asked, a confused smile on his face.

"If you want it, that is," David said quickly.

"Yeah, of course!" Tucker said, nodding enthusiastically. "How did you manage that?"

"Shane finally listened to what I had to say about what happened with Adrian, and he agreed that it wasn't your fault. Once I told him you wouldn't be as busy with school now, he finally gave in."

"David, that's amazing! Thank you!" Tucker said, pulling him in for a kiss.

"It was kind of my fault, so I felt like it was the least I could do," he replied. "*And*, Shane got Adrian banned from the bar!" he smiled triumphantly, and Tucker kissed him again. He didn't have to say anything about that for David to know how appreciative he was for that added support.

The two spent the rest of the afternoon together in David's apartment; cleaning up the remnants of brunch while listening to music, watching a movie together on the couch, until Tucker eventually bid David farewell and drove back to his dorm. He called his mom and told her all the good news he'd received today, and did the same for Kiara afterwards.

"Wait, so you're staying here this summer?" Kiara asked.

"I guess so!" Tucker said, holding the phone to his ear with his shoulder as he started taking down the clothes in his closet to pack.

"Where are you going to stay? We can only stay in the dorms until the end of the month!" she pressed.

"I don't know," he replied thoughtfully, throwing the clothes on the empty bed he used as a desk. "I hadn't really thought of that, I guess."

"I'm coming over," Kiara huffed, ending the call abruptly.

There was a sharp rap at the door two minutes later, and Kiara barged into the room once Tucker opened the door.

"What do you mean, you don't know? You're going to be homeless, Tucker!" she said, turning to face where he stood at the door.

"Hi to you too!" he replied, closing the door.

"No, we're past pleasantries," Kiara said, looking around the room. "Jesus, you aren't even packed yet?"

"I will be!" Tucker said indignantly.

Without a word, Kiara took the posters off of Tucker's walls, laying them on top of each other on the floor, and moved to his closet.

"Ki, I got it," he said, moving in between her and the half-empty closet.

"I'm here to help!" she snapped, trying to move around him.

"I got it," Tucker repeated firmly. Kiara gave him a dirty look, but moved away from the closet.

"Fine," she said, throwing her hands up in defeat. "Don't say I didn't try."

"You're so dramatic!" Tucker laughed, stooping to pick up the posters and moving to place them on top of his dresser.

"You've got, like, *no* time to find a place to live for the summer if you're going to stay and work, Tucker! You're not being dramatic enough," Kiara huffed.

CHAPTER 28

"Hey, what are you doing tonight?" Tucker asked, desperate to change the subject.

"Nothing, now that the semester's finally done. Why?"

"You want to come to my show?" he asked, leaning against his bed.

"You have a show tonight and you didn't tell me?" Kiara gasped, smacking Tucker's arm. "Of course I want to go!"

"Okay, good," Tucker grinned. "You can just drive with me if you want to hang out while I get ready."

Kiara hopped up on Tucker's bed, laying on her side, and pulled out her phone. "I'll be here when you're ready."

Tucker laughed and moved to his closet to pull out the cheap makeup case he'd bought online that now held all of his products. He dragged a chair to the bathroom counter, sitting down and beginning the now-familiar process of painting—shaving, primer, glue, powder, foundation, highlight, contour, blush, eyes, lips, and lashes.

During the time Tucker was painting, Kiara ran back to her dorm to change, and was now knocking on his door again, just as he finished his last step. He moved his face around, analyzing his makeup from different sides in the mirror, and opened the door when he was satisfied.

Kiara stood in the hall in a tight black velvet mini-dress and matching black heels, a bright red lip and gold eyeshadow on her lids, and her hair slicked back into a bun on the crown of her head. When the door opened enough for her to see Tucker's makeup, her jaw dropped and quickly morphed into a huge grin.

"You look amazing!" she said, moving inside.

"So do you!" Tucker said, closing the door behind her. "I'm just about ready—let me go change and I'll be good to go."

Tucker hurried back to his closet, pulling out a similar pair of black heels and a sequined black dress with gold accents along the sides and the chest area, a few pairs of tights, his pair of foam hip and butt pads, and a black spandex waist shaper and stepped into the bathroom to change. He stepped out again a few minutes later, fully dressed, and moved back to the closet once more to pull out a tall black wig Jamie'd gifted him previously.

"Where did you get that?" Kiara gasped once Tucker was fully dressed.

"Mostly online, but the wig came from my drag mom," Tucker murmured, looking in the mirror and securing the wig on his head with bobby pins. He turned and looked at Kiara, smiling. "What do you think?"

"You look amazing!" she replied in awe. "I can't believe I'm finally getting to see you perform—I haven't even seen you in full drag before!"

The two hurried down to Tucker's car in the parking lot behind his building, and Tucker maneuvered his way through Saturday night traffic all around UCF as he drove to Haven. Once they were on the highway, they were free of the traffic on the streets and made it into Haven's parking lot without any issues.

The two strutted into the lobby, Tucker waving and winking at everyone who looked at him or said hello. They handed their IDs to Ned, who nodded at Tucker with a smile before handing them back. The two moved further inside the building, stopping to check their reflections in the mirror-lined hallway before emerging in the dark, booming club.

It being a Saturday night, the club was packed and the dance floor was full of shirtless men, drag queens, and women dancing to a remixed song the DJ was blasting through the speakers. Tucker and Kiara strode to the bar where David was moving to the music as he poured drinks for some women. After they paid and walked away with their cocktails, David turned to them and grinned.

"Wow, look at you two!" he exclaimed. He took Tucker's hand and kissed the back of his palm, winking at him. "Looking especially dazzling, Ms. Kahlo."

Tucker blushed, and Kiara squealed with delight as she looked between the two.

"Jamie's already back in the dressing room if you want to go join her," David advised.

"Are you going to be alright while I get ready for the show?" Tucker asked Kiara.

"I'm not a child!" Kiara scoffed. "I'll be fine—and I can hang out with David in the meantime."

CHAPTER 28

"You'd better be careful or else he'll put you to work!" Tucker warned playfully. "I'm headed to the dressing room, so I'll see you after the show!"

"Break a heel!" Kiara yelled over the music as Tucker walked away. "Like how people say 'break a leg' before a show," she explained, noticing David's confused expression.

Tucker strode toward the dressing room, reminding himself to exude confidence. He was proud of how he looked, so it wasn't hard for him as he walked by a pair of drag queens walking the other way, noticing how they looked him up and down before offering a half-hearted smile. He returned it, but didn't say anything to them. He remembered something similar happening to him at his last gig and could hear Kitty's words of advice ring in his ears—"Just ignore those whores."

As he approached the dressing room door, he made sure to knock first before opening, not wanting to hit Jamie with it like he had each time before. He scooted inside and shut the door, maneuvering around the chair Jamie was sitting in to get to the other side of the room.

"Hey, girl," she murmured, her eyes opened wide as she applied mascara to her top and bottom lashes.

"Hey," he greeted. "Let me ask you something—what is with these queens being so judgy for no reason? I just saw two of them on my way here looking me up and down, and I just don't get it. I don't even know them!"

"Because you're a baby queen that got a spot in the show," Jamie replied simply, turning to look at him. "You look good, by the way."

"Thanks," Tucker said with a smile. He knew how honest Jamie was, so any time she gave a compliment he knew she meant it. "I get that I'm newer, but I just don't understand why someone wouldn't like me because I get to perform."

"Girl, welcome to drag," Jamie said, rolling her eyes and turning her attention back to the mirror. She picked up a large fluffy brush from the counter, brushed it against her cheekbones, and set it down again with a satisfied sigh. Jamie stood, moving to a rack behind Tucker and pulling out a black leotard with gold accents that looked similar to Tucker's dress and a pair of shiny black thigh-high boots.

Jamie carefully pulled the tank top she was wearing over her head to avoid it touching her freshly painted face, giving Tucker no warning before her breasts were fully exposed as she stepped into the leotard. He looked away quickly, and Jamie scoffed at his modesty.

"What, you haven't seen tits before? I paid enough for them, so I don't care who sees them!" Jamie said.

"Not in-person," Tucker muttered, staring straight at the door. He heard the sound of zippers closing, but didn't dare look away in case she wasn't ready.

"Relax, Mary," she laughed. "You can look now. I'm all done."

Jamie's leotard had a plunging v-shaped neckline that accentuated her cleavage, outlined in gold. Her hair was slicked back into a tight ponytail, which was long enough to brush against her lower back.

"You ready?" she asked. Tucker nodded, ignoring how his heart rate began to pick up. He followed her out to the familiar spot outside behind the dance floor, making sure to smile at everyone he passed. Even if the other queens were going to be cold and judgmental, Tucker was determined to kill them with kindness.

The show began shortly after, and Tucker could hear a queen he didn't recognize, who introduced herself on the microphone as Minnie Corndog, hosting the show that evening as each performer was introduced. Finally, Tucker was next, and he stood ready by the door.

"Up next," the host's voice boomed through the speakers, "please help me welcome to the stage, the lovely Karma Kahlo!"

Lady Gaga's "Telephone" began to play as Tucker entered the room, the crowd cheering once they caught sight of him. He mouthed along to the words, making sure to interact with the audience, and moved back to toward the door to make sure they saw Jamie's entrance when Beyoncé's verse started. They went wild, cheering and throwing dollar bills at the two as they moved around the room, dancing with audience members and with each other.

Kiara had made her way to the front of the crowd and was recording the performance on her phone with one hand while holding money in the other.

CHAPTER 28

As Tucker made his way around the audience and got to Kiara, she shoved the dollar bills into his bra and cackled with delight. The song ended, and the crowd cheered once more as Tucker blew them kisses with wadded up dollar bills in his hands while he exited the room.

"That was so fun!" Tucker exclaimed as he and Jamie made their way back to the dressing room.

"I'm really proud of you," Jamie said, patting Tucker on the back. "You did a great job tonight."

Tucker stopped and looked at Jamie, feeling touched. Without a warning, Tucker pulled her into a hug for a few moments before setting her free.

"Bitch, I still have another number to do! Watch the makeup!" Jamie chastised, smiling despite herself.

"Sorry, I'm just really happy you're my drag mother. Thank you for helping me," Tucker said.

"You're welcome," she replied proudly. "You're doing really well, so I can't wait to see where you'll go." With that, she strutted back to the dance floor doors, ready for her next number.

In the dressing room, Tucker folded all the dollars he'd been gifted and hid them in his bra, kicking himself for not bringing a bag or a change of clothes. He headed back to the bar, overhearing the host wrapping up the show through the speakers, where Kiara and David were in deep conversation as he approached.

"You did amazing!" Kiara gasped when she noticed Tucker. "That was so much fun! I just showed David the video."

"Oh, yeah?" Tucker asked, looking at David. "What'd you think?"

"Kiara took the words out of my mouth. You did amazing, babe," David said, leaning across the bar to lightly kiss Tucker's lips. Tucker wiped his ruby-red lipstick off of David's mouth, laughing.

"David," Kiara said, pulling on Tucker's hand and slowly walking away, "we'll finish our conversation later, okay? It's time to go dance!"

Tucker opened his mouth to ask what they were talking about, but was yanked toward the dance floor before he could ask. The two maneuvered their way through the crowd until they found a space for them, and danced until neither of them could feel their feet in their heels any longer.

Tucker drove them back to campus, the streets now quiet late in the night, and the two parted ways as Tucker went back to his room to take off his makeup and shower. When he was dressed, he checked his phone and opened a pending text from David.

DAVID: If you're still up, want to sleep over at my apartment tonight?

Tucker grinned as he read, typing back a fast yes and rushing to pack an overnight bag. Aside from when they shared a bed at Tucker's parents' house and the fiasco in December, the two had yet to sleep over at each other's places, both having agreed to take things slow and keep school as their priority. Tucker hurried down the steps and out the door to his car, jumping back into the driver's seat and driving out of the parking lot.

David met him at the door when Tucker arrived at his apartment building, and the two unwound on his couch before they trudged to bed, feeling exhausted. They undressed down to their underwear, but neither tried anything sexual as they got into bed, both too tired.

Once their bodies were pressed together, however, they both seemed to change their minds and their lips crashed together in the dark, hands roaming all over each other's bodies. David rolled on his back, pulling Tucker on top of him, and the two gyrated as they kissed, their tongues dancing together while Tucker moved his hips in a clockwise motion on David's crotch. David threw Tucker off of him onto his back, switching positions so he loomed over Tucker, and pulled his underwear down as he placed hungry kisses down his torso, eager to get below his waistline. Tucker yanked at David's briefs from where he laid, his mouth opening in shock as he admired David's naked body in the dark and let his hands wander down David's chest and abdomen until they were wrapped around his impressive erection, earning a satisfying groan from David as he leaned in to Tucker's

CHAPTER 28

touch.

Too exhausted to move after they'd both finished, Tucker rolled on his side and David wrapped his arms around him, and the two fell into a deep blissful sleep together, a satisfied smile on both of their faces.

Chapter 29

"So, what were you and Kiara talking about last night after my number?" Tucker asked from one of David's barstools the next morning as David prepared them breakfast. The two had spent the morning in bed together, chatting and exploring each other's bodies for the first time, and David eventually forced Tucker into some clothes and into the kitchen so they could eat something.

"Oh, right!" David said. "I totally forgot—she was talking to me about how you guys were looking for a place to live, and I told her my neighbor downstairs is looking to sublet her apartment! She told me her boyfriend dumped her, so she's moving into something smaller on her own."

"Wait, you said she told you *we* were looking for a place?" Tucker asked, his face confused.

"Yeah, she told me while you were in the dressing room. I told her I could probably get her a job if she was interested, so I'm going to talk to Shane about that later today and call her after. It'd work out well, right?" David smiled, looking proud of himself.

"I can't believe she didn't tell me any of this," Tucker muttered to himself.

"Nothing's official, so I'm sure she was just waiting to figure things out first," David said, placing a plate of eggs and hash browns in front of Tucker. "Relax, this could be a good thing!"

"I'm relaxed, I promise," Tucker said as he scooped up some potatoes on his fork. "This is just big news, so I'm shocked she didn't tell me as soon as you told her, is all."

There was a knock at the door, and David and Tucker gave each other

CHAPTER 29

confused looks before David rose to answer it.

"Oh, hi," David said, sounding surprised as he opened the door wider. Tucker was just as surprised as Kiara walked into the apartment in a burgundy pantsuit and a matching pair of glasses, her hair at her shoulders in beautifully defined curls.

"Ki, what are you doing here?" Tucker asked, bewildered. "How did you even get here?"

"My roommate Vanessa drove me. She's waiting in the parking lot," Kiara said simply, sitting down on the couch casually. "David told me about his neighbor downstairs looking to sublet last night, so I just paid her a visit and got all the information for it."

David looked surprised, but he said nothing as he sat back down on his barstool. Tucker, however, stood and began to pace.

"You just knocked on her door and said, 'I heard from your neighbor that you want to sublet, so here I am'?" Tucker asked, turning to look at Kiara.

"Well, not like that," Kiara chuckled. "That'd be kind of rude. I just told her I knew David and if she was interested in subletting to call me, but she just gave me all of her information right then and there!"

Tucker turned to David, speechless at Kiara's boldness. David shrugged and shoved another forkful of egg in his mouth so he didn't have to get involved in their conversation.

"I took some pictures of the place if you want to see," Kiara said, pointing her phone at Tucker.

He stared at her for a moment, dumbfounded, but moved to sit next to her on the couch. "Fine, show me," Tucker grumbled.

Kiara swiped through the photos she'd taken, and Tucker couldn't deny that it was a beautiful apartment. She gave him all the information the tenant, Jasmine, had given her, and found that it was in his price range now that he was working again.

"Are we about to be roommates?" Tucker asked Kiara, still feeling confused about the whole situation but quickly getting excited.

"I think so," Kiara giggled. "But it depends on if I get this job," she added loudly, looking directly at David.

PAINT

"You are so pushy!" David laughed, pulling out his phone. "Let me go call Shane and see what he thinks."

"I'm not pushy, I'm driven!" Kiara called after him as he stepped into his bedroom and closed the door.

David emerged ten minutes later, his face unreadable as Kiara and Tucker looked at him expectedly.

"Well?" she asked, her voice hopeful.

"Unfortunately, I couldn't get you the same job as Tucker," David sighed. Kiara looked crestfallen for a moment, but composed herself quickly.

"That's okay. I'll just keep hunting for a job, then. Thanks for asking, David," she said.

"I'm not finished," he said quickly. "I couldn't get you the same job as Tucker, but I *did* talk Shane into letting you work as a shot girl part time and Assistant Stage Manager part-time for the shows on the weekends!" David beamed, looking proud of himself. "I told him you were going to school for theatre, and it was actually his idea! Isn't that awesome?"

"That's amazing!" Kiara gasped, clapping her hands over her mouth excitedly. She jumped to her feet and ran to give David a hug, quietly squealing with excitement. "I have to tell my parents," she said when she let go. "And I have to tell Jasmine we want the place!"

She grabbed her phone from the couch, blowing an air kiss to Tucker on the couch and another to David as she passed, and walked out the door without another word. David turned to Tucker, looking very confused. Tucker opened his mouth to speak, but just shook his head in exasperation.

"That's my best friend," was all Tucker could manage, smiling.

David sat next to Tucker on the couch, and not even five minutes later Tucker's phone buzzed with a new text notification from Kiara.

CHAPTER 29

KIARA: *We're good to go, roomie!*

Tucker showed the text to David, laughing. He'd known Kiara was a go-getter, but she had truly outdone herself with how fast she'd handled their living situation.

"I guess we're neighbors now," David said, taking Tucker's hand in his.

"Maybe you can sleep over at my place next time," Tucker suggested. "It's not too far from here."

"Sounds fun," David replied, smiling as he kissed the back of Tucker's hand. Tucker laid his head on David's shoulder, and the two sat together in contented silence, happy just to be together.

* * *

As summer progressed over the next few months, Tucker somehow kept himself just as busy as he was during the Spring semester. David had left him in charge of training Kiara in her new position as shot girl at Haven a few days after she'd accepted the position, and she'd demanded to be signed off on her training after an hour and a half on her first night. Whereas Tucker took the shy-but-friendly approach when selling shots, Kiara made her money by walking up to patrons and telling them to buy her shots, which worked almost every time.

"Everybody loves a powerful woman—especially the gays," she'd told Tucker with a confident smirk after selling the contents of her first tray in record time.

Kiara had quickly become a favorite around the club; chatting with the drag queens before the show and getting their drinks for them, tag-teaming shot sales with Tucker on especially busy nights, and even helping Ned with his love life (by taking his phone and texting the woman he was interested in to ask her on a date on his behalf).

She'd also stepped into her duties as Assistant Stage Manager with ease, barking set lineups and call times to the queens before every weekend show.

By the end of May, Tanya, the Stage Manager, demanded Shane let Kiara work with her full-time and he eventually gave in to her request.

When they weren't working together at the club, Tucker and Kiara spent their time together in their joint apartment. When they'd first moved in, Tucker had been worried that being together all the time would put a serious strain on their friendship, but it seemed to only strengthen it even more. They had their own rooms, so boundaries could be set if they weren't feeling social (not that Kiara ever cared about boundaries), but it was rare that they wouldn't come home and watch a movie or just chat about nothing. Kiara's parents had gifted her an end-of-first-year-of-college present, a reusable gift card with a thousand dollars on it that was used to purchase some second-hand furniture from a local thrift store, so they now had a bright red couch, two dark blue cushioned chairs on either side, a black coffee table in front, and a lime green dinner table that was usually covered in paperwork Kiara'd pour over before work each day. None of the furniture matched, and actually clashed quite a bit, but neither of them cared and agreed that it gave their apartment character.

When he wasn't working or at home with Kiara, Tucker was usually with David at his apartment a floor above or on dates around the city. Though he'd been in Orlando for almost a full year, he hadn't been out to explore his surroundings much during the two semesters, and David made it his mission to fix that. They'd taken day trips to all the major theme parks, two different botanical gardens, visited various clubs downtown (and a Hamburger Mary's, which Tucker was delighted to learn also had drag performances at night), but Tucker still loved sitting on the couch with David at the end of the night the most.

He hadn't been in touch with his parents a lot while the busy semester progressed, feeling stressed out enough with the workload he had to deal with without adding familial drama on top of that, but had received a brief phone call from his father shortly after he'd moved in with Kiara that surprised Tucker.

"Hey, Dad," he'd answered the phone, his tone cautious. The two had barely spoken to each other the last time they were together on Christmas,

CHAPTER 29

and there hadn't been any real communication since that wasn't orchestrated by his mother.

"Hey, Tucker, do you have a minute?" his dad replied, sounding gruff as ever.

"Yeah, what's up?"

"I've been doing a lot of thinking, son, and I owe you an apology," Ken said. Tucker said nothing, allowing his father to collect his thoughts and continue without interruption.

"I know you know this is all new for me, you being gay and all, but how I reacted was unfair to you. I wanted to tell you that I love you and that I'm sorry." His father's voice cracked, and Tucker could hear him sniffling quietly as he spoke. "I should have said this ages ago, but who you love doesn't mean a damn thing to me. I love you no matter what, you hear that?"

"Yeah, I hear you, Dad. I love you too," Tucker replied, tears pooling in his eyes as well.

"Your mother told me that you're seeing David now. He's a good kid. You two will have to come visit again sometime," he invited.

"I'd like that," Tucker replied, smiling.

Kiara wasn't the only one to earn a promotion at work that summer, and Tucker had officially joined the cast of the Monday Madness drag show at Haven by July. Jamie hadn't even asked if he wanted the position, but had left a voicemail for him that said, "Hey, girl, one of the queens in the Monday show is moving to L.A., so I'm giving you her slot. Don't fuck it up!"

At first, Tucker had been hesitant to fill the position. He'd called Jamie back and confessed that he felt he didn't deserve it because he was so new, but was told to "shut the hell up and say thank you", so he did just that and accepted the role as a permanent cast member. The other queens in the cast—Jamie, Crystal Waters, Kitty Dupree, and two queens named Anna Biotics and Anita Cocktail that Tucker learned were a couple in real life—were all welcoming to him, and any hesitancy Tucker felt melted away before the first Monday show he was a part of even began. Working each week had given Tucker a lot of experience with drag and helped to form a more sophisticated perspective of what he wanted to do with it, finally able to go beyond simply dressing up and going onstage—he saw it for what it was, an art form; an expression of the self that could be anything and anything he wanted it to be.

He'd also used the summer break as an opportunity to learn more about becoming more creative with drag, watching the other queens in the dressing room and videos online to learn how to style wigs and sew, and could now make outfits for his performances. Tucker knew he still had a lot to learn, but was proud of himself for becoming more self-sufficient with his drag and no longer relied on Jamie to help put him together. When Kiara saw him attempting to style a wig in his room one night, she'd suggested/demanded that he enroll in some technical theatre courses in the Fall semester so he could learn more about stage makeup, costume design and construction, and wig styling, and had him signed up before he'd finished putting the wig in curlers. After considering the training he'd receive in the courses, Tucker realized that he finally felt excited to be at UCF and the future paths it would lead him if he committed to a technical theatre major. He couldn't believe he hadn't seen the correlation between the technical theatre major and his love of drag before, but it seemed so obvious now that Kiara had pointed it out.

Tucker now sat in the dressing room at Haven by himself, the room only lit by the lights on the vanity mirror he was using, as he slowly began the process of becoming Karma Kahlo. Due to the size of the small dressing room versus the large size of the cast, a majority of the queens elected to get ready at home before the show, so Tucker typically had the dressing room to himself. He had only begun slathering foundation all over his face before David joined him, having some time to kill before his shift began, followed closely by Jamie, who was already in makeup when she entered. He watched Tucker quietly, entranced with Tucker's process. Once Tucker had coated his face in powder, David began to chuckle quietly to himself.

"What?" Tucker said with a curious smile, turning to look at David.

"It's just really entertaining seeing your process, is all," David said. "I know the final product is beautiful, but you look crazy right now—no eyebrows, no lips, no nothing."

"Girl, she looks crazy when she's done, too," Jamie interjected with a laugh,

CHAPTER 29

brushing more blush onto her already contoured cheeks.

"Beauty is in the eye of the beholder," Tucker replied, turning his attention back to the mirror as he started his eye makeup. David nodded in acknowledgement, but said nothing, watching Tucker work, and Jamie rolled her eyes in the mirror with a playful smirk on her face.

"I read that in one of my English Composition classes," Tucker said after he'd finished one eye. "An author named Margaret Wolfe Hungerford wrote it in the late 1800s, and it's still one of the most celebrated phrases used today."

Tucker paused, shifting his attention back to his reflection and working on his other eye. "I think that applies to a lot of things in my life," he resumed after his other eye matched, "like the way I decorate my room, what I wear, and of course, my drag."

"Very true," David affirmed, still watching. "I like how you do drag—I've seen a lot of different kinds of drag queens come through the club since I've started working here, so it's cool to see how everyone interprets it."

"Exactly!" Tucker agreed, brushing warm brown contour along his cheeks, temples, jaw, and sides of his nose. "I see drag as an art form, but I think a lot of people forget about that and expect very cookie-cutter looks and performances now that it's become so mainstream. They see drag on TV and think that's how it should be for everyone in the world. But drag, at least to me, is self-expression and doing what you want, not fitting into a mold to look like everyone else. I've seen a lot of different kinds of performers even in the short time I've been here—men, women, non-binary people, trans women, trans men; all doing different kinds of drag, and all of it really cool to see. It's about standing out, being you, pushing the envelope. And it certainly doesn't matter what's in your pants."

"Give the girl a cast spot and she's got a lot to say about drag now, darling!" Jamie teased, getting up from the mirror and pulling her tights up over her legs until they snapped around her waist.

Tucker quickly followed those same contoured areas with a light layer of blush, drew on a bright red lip, and glued his fake lashes on before continuing his thoughts as he pulled up his tights. "I've learned a lot in a short amount of time!" Tucker finally replied, looking at Jamie in the mirror as she dressed. "As I'm sure you've seen plenty, Mary, people in the drag scene are really quick to judge others on what they look like and what they wear. I know it's happened to me, and most of the time it was by people I'd never even met before!"

"Oh, I've seen it," David confirmed, chuckling. "Someone tried to make fun of something Jamie was wearing a year or so ago, and I watched her rip their eyelashes off and smudge their lipstick right as they were being announced to go onstage. These queens are ruthless!"

"And I'd do it again, bitch! Don't try it with me!" Jamie replied, clicking her nails on every word at David, making him laugh.

"My point exactly," Tucker laughed, imagining the scene David described. He could almost hear Jamie yelling insults at the queen, which made him laugh more. "So, that's what I'm saying," he said, pulling a tight gold leotard he'd sewn earlier that week, "beauty is in the eye of the beholder. I like to remind the girls every time we're here, because as long as we know we look good, it doesn't matter what those bitchy gays in the audience think."

"She says it every fucking week," Jamie interjected, rolling her eyes again. She was now fully dressed, sporting a tight bun on top of her head, a black lip and matching dark eyeshadow, and was wearing a slick black latex leotard with matching black thigh-high boots.

Tucker turned back to the counter, grabbing the coiffed brown wig that sat on a styrofoam wig head next to his makeup and positioning it on his head. When he was happy with it, he stepped into some matching gold sequined boots and zipped the sides. He took a step back, examining his look as a whole, and turned to look at David. As if on cue, David held up his phone and took a picture of Tucker and Jamie, who moved into the frame and wrapped her arm around Tucker's waist, smiling at the picture and showing it to them.

"That's what I'm talking about!" Tucker said, pointing his painted fingernail at the screen. "I think we look damn good tonight, so it doesn't matter what they think."

Satisfied, Tucker turned off the vanity lights and opened the door for the

CHAPTER 29

three of them to leave the room.

"After all," he added with a wink as David and Jamie exited, following behind them, "this is my paint, darling."

About the Author

Colin Brooks is a queer author currently living in Orlando, Florida. He is a graduate of the University of Central Florida, where he earned his two BA degrees in English and Theatre Studies, and now lives with his partner, Ryan, and their pets—the best dog in the world, Ryder, and a demon in cat's clothing, Nellie.

You can connect with me on:
- https://colinbrooksauthor.com
- https://twitter.com/colinbrooksauth
- https://www.facebook.com/colinbrooksauthor
- https://www.instagram.com/colinbrooksauthor

Made in the USA
Columbia, SC
11 January 2023

10059127R00167